Short Order Frame Up

Ron Jacobs

Fomite
Burlington, Vermont

This book is a work of fiction. The events and people are not real. The racism and injustice is.

First published by MAINSTAY PRESS
Copyright © 2007 by Ron Jacobs

ISBN: 978-1-937677-40-4
Library of Congress Control Number: 2013932825
Fomite
58 Peru Street
Burlington, VT 05401
www.fomitepress.com
Cover by Eric Gulliver
Author photograph by Donna Bister

Many thanks go to those who critiqued and encouraged me to continue this project, especially Wendy Gunther, Holly Thistle and Kathleen Brown. Also, much gratitude to Tony Christini of Mainstay Press for his original interest and suggestions. Of course, I can't thank Donna Bister and Marc Estrin of Fomite Press enough for publishing this edition

As for the inspiration, all the credit goes to the pancake house crew I worked with back in 1974-1976.

And, of course, thanks to my family and its multitude of members.

To R, who rarely suffered fools

Crime Fiction and Capitalist Reality

The novel is generally acknowledged to be a bourgeois form of literature. It wasn't until there were enough literate people with time for leisurely reading that this entertainment came along. The crime novel reflects the bourgeois obsession with order and usually represents the concerns of that class. There is a crime against an individual that shakes up bourgeois society. A detective from the police force or a private investigator hunts down the perpetrator through a series of clues, makes the arrest and all is well again. Agatha Christie's novels are perfect examples of this. Then there are the tough guy novels featuring men like Mike Hammer. In this type of story, the protagonist easily forsakes the niceties of bourgeois society in his crime solving. Naturally, this alienates the police and the bourgeoisie, but he still gets the job done, captures (or kills) the criminal, and allows the middle class to get on with their lives. This representation is occasionally turned around and the protectors of order -- the police and courts -- are the criminals and by association so is the system they work for. This is noir. Noir does not pretend that the society their protagonists operate in is worth saving. It's just the only one we have. This is where the novels of a few current writers exist, and where mine are intentionally placed.

Writing about Italian noir for *World Literature Today* critic Madison J. Davis noted :

> The traditional mystery, deriving from Poe's "The Murders in the Rue Morgue" and evolving through Conan Doyle and Agatha Christie to contemporary practitioners like Carolyn G. Hart and Simon Brett, requires a certain faith in the legal system—or at least in a measure of justice parceled out to those who commit crimes. We live, however, in a skeptical world, in which even those who enjoy the puzzles and deductions of the traditional whodunit cannot see them as realistic. The events of the twentieth century have cracked, often splintered, our faith in the legal system and the triumph of justice, even in the good ole U. S. of A.

I would argue that the twenty-first century has brought us beyond even the skepticism Davis acknowledges. Indeed, skepticism seems almost quaint, when we read about hundreds of men being released from prison because they were jailed they for crimes they did not commit. Their incarceration was not due to a mistake, but a conscious decision by authorities to match a crime to the victim they chose. Every time news like this comes out, the credibility of the police as protectors of society diminishes. When working people see their friends and children going to prison for drug offenses while the wealthy usually avoid doing time, their perception of the legal system being rigged in favor of the wealthy and powerful is rein-

forced. Since the police are the most obvious represen-
tatives of that system (and the individuals most citizens encounter) they are no longer perceived as much
more than enforcers of the rights of the wealthy and
powerful. This perception, long held by those considered The Other in society, is now part of the common
parlance. Indeed, television crime shows assume this
in their portrayals of police departments and individual cops. Certain series, most notably David Simon's
depressingly exquisite take on the corruption rampant
in an entire city's political and legal system called *The
Wire*, create a world where the incorruptible individual has no place.

This does not mean that the police don't enjoy at
least tacit support by a majority of the population; it
does mean that the number of people who believe the
police are not above criminality is much diminished
from just a few decades ago. The abuse of power by
police during the protests of the 1960s and onwards;
the revelations of individual cops like New York's
Serpico regarding corruption and illegal arrests
(among other things); the militarization of most police
forces in cities and towns large and small; and the
continued abrogation of civil liberties in the name of
the war on drugs and the war on terrorism. All of
these make the line between the police and the criminals they supposedly oppose very thin. Despite the
multitude of cop shows on television attempting to
present police as protectors of order and the innocent

and even the presence of movies like Clint Eastwood's Dirty Harry series (which serve as propaganda for authoritarianism), many residents of modern society are convinced the police are not there for their sake.

Nor is the legal system. Occasionally a clever lawyer is able to keep an innocent person out of prison -- in real life and in fiction. Indeed, certain authors have made a good living writing legal thrillers that feature these kinds of stories. More often than not, however, the police and the courts conspire to convict the person in the docket no matter what. It's not that the conspiracy is intentional; it's just how the system works. Police arrest a person for a crime and the courts do the rest. Without a good attorney -- something very few can afford -- the suspect's options are very limited. If one adds a cop with a grudge, a judge with an agenda, or a politician with a law and order platform to the equation, that person in the docket does not stand a chance.

A few decades ago I was charged with "possession with the intent to sell" because I was sitting in an automobile when an acquaintance sold a small amount of marijuana to an undercover cop. This all went down not long after the state I was living in had passed a law that rendered the U.S. Constitution's prohibition on unreasonable search and seizure null and void. Anyone who was in the vicinity of anything having to do with illegal drugs was as culpable as the person actually involved with the drugs. So, since I was in the car when the drug deal occurred, I was also involved in the sale. When I showed up at court on the charge, I asked my public defender if I should challenge the charge and plead not guilty. His response was simple. If I challenged the charge I would not win. He advised me to take a plea deal and do community service. I took his advice. The law was not interested in justice, just in throwing people in jail.

Much anti-capitalist and antiwar activity is already labeled criminal in an imperial society. This in itself means that characters participating in activities that fall into this category are already suspect. Meanwhile, the forces of law and order trying to stifle such characters have a leeway not provided the citizen, no matter what he or she is involved in. The often violent reaction of the authorities to the Occupy Wall Street protests in Fall 2011 provides a recent example of this fact. A greater contradiction occurs when the forces of authority engage in criminal behavior in the pursuit of the forces aligned against the rulers the police are hired to protect. A further complication comes into play when criminal actions by the police are ignored or sanctioned while criminal acts by the targets of the authorities are not. In a line quite familiar to most rock and roll fans (especially those who listen to the Rolling Stones) that calls every cop a criminal, this contradiction is even clearer.

Back to that incorruptible individual. Most noir features a private investigator. Like the accused, he or she is an individual who lives on the edges of the law. In a world where the law itself can be unjust, only those not in debt to the system designed to bring justice can find that justice. Most often the investigator is one who works for hire with a set of morals that are immutable. In certain cases, like two of the novels in my 1970s trilogy, the investigators are regular folks determined to help a friend. Still, they are not without faults. Alcohol is often a vice these characters deal with. Most recently, in Thomas Pynchon's foray into the genre with a book titled *Inherent Vice,* his private eye smokes a lot of marijuana. Early on, many of the so-called tough guys like Mike Hammer were sexist and racist. As the genre has evolved, so have the investigators. Like the society they operate in, today's investigators include Blacks, Latinos, Asians, and women.

Today's noir fiction is the story of a system and society in decline. Marxist Ernest Mandel published a book on crime fiction in 1986 titled *Delightful Murder.* In this book, Mandel looks at the genesis and development of crime fiction. We see the development of the criminal from a lone individual whose exploits shock and dismay, but whom heroic police agents can capture. As capitalism moves into its monopoly phase, the lone criminal remains a problem, yet the real problem developing is an entire class of criminals. These are what Marx labeled the lumpenproletariat: that part of society whose sole task is surviving no matter what it takes. Usually extremely poor, only occasionally employed in conventional jobs, and existing literally outside of society, the lumpen are the truly dangerous ones in the bourgeoisie's midst. They provide respectable society with their entertainments such as illegal drugs and sex, but must be controlled at all cost. The investigator's position in society is closer to that of the lumpen than to any other stratum. He or she understands the justice of the streets is often not the justice of the courtroom. Of course, this position outside of society means there is nothing to lose in fighting the wealthy and powerful.

Mandel published his book before capitalism's latest phase was truly underway. That is, neoliberalism. This stage of monopoly capitalism is the nightmare that Rosa Luxembourg warned us about. Financiers who produce no product run the world. Instead of creating work, their actions profit from the destruction of jobs and the impoverishment of millions. They launder the millions made by international drug lords while financing politicians who want to build more prisons and lock up those who use the drugs. As far as the financiers are concerned, the working class itself is now a criminal class. Yet, we know better. It is the financiers and their class that are the true criminals. Still, they go free while workers go to jail for the crime of being poor. The conspiracy of the super rich is not an accident. They built the world that way.

Writers can choose to point this out or they can go

along with the status quo. Good crime fiction on a neoliberal planet chooses the former. The task of those who write these tales is to point the finger at the true criminals. The police are only heroes when they bust the big guys. The system can only be just when it turns on its own. At this juncture in time, this only seems to happen in stories. Unfortunately.

He believed in his heart that Snowdon was one of the most racist places on earth.

Peter still remembered the response in the junior high when Martin Luther King was killed. Some of the greaser types walked around the next day picking fights with the black kids. Shit, they even tried to fight him because he said that the world had lost a great man during a discussion in homeroom. The only reason he didn't get his ass kicked was because he knew some of the kids picking the fights.

There were unwritten rules in this town about race and gender. The black kids grew up knowing them and the white kids grew up enforcing them just like their parents had.

He remembered the first time he realized what the "Whites Only" and "Colored Only" signs meant at the drinking fountains in the shopping center. His dad almost shit a brick when Peter took a drink from the Coloreds fountain because there wasn't a line like there was at the one for whites.

Hell, even hanging out in the local watering hole,

as Peter was known to do on occasion, with two white women and a black man who squeezes their butts every time they come back from the bar is pushing the limits. That's putting the two greatest fears of the crackers together. Black men and white women. And this is 1975. We're supposed to be beyond that. Not in Snowdon, we ain't. You gotta remember, thought Peter, John Wilkes Booth was given shelter not far from here after he killed Lincoln. The legacy of racism is in the blood of a lot of these white folks. It's only the influx of government workers from more enlightened parts of the country that's made this place better than Mississippi in the last few years.

1

Peter headed out the back door of the pancake house, glad to be through with work. Sniffing his shirt, all he could smell was the odor of bacon grease.

That's okay, he thought, as soon as he got home he knew he could take these clothes off and take a shower. Then listen to some tunes, drink a couple beers, and head to Mac's Tavern for some drinks and a sandwich with Art. But first it was time to light up this joint for the walk home. It's funny how you can do that these days—walk right up the street smoking a joint. People driving by and just smiling while they whistle the tune on the radio.

As for this job. Well, he'd had worse. At least most of the people he worked with were cool. Everyone knew they were in the same boat. Trying to make enough to pay rent and stay reasonably happy. That meant enough beer and weed to get by. He could eat all he wanted at work, although pancakes and their accoutrement did get old. Man did the weed feel good. Almost home and the joint still had an inch and a half to go.

He picked up the mail, rifled through it, saw a letter from his mom who was over in Germany on a military base with dad, and a lot of bills. Then he opened the door, scratched Fred the dog and headed toward the shower, removing his grease-soaked clothing as he progressed. Just as he reached the bathroom door the phone rang.

"Hey." Peter stood in the bathroom doorway.

"Hi, man. This is Jeremy."

"Yeah?"

"I'm in deep shit, man. I spent Malcolm's money that he gave me for some pot and I know he's gonna want to kill me It was like 200 bucks."

"So why are you telling me, Jeremy?"

"Cause you're like friends with his uncle and maybe you can tell him to give me another day or so?"

"I'll try, Jeremy. But you always do this shit and Malcolm don't like you anyway."

"Fuck that nigger."

"Hey, you say that around me again and I'll tell Malcolm you spent the cash on dope for you and Josey." Josey was one of Malcolm's old girlfriends. "He'll definitely kill you then."

"Whatever."

"I'll help you out Jeremy, but you shouldn't let people talk you into fronting their money to you since you always fuck up."

He felt a little bad for the kid. He had been on his

own since he was twelve when his mom's white trash boyfriend tried to sodomize him and Jeremy sliced the guy up. Unfortunately, his mom testified against him and said he was incorrigible, so Jeremy ended up in juvey. When he got out, Art gave him a job as a dishwasher at the pancake house where we all worked and Peter let him crash in the shed out back of where he used to live until the other folks in the house made Peter tell him to leave. He was living with a college girl these days. She liked his easy access to dope and the way he catered to her every whim. She also slept around on him a little without him knowing. Hell, Peter had spent an afternoon or two with her himself. If Jeremy knew, he would definitely freak out, having the self-esteem of a beaten puppy.

He was always trying to deal pot and acid and always failing. Usually he failed because he smoked the stuff himself or gave away the acid to his buddies who were still in high school and came over to where Jeremy lived instead of going to school. It was suburbia, what else was there to do but skip school and get high? It was better than breaking into houses or setting fires, like some of the kids in town. Like every other white kid who worked at the pancake house, Jeremy almost always used the n-word when talking about black people. It drove Peter crazy, having been involved with the Panthers the year he was in the service and feeling more like a brother than a white guy half the time. Some might say Peter was confused, but he would say it was the whole fuckin' country that was, not just him. Art and the other blacks who worked at the restaurant made it clear they would kick anybody's ass if they heard them using that word around them, so he knew these kids could control their tongue. Peter guessed they figured that since he was white that he wouldn't care since every white person they knew used it liberally.

Snowdon was southern, despite it's best intentions to appear otherwise. Like most of this part of Maryland, it had been slaveholders' turf until the end of the Civil War. Since that time the politicians were about half out and out racist and the other half were intent on trying to rid the area of that image. You know, naming one of the schools after Benjamin Banneker and another after Martin Luther King. No matter what though, the town was still a racist pit. Shit, only five years ago the klan tried to burn down a church and, failing that, tried to burn down the house next door. Then, when the blacks who lived in the neighborhood wanted to hold a march they were told that they couldn't because it would stir up trouble. This was a year before Martin Luther King was killed down in Memphis. Then, a week later the klan was given a permit to march right through the main street of the black neighborhood, which was known locally as the grove. Of course, they got full police protection.

Peter took a shower, dried himself off, brushed

his hair and put on some clean jeans and a shirt, and headed out to the tavern to meet up with Art. He heard the phone ring as he locked the door. He didn't answer it.

Peter got there first. After putting his denim jacket in a booth, he ordered a Miller High Life and a shot of JD, paid the bartender and went back to the booth. He drained the shot and sat back to enjoy the beer. There was this one chick he worked with named Lucy who was always in the place. Like usual, she had on a tight top and jeans and was drinking whatever someone would buy her. She was pretty damn cute but also acted pretty crazy. In the past, Peter had always tried to stay away from her in any sexual way 'cause he didn't want the hassle. At least that's what he told himself. They talked a lot though about the days when they were both in junior high together. They had the same homeroom teacher and loved to give her hell. Lucy was super smart but just didn't give a shit. Now or back then. Maybe she didn't give a shit because she was so smart.

"Hey, Peter." She began. "When you gonna let me take you home?" This was their running joke since high school. Peter always said, "Never," but knew that someday he would say, "How about right now?" Who knows what her reply would be when that happened? Just as he was getting ready to give her his all too familiar response, Peter noticed Art coming into the place. He was truly styling today. Always a fan of a certain combination of Sly Stone's flamboyant costumes, James Brown's Godfather of Soul getup, and Superfly, Art was dressed to the hilt in a pair of button-down navy blue bellbottoms, a loud paisley shirt like the one Jimi Hendrix is wearing on the cover of his first Experience album, and a floor length leather coat, just like Ron O'Neal in Superfly. Peter moved over in the booth to make room for him. Lucy was already sitting opposite Peter.

"Hey all," said Art as he slipped into the booth. "What are y'all drinking? My treat."

"Miller," said Peter. "And JD straight up."

"White wine," said Lucy as she leaned over and gave Art a kiss for a greeting. He always liked it when the ladies did that. The waitress came over and took the drink orders. Art was drinking Chivas tonight, with water on the side. When she came back with the goodies, Peter ordered a steak sandwich with fries. Art asked the waitress if the bartender could turn the television to the ball game. Peter hated the Orioles but loved baseball and watched it anywhere and anytime. He could always root for the other team.

"Malcolm's gonna get his ass in a lot of trouble, Peter," began Art. He actually looked a little worried about his nephew. Peter knew Art had promised his mom that he would watch over the guy, but he had always acted as if all that meant was getting him a job and a place to live—both of which he had done. Otherwise, he let the guy do his own thing and didn't seem too concerned about what that thing was. This concern was new.

The game was starting. The Indians were on the field and the Orioles were up to bat. What's his name Raich was pitching for the Indians. Singleton was leading off for the O's, of course. It was easy to root for the Indians in this instance although there wasn't much to root for. Maybe this new pitcher Dennis Eckersley. At least he looked cool. Oh yeah, Frank Robinson was their player-manager. That made it a little more interesting. The former Oriole managing his new team against his old team.

Lucy got up and went to the bathroom. When she came back, Peter and Art were eating. She squeezed Art's arm and asked him to switch seats. Art told her to let him finish his sandwich. She sat down opposite Peter again and before he knew it she had her feet on his legs trying to worm them in between. After first trying to ignore what he figured was just Lucy's drunken teasing, Peter opened his thighs and let her place her foot where she wanted. Mike Cuellar was on the mound for the Orioles. They were ahead 1 to zip. It was Singleton who scored. When the waitress came back over, they ordered another round of drinks. Art lit a cigarette and traded seats with Lucy, who put her arm around Peter's waist and kissed his neck. He wasn't used to this type of attention from her. Usually (in fact, ever since seventh grade), they just played at playing around. He never thought of her touches as anything but a tomboyish joke. Perhaps he was wrong.

Just as Peter began to slip deeper into his reverie, Art pounded the table. "Damnit!" he shouted. "That stupid shit can't hit worth a damn!" Apparently, the Indians second basemen Kuiper had just hit into a double play, quashing a potential rally. Art was a big fan of any team from the Midwest, having grown up in East St. Louis. After his outburst, he drained his drink and called the waitress over for another one. Peter had been ignoring his second beer, thanks to Lucy's manipulations. He quickly drained the glass, though, and asked for another, too. Lucy got up to go to the bathroom.

"Anyhow, Peter, like I was saying," began Art. "Malcolm is gonna get his ass in some serious trouble. I told him to just let his trip with Jeremy go for a couple days since Jeremy usually figures something out, but Malcolm sees it as a racial thing."

"It could be, you know," Peter reminded him. "Jeremy ain't the most enlightened kid in the world."

"Yeah," said Art. "But still, it ain't worth gettin' so pissed off about. If nothin' else, I'll give Malcolm his money and talk to Jeremy myself about payback. I mean, shit, we all been ripped off at least once and survived."

"Tell me about it," agreed Peter. "I always figure

that karma takes care of it." He was thinking of a recent episode with this brother named Joe who had worked for a week at the pancake house washing dishes. He had borrowed twenty bucks from him to pick up some weed, or so he said, and never produced shit except for a ton of excuses.

"You talkin' about that jerk Joe?" laughed Art. "Now he's shovelin' shit at the track." Snowdon had a horse track where one could always get a job cleaning the stalls when the horses were running. Peter did the gig for a week once but just couldn't handle the smell. It was the urine that killed him, not the manure. Joe fancied himself a gambler and a hustler, so he liked to hang out at the track. Art, who really was a hustler, laughed at Joe's feeble attempts to be a con man. If Joe weren't so full of himself, Art would teach him a trick or two. Unfortunately for Joe, his ego got in the way of his better sense and he would probably end up doing some serious time just for being stupid.

"Yeah, that's the guy. What a screw-up. You know, after he took my money and lied to me about what happened to it for at least two weeks until I finally told him I didn't give a shit about it just because it was gettin' so pathetic, he came back around and tried to talk me into fronting him some more cash." Peter laughed. "I just looked at him and told him to get the hell out of my face. He did." The waitress came back with the drinks and Art paid her. Lucy was making her way back to the table. Art nodded his head towards her and asked what was up with her.

"I don't know, man. All of sudden she's gettin' sweet on me."

"You oughta jump on it if you can, you know," he counseled. "She's a great kid and not bad lookin' either. Even if it's only for the night." Art called everybody under thirty a kid—which was most everyone he knew in the area.

Peter knew Art was right, but at the same time he was pretty tentative about the possibility. "We'll see how it goes tonight." She slid in next to Peter. "You know, Art, I wouldn't worry about Malcolm. He'll go to Baltimore and hang out with his bros down there and forget all about Jeremy until he comes back to town. That's what always happens. He'll realize it ain't worth gettin' so worked up over. Yes! Robinson just hit a fuckin' homer!" The Indians were in their half of the second and had just tied the game on two home runs. Art raised his glass. He was beginning to put away the drinks quicker—something he always did once he had finished the first two. He had an amazing capacity, however, for a guy who only weighed about 140 and stood maybe five foot eight not counting his afro.

The tavern was beginning to get noisy with the sounds of a summer night. The jukebox had been turned on and the television's sound was off. This happened every night. Two construction workers with long hair and dirty t-shirts were over by the box now making their selections. Hopefully they would choose something worth their quarter. Art was joking with Lucy about their boss.

The Allman Brothers "Blue Sky" came on. Well, at least it wasn't Glen Campbell or Grand Funk Railroad. While Peter dug the Allmans, he had a feeling Art would have preferred something by the Ohio Players or Earth, Wind and Fire. While Lucy was open to anything you could dance to—which meant she liked the disco stuff a hell of a lot more than Peter—her record collection was mostly made up of Grateful Dead and Stones records. The more he drank tonight, though, the less the music mattered. The idea of sleeping with Lucy sounded better and better.

It looked like the three of them would be taking a detour through the carnival first, though. Art wanted to go over to the lot where it was being held and do some gambling and he was getting tired of the ballgame. Lucy wrapped her arm around Peter's waist, licked his neck and finished her drink. Art stood up and the three of them headed out the door. Peter was hoping they didn't spend too much time there. He had been going to these things since he was a kid and still found them boring. Art wanted to gamble though and he was always fun to hang around with when he was on a roll. The game was in the bottom of the fourth and the score was still tied at two. He figured he'd catch up with the score later.

"You know, I wish everyone was as easy to deal with as you two guys," commented Lucy out of the blue. They were walking in the direction of the carnival, which was set up on a huge parking lot next to the Sears store which lay behind the shopping center. The tavern they had been drinking in was in the shopping center in the exact opposite direction. If he had to, Peter would say the distance was about 500 yards as the crow flies. "It's like you never get too upset about anything. Meanwhile, everyone else is flipping out over such stupid shit." Peter appreciated the observation, although he wasn't sure how true it was.

"Yeah, we're just mellow guys," said Art. "As long as we can have a drink and a hit or two of weed we can maintain anywhere and anytime. Oh shit, I just remembered I have to go cook dinner for my Mom. I'll see you all in an hour or so." Art's mom had been in town for a week or two. She had come in from Kansas City, Missouri just to check up on her boy. At least that was how she put it. Art didn't seem to mind her presence. In fact, he seemed to like having her around. Art headed off to the apartment he lived in with Malcolm. Lucy and Peter traded drunken grins and continued on their way.

"Where do you wanna stop first?" joked Peter. "The little fish with the magnets on the end of the line? Or the booth where you shoot at those ducks that keep going around?"

"Let's go get a drink," replied Lucy.

"Now that's my kind of ride." They found the beer tent and ordered a couple plastic cups full of alcohol. The evening sky was turning dark as we sat at a table in a corner near the bar. Their corner was even darker.

"You know, Peter, I think you've wanted to sleep with me since seventh grade. The way you used to poke my butt every day with your feet and then act like it was an accident." Peter had sat directly behind her in homeroom. "I liked the attention even though I pretended I was pissed off."

"Hell, I didn't even know what sleeping with someone was then. But I did fantasize about kissing you a lot." Isn't it too bad our thoughts don't remain as innocent as they once were, thought Peter.

"I could have helped you out on your ignorance. Not that I was having sex in seventh grade but my big sister did bring a few boy friends home from college. I learned a lot from watching her."

"It's better this way," Peter joked. "I was saving myself for you." He placed his hand on her thigh and squeezed. She responded in kind and they kissed. After finishing their drinks, they left the tent, walked back to the tavern, found Lucy's car and went to her place. They planned to meet up with Art in an hour or so.

Art's mom was in the tub when he got to the

apartment. Malcolm was sleeping on the couch still in his work clothes. There was a half-empty pint bottle of Smirnoff's next to him and a jug of orange juice. Art took off his shoes so as not to wake him and headed into the kitchen. He took some chicken legs, breading, and eggs out of the refrigerator and began preparing dinner. After turning on the oven and breading the chicken, he tiptoed over to the couch and gently took the bottle of Smirnoff's from his nephew. Ignoring the orange juice, he unscrewed the cap and took a drink. The little light on the oven that went dark when the oven was preheated was dark so he put the chicken in the oven and began to prepare the salad. He could hear the water drain from the tub and his mom drying herself off.

While Art set the table and continued to drink from the almost empty pint bottle, Malcolm woke up. After a couple attempts to return to his nap he sat up slowly and said hi to Art. Then he lit a cigarette.

"What are you doin' tonight, Malcolm?" asked his uncle. "I got your bottle. I'll buy you another if you want since I almost finished this one."

"I don't know, man. I wanna go to Baltimore and check out this cousin of Antoine's. She looks real fine in her pictures. But I gotta get my money from that little white chump."

Art's mom came out and sat down at the table. Art poured her a glass of wine and motioned to Malcolm to come sit down. He found a couple beers in the back of the fridge, opened them and gave one to Malcolm. He took a sip from the other.

"Dinner should be ready in a half hour or so. Have some salad in the meantime."

"Mom," began Art, "I'm goin' to that carnival after dinner if you wanna come along. It's within walking distance so if you get tired of my playing you can come home. Malcolm's going to Baltimore."

"Actually, I think I'll just relax by myself. Watch a little TV and a have a quiet evening if that's okay." She took a sip of her wine as Art checked the chicken's progress. Malcolm finished off his beer and looked in the fridge for another. Somewhere behind the salad greens he found two more and handed one to Art. For a few minutes, the only sounds one heard were that of salad being eaten and beer being drunk from a can. Then Art took the chicken from the oven and served it along with some potato salad he had made earlier.

"Malcolm, you be careful in Baltimore. I don't like some of those boys you been bringing back from there. They remind me of the fellers your father fell in with and got him in prison." Malcolm's dad had run with a pretty tough group of young men after he got out of the Army back in 1954. Sure, Malcolm's father had been in Korea and seen some pretty ugly shit over there but he'd never knowingly killed a man. Then, not three weeks after Malcolm's birth, his dad had got involved in a fight with a bunch of street hustlers and crapshooters over a fifty dollar debt. Malcolm's dad hit one of them on the head with a wine bottle and that one died a week later, never regaining consciousness. Malcolm's mom began a downward spiral of drugs and alcohol soon afterwards and Art's mom took Malcolm in. His dad's parents were both dead and Malcolm's mother's parents didn't want nothing to do with him. He called her Auntie Grace. She raised him until he was drafted into the Army in 1972—the last year they drafted young men and sent them to Vietnam. Malcolm had been lucky and ended up in Japan instead.

"Don't worry, Auntie. I got it under control." Like always, Malcolm wanted to reassure her, although lately he didn't think she believed him like she did back when he was in high school. "Hey, Art, can I borrow twenty bucks from you? I'll pay you back when I get paid again."

"Yeah." Art pulled a roll of bills from his pocket and peeled off a twenty. "Just give that kid a couple more days to make good."

"I'll try but I ain't making no promises, Art," Malcolm said. "We'll see how the night goes." Auntie Grace finished her chicken and brought her dishes over to the sink, where she rinsed them off and placed them in the dishwasher. Malcolm picked up his wallet and money from the couch he had been sleeping on before dinner, put on his shoes and told his aunt and Art goodbye. Then he left. Grace refilled her glass. Art got up and turned on the TV hoping to catch the score of the game he'd been watching earlier. He turned the dial just in time to catch the score on Channel 2. Indians 3, Orioles 5. His mom made some room for herself on the couch and asked Art to flip through the channels for her. He found a show she liked, set her bottle of wine next to the couch, and left for the carnival. It was time to party a little.

2

"Come on, Jeremy," begged Julie. "Just take this money and give it to Malcolm. Shit, you can pay me back later." She pushed her long blond hair away from her face and thrust the money into Jeremy's pants pocket. While she had her hand there she gently squeezed his balls. Jeremy smiled, his light blue eyes losing their angry, scared edge. He put his skinny arms around her, pulled her towards him and kissed her thin lips. Julie stroked his platinum, almost white hair and put her hands in the back of his pants, grabbing what little flesh was on his ass. He grabbed her hand and walked back into the bedroom.

When both were sufficiently pleasured, they rolled over on their backs. Julie turned on to her side, laid her head on Jeremy's small chest and stroked his legs. Jeremy felt a little better, but his mind began to wander back towards the situation with Malcolm and the cash. He sat up and pushed Julie's hands gently away.

"I can't take your money, Julie. That's for your school. Shit, I need to get someone to front me the weed for that asshole."

"No really, babe, it's okay. I can borrow some cash from my mom. She's got plenty since she married that rich jerk."

"I don't want you takin' his money, not after he came on to you like he did. Fuck him."

"Hell, the way I look at it, that's a good reason to take it and never pay him back. Or I could borrow some from Lucy. She's cool as long as I don't tell her why I need it." Julie worked at the pancake house where Lucy was the head waitress. Even though Julie was two years younger, they had been in the same dance class through most of high school and still went dancing sometimes, although since Jeremy had moved in, their relationship had been strained some due to Jeremy's notions about certain things, interracial relation-ships being one of them.

"Shit, she'll probably tell Malcolm the next time she fucks him."

"That's not fair, Jeremy. She doesn't see him any more and only went out with him a couple times. He's too crazy for her. Besides, what difference does it make?" Julie put her lips on Jeremy's stomach and began to move them down-ward. He slid out from underneath her advances and began to get dressed. Once he had tied his sneakers, he left out the door, telling Julie he would see her at the carnival later. He didn't tell her he was going over to Rock's house.

Rock and Jeremy had known each other since they were in preschool together. When his mom had let that asshole boyfriend of hers move in, Jeremy had spent most of his time at Rock's. His parents didn't mind since they thought his mom was crazy as a loon. He and Rock used to break into houses when they were eleven until Rock's dad found out and whipped the shit out of both of them. After that, Rock's parents weren't so big on him coming over as much. Still, they were decent to him when he did and Rock's mom always fed him well. She thought he was way too skinny, but only because Rock was already about 190 pounds and over six feet tall. Of course, Rock's dad was at least 220 and easily 6'6". He worked for the fire department and wanted Rock to do the same, but Rock hated school and was always skipping class. Julie trusted him about as far as she could see him. He worked at the pancake house, too. About the only ambition he had was to drive a "fuckin' Camaro." Still, Jeremy knew that's where he had to go. Rock and him could figure something out.

Jeremy knocked on Rock's window, then opened it and crawled in. This was his usual method of entry when he was trying to stay away from Rock's parents. They usually never bothered Rock in his room. Rock was on his bed with a pair of headphones on. He looked over at Jeremy and nodded. Jeremy turned down the volume on Rock's stereo, noticing that the album spinning on the turntable was Get Your Wings by Aerosmith. Rock took the headphones off his head.

"Hey, man," muttered Rock. "What's up?"

"Man, I'm in some deep shit, Rock. You gotta help me."

"What? Is this about that money Malcolm fronted you?" Rock turned off the turntable and reached under his bed for the shoebox that he kept his weed in. He opened the box and began to roll a joint.

"Yeah."

"When do you have to give him the dope?" asked Rock.

"I was supposed to give it to him last week and now he's startin' to threaten me and shit. I ain't scared of him but those niggers from Baltimore kind of freak me out."

"Fuck 'em, man. We can deal with 'em."

That's easy for you to say, thought Jeremy. You're six feet tall. Me, I'm just a skinny little fucker. "Yeah right," said Jeremy skeptically.

"No seriously, man. I don't mean by fighting or nothing. I know you're not into that. But there's another way."

"Oh yeah? What's that?"

Rock finished rolling the joint and returned the rest of the weed back to the baggie it came from. He put the baggie back in the box and returned the box to its place under the bed. He looked up at Jeremy and said, "Let's go outside for a walk and I'll tell you my plan. We can smoke this while we're at it."

"Cool."

The two climbed out the bedroom window and headed to the small park a half block from Rock's house. Rock sparked up the joint and took a deep draw. He handed it to Jeremy.

"My idea," began Rock, speaking between exhalations of smoke, "is to break into Samson's house and steal some of his weed. He's got four or five pounds of this stuff we're smoking and it kicks ass." Just as Rock said this, Jeremy began coughing, not being used to the strength of the pot. Samson was Rock and Jeremy's main pot supplier.

"Shit," said Jeremy, still coughing. "This weed kicks. What is it?"

"Samson calls it Panama Red and it's really fuckin' red." The two had reached the park and were sitting on a bench. They sat in silence, smoking the joint and keeping a lookout for police who might be cruising by. Occasionally the silence was interrupted by an uncontrollable cough.

"Shit," coughed Jeremy. "If someone heard us they would think we were fuckin' dyin' from some lung disease or somethin'. This weed kicks ass. How hard would it be to break in to Samson's, do ya think?" The more stoned he got, the better Rock's idea sounded. It would not only solve the problem of getting his ass kicked by Malcolm's bros and if anyone could afford it, Samson could. He must move ten pounds of fuckin' herb a week. What's a quarter pound to him?

Rock was quietly thinking out the strategy he and Jeremy would use to steal the pot. Samson lived in a small house on an acre or two of woods about five miles from the center of Snowdon. They would need to ride bikes over there and hide them somewhere near. Then, like always, Jeremy could climb in the window since he was so little. The problem would be finding where Samson hid his stash. It was usually in the bathroom under the sink in a locked cabinet. That would be the hassle. Jeremy wasn't really good at breaking shit up since he was pretty weak. Usually, Rock just hit something that needed breaking with his fist and they were in. That was when they didn't have a key to get in. If they had a day or two, Rock could go over to Samson's place and buy some weed. Then he could watch where his key and stash were.

"When do you need to get the shit to Malcolm, Jeremy?" asked Rock. Maybe Jeremy wasn't in as much of a hurry as he seemed to be.

"Tonight, man. Malcolm said he was going to Baltimore to get his boys together. Can we do it, you think?"

Rock searched his memory, trying to recall whether or not Samson had mentioned where he would be tonight. He wasn't sure, but thought he had said he and his dogs were going to Pennsylvania for the week. His mom had a cabin in the Poconos where

Samson liked to go and relax.

"You know," began Rock. "I think he said he was going away for the week. We can get our bikes and check it out. I know you can climb in his window and stuff, but I don't know how you're going to get in to his stash. Shit, I'm not even sure where he keeps it these days."

"Fuck it," said Jeremy. "I'll figure it out."

Now quite stoned from the Panama Red, Jeremy and Rock went back to Rock's house. They opened the garage door and grabbed their bikes. Jeremy always kept one of his bikes in Rock's garage. He had been doing it since he stole his first bike back when he was ten. Quietly, so as not to arouse the attention of Rock's parents, they rode away towards Samson's place.

Peter untangled himself from Lucy's arms and rolled over on his back. Re-orienting his thoughts, he realized he was laying on the green shag carpet that covered Lucy's living room floor. She was still asleep, her arms stretched in front of her and her reddish-blond hair covering half her face, which made her look even cuter than she already did. Peter thought about waking her up and starting the last hour or so all over when he remembered Art.

"Oh shit!" he shouted. "What the hell time is it?" Lucy opened her eyes halfway and put her hands on his thigh.

"There's a clock in the kitchen." Peter stood up and found his way in the dark. The clock said 9:00. He went back into the living room and felt around for his clothes. Lucy stood up slowly, went over to the wall nearest the kitchen door and switched on the light. Peter blinked and then thought, man did she look good naked. Then he got dressed. Lucy went to the bathroom. When she returned Peter was dressed and ready to go. Lucy put her clothes on quickly. Once dressed, she leaned over and kissed Peter on the cheek.

"We should do that again, cutie." Peter nodded his head in agreement. The two left the apartment.

Julie knew what she had to do. She was going to find Malcolm and give him two hundred bucks. She didn't want Jeremy to get hurt. Sometimes she hated herself for feeling so maternal about the guy, but he just made her feel that way. Jeremy would get pissed when he found out, but she could take care of that. A little lovemaking went pretty far with him. Probably 'cause he never knew what love was with such an asshole for a mother. She finished getting dressed, put the money in her purse, and left the apartment. After backing her car out of the parking space, she pushed the Little Feat tape into the player and went off in the direction of the carnival. She turned up the volume on the tape. "Dixie Chicken" was one of her favorite songs. Peter had turned her on to the band.

He knew his fuckin' music. Sometimes Jeremy and Rock made fun of his taste, but sooner or later they all bought the records he talked about. Springsteen, the Dead, Little Feat, Dylan, Parliament/Funkadelic — all good music that said something too.

The carnival was five minutes from her place. Once she arrived at the shopping center she found a place to park. She got out of the car and walked towards the carnival, thinking about where she might find Malcolm. Hopefully, he'd be cool to taking the money from her. Knowing Malcolm, though, that wouldn't be much of a problem. He was into the money thing. It's funny, she thought, how all these guys were so into money and they never had much. After all, how much money were you going to make washing dishes or frying eggs for a living? Plus, the way they dealt dope wasn't going to make 'em rich, either.

This whole exercise was symptomatic of how it usually went. Either they smoked up their weed and had none to sell or they smoked up somebody else's and had to borrow money to pay them back. It was too bad Malcolm was being such a pain in the ass about it this time, but she kind of understood his reasoning. After all, Jeremy had done this before and his reputation with Malcolm was not in good standing, to say the least. Still, she loved the skinny little guy.

Julie saw the beer tent and figured that's where she would find Malcolm or somebody else she knew. So she went in that direction. Of course, the noise got louder as she neared the entrance. She showed her ID to the big fat guy at the door and went into the tent. The lights were bare and consequently quite bright. Once her eyes adjusted to them she looked around for a familiar face. It looked like Art was over by the bar. Might as well go talk to him. He was always good for a laugh. Plus, he might know what was up with Malcolm and this mess between him and Jeremy. Hell, maybe he could help her find Malcolm.

"Hey Art," said Julie. "What's up?"

"Hey girl, you wanna beer or something? You lookin' mighty fine." Art was in fine form already.

"I'll have a beer, thanks." Julie gave Art a peck on the cheek. He smiled and squeezed her arm. The bartender gave him a plastic cup of beer and waved him away when he attempted to pay.

"Hey, Art, you done paid enough money tonight. Plus this here pretty girl deserves one on the house." The bartender flashed Julie a quick smile and turned back to the tap to fill another couple cups for his next customers. Julie said thanks and took a sip. She yanked on Art's arm and pulled him towards an empty table.

"Hey Art. I need to talk to you." They sat down.

"What's up Julie, baby."

"It's about Malcolm and Jeremy. I don't want them to do something stupid over this fuckin' money."

"Me neither. But they both actin' like fools, you know."

"I agree. Them and their stupid little egos."

"How come you can see it and I can see it but they can't?" Art knew the answer. Young men always got hung up on that kind of stuff. Hell, he'd done time trying to prove how bad he was when he was 19. Two years in prison was enough to convince almost anybody that all that male ego shit was just that. Too bad so many youngsters had to learn the hard way. As the song said, though, that's the way of the world. The tent was beginning to fill up with folks. Art looked at his watch. It was going on 9:30. He wondered where the hell Peter and Lucy were. They must have fallen to their lust, as the bible thumpers liked to say. Good for them.

Just as he finished that thought he noticed Peter walking into the tent. Lucy followed. They headed directly to the bar. Art pointed them out to Julie, who smiled and went over to ask them to join her and Art. It was easy to see that their relationship had changed since Art had seen them last. Julie picked up on the vibe, too. She grinned. It was no secret to her that Lucy had wanted Peter for a while and that Peter was open to the possibility. It was just a question of when the two of them would quit pretending that they weren't interested in each other.

"Where the hell you been, man? I been waiting for you for a while," Art ribbed. "Me an' Julie been wonderin' what the hell happened, right Julie?"

"That's right, Art."

"We had some business to attend to," answered Lucy.

"Some pleasant business, I bet," said Art.

"Yep." Peter looked at Art and grinned. "Malcolm or Jeremy been around?"

"No, I ain't seen 'em," said Art.

The four sat at the table for a while, drinking and talking. Every once in a while someone they knew would stop and talk for a few minutes. The fate of Jeremy and Malcolm lingered in the back of each of their minds. What were those dumb asses gonna do next? The beer continued to flow.

"How's your mom liking Maryland, Art?" asked Peter.

"I think she might stay. It's less urban than KC and she likes the minister over at the Zion Church. That's good enough for her."

"And she's near her boys," teased Lucy.

"Yeah. 'Cept Malcolm's givin' her gray hairs."

"I'm sure you gave her your share."

"Oh yeah. She spent a lot of extra time in church when I was doing my wine and crap shooting gig. She knew it was trouble every which way if for no other reason than the police didn't like no uppity brothers. But it was nothing compared to Malcolm's dad. One night he just went freakin' crazy on everyone who he played around with. It wasn't over nothing but a few bucks, but Malcolm Sr. lost it. I agree with Mom who thinks it was the stress of the war finally catchin' up with him. That, and this fine little conky hair bitch he was seein'. That little girl wasn't nothing but 16 at the most and she played all these older guys offa each other. Them dumb boys was only thinkin' with their dicks, which meant she had the advantage. Sweet little 16…oh my my."

"Do you want her to stay, Art?" asked Julie.

"Yeah. We'd have to find a bigger place, but Mom said she'd sell her house in KC and we could find a place out in the country a bit as long as I drove her to church. Malcolm could use her around, too, even though he don't know it."

"Hey Art, who won that ball game you was watching?" asked Peter.

"Baltimore. 5 - 3."

"I tell you Cleveland ain't goin' nowhere. It's Boston all the way."

"Shit, that racist place. Kids can't even go to school without gettin' spit on."

"It's racist everywhere."

"Yeah. You right. But Black kids ain't gettin' spit on in Snowdon for goin' to school like they is in Boston." For the past year or so, the papers had been full of news about attacks by whites on poor black kids who were being bused into poor white neighborhoods in Boston.

Jeremy and Rock rode their bikes into the woods off Route 216. They were now about a mile from Samson's place. A dirt road without a name would bring them to his driveway, which was really just a couple ruts in the dirt from his truck. They were dressed in dark clothes and wore Chuck Taylor sneakers. The plan was to try all the windows in Samson's house until they found an open one. Then Jeremy would climb in since he was the smaller of the two. He would go directly to the bathroom and use a crowbar to smash open the cabinet under the sink where Samson kept most of his stash. Then they would get the hell out of there. Jeremy had only been inside the house once, but Rock was a regular visitor and had drawn a rough sketch of the house's inside layout. Jeremy was pretty confident that he could find the herb and get out quickly. Of course, the entire plan assumed that Samson really was out of town and neither his dogs or a friend were staying at the house. Otherwise, the two young men did not have an alternate plan.

They were really near Samson's driveway, now. They put their bikes into the woods as silently as they possibly could and crept into the woods along the road. Soon they were at Samson's driveway. Still no barking dogs. That was a good sign. The two continued to sneak towards the house. The distance was perhaps 200 yards. No trucks or cars in the driveway or in front of the building. Still no barking dogs. Jeremy and Rock ran with their heads down towards the back of the house. They tried one window. No go. Then another. It went up about halfway. Samson must have had some kind of locking mechanism on the window. Still, it was open enough for Jeremy to squeeze in. Rock held him up and pushed him in. Jeremy stood up inside the room where he had landed and stuck his arm out the window. Rock handed him the crowbar. Jeremy thought about his location and that of the bathroom for a minute, recalling the sketch Rock had drawn. Then he tiptoed towards his destination. In the dark. He found the bathroom without any trouble. He crawled towards the cabinet and pulled on the lock, just in case Samson had left it open. Jeremy couldn't believe his luck when he discovered the padlock was not secure. He quickly lifted it off the latch and opened the doors. Just as quickly, he found two garbage bags. Opening the first one, he saw several large baggies of herb. That must be divided into quarter-pounds for sale thought Jeremy. I'll leave that one alone. He opened the other garbage bag and saw a brick of weed that was partially broken up. Estimating what he assumed was a little more than a quarter-pound, he pulled a plastic bag from his pants pocket and stuffed it with the weed in his hand. Then he returned everything back to where he had found it, trying to make it look completely undisturbed. He closed the doors to the cabinet and put the padlock back into the latch. Not sure whether to lock it or not, he decided to lock it. Then he left the same way he came in. Once outside, Rock pulled the window shut and the two walked quickly back towards their bikes. Once they had left the woods, they headed back to Rock's parents' house

When they were back in Rock's room, Rock took out his scales and measured out four ounces for Malcolm. To their joy, Jeremy and Rock discovered they still had at least another half ounce for themselves.

3

Malcolm pushed the MFSB 8-track into the system he had just had installed in the dash. The sweet sounds of "The Sound of Philadelphia" filled the interior of his Pontiac Sunbird. He bought the car after his second month working for his uncle Art at that honky motherfucker's pancake house. The only thing that made it cool was Art, Peter and a couple of the chicks they had working as waitresses. Otherwise, it was just like the army. Lots of crackers coming in and telling him what to do. His uncle and his cousin Jimmy could deal with the shit, but they was from a different generation that grew up playing like they liked white people even though they thought most of 'em was better off dead. Not Malcolm though. And that little peckerwood Jeremy thinking he can take my money and use it for his own shit. I just don't play it that way and he's gonna find that out. Fuck Art and his warnings about the police in this town. They white just like most cops and they don't like us black folk. How is that different from Kansas City?

Malcolm put the car into reverse, backed out of his parking space in front of the apartment he shared with his uncle and now his great-aunt, put it into first and drove off. His first stop would be the liquor store to pick up a pint of rum. Once he did that, it was off to Baltimore. He liked the idea that there might be some nice ladies down that way just lookin' for somebody to spend some money and lovin' on them. He loved cruising on a weekday night. Lots of cars were out, especially since it was so damn hot, but none of them seemed to be going anywhere special. Fuck, this tape is too mellow. Where's that Sly tape? Thank ya falettinme be myself, fuck yeah. Malcolm lit up a reefer he had rolled and drew long. The smoke felt good in his lungs and head. Traffic was light and it looked like he'd be at his bro' Antoine's crib in less than an hour.

On to Pratt Street and past the harbor which always looks so cool, then get over to Central Ave. Now I just got to remember which one of these streets is one way so's I can get over to South Chapel. There we go. What's them pigs doin' up there? Just a traffic stop. Cool. I'll just drive on by. Finished that joint back by Saint Denis or whatever that place is called.

Malcolm found a place to park, secured his car

and walked the half block to Antoine's place. Folks were sitting on the steps drinking and talking. Antoine wasn't with them. His little sister Karin saw Malcolm coming and ran up to him. She wasn't but ten years old and had a kid's crush on most of Antoine's friends, especially Malcolm.

"Hi Malcolm," she jumped up on him and gave him a hug. "Antoine's inside with my cousin and Leah. They waitin' for you." Malcolm put her down. The other kids on the steps started teasing Karin about Malcolm being her boyfriend as kids do.

"Thanks sweetie. See ya later." Malcolm went inside the rowhouse. Once inside, he found Antoine and two nice looking women sitting back drinking wine and listening to Harold Melvin and the Blue Notes. After greeting Antoine, Malcolm sat down and Antoine introduced the women.

"This here's Leah," said Antoine, pointing to a small women with a four or five inch high afro, a gold African style wraparound dress and blue platform shoes. Her skin was a fine mellow brown and her body just curved when and where you wanted it to. Malcolm took her hand and kissed it. Although she knew it was just a jive show off kind of thing, Leah giggled and sat back down on the couch.

"And this here is my cousin Marion." Antoine introduced the other woman, who was every bit as beautiful as Leah, except maybe six inches taller. She was wearing a leather skirt that showed most of her long ebony legs and a black halter top. Malcolm took her hand and kissed it, as well. Then everyone sat down. Malcolm pulled the rum he had purchased out of his back pocket and asked Antoine for some glasses.

"Shit, you know where they at, brother. Go get them yourself." Malcolm laughed and got up. He came back with two more glasses.

"This is all I could find," he wiped the dust from them with his shirttail. "Who wants some rum?"

Leah finished her wine and gave Malcolm her glass. Antoine got up and went to the kitchen. He returned with a bottle of RC Cola. Malcolm poured a couple fingers of rum into the glass. Leah took the RC from Antoine and topped off the drink. Malcolm followed suit. Marion was satisfied with her current drink.

Leah raised her glass. "To Kareem and his new team."

Malcolm looked at her, puzzled. "What you mean? His new team?"

"The Bucks traded him, man. Ain't you heard?"

"No man. To who?"

"The Lakers. The Bucks got Elmore Smith, Brian Winters and a couple draft picks."

"Jabbar is back in LA. How about that?" Malcolm clinked his glass and took a drink.

"I wonder what he thinks about the Muslims

changin' their attitude 'bout white folks?" said Marion. "I read in the paper today that Brother Elijah's son Wallace said they ain't devils no more."

"Shit, some of them always gonna be devils," laughed Leah.

"That's for damn sure," agreed the others.

"I'm more of a Panther supporter myself," said Leah. "They just had more style."

"And now they all dead or in jail," said Antoine. "That's where their style got them."

"That's fuckin' J. Edgar and the rest of them pigs." Leah took another sip from her glass. She leaned back on the couch and hummed along to the music.

"I work with this white dude who says the same thing," said Malcolm. "He used to hang with some Panthers over in Germany when he was over there. There's this brother who works with us who's a Muslim and him and this white guy are always arguing politics like that. I think they both a little crazy. The Muslim brother is on work-release. That's where he joined the Muslims. He's one big motherfucker."

"What's he in for?" asked Marion.

"Armed robbery. He's always telling the younger brothers that it's a dumb way to go. He got ten years and 35,000 dollars. Like he tells it, that's only 3500 bucks a year, which ain't shit."

"He's got a point there," Marion noted. Her

drink was gone. She took the bottle of wine off the table near the couch and poured herself another glass. "You got any dance music here, Antoine?"

"Is Richard Nixon a crook? How 'bout some Ohio Players? That'll get your body shakin'." Antoine walked over to his record collection, pulled the Ohio Players' record Fire out of the stack and put it on the turntable. The opening bass line of the title track boomed out of the speakers. Marion began to dance. She pulled Malcolm up off the couch and the two got to work. Leah poured herself another drink. Antoine did the same. By the time the album had shifted into the third song, "Runnin' From the Devil," Leah and Antoine were up and dancin' too. After that song Malcolm sat down and Marion took a spot on his lap. She gave him a little kiss and picked up her drink. It was their turn to watch Leah and Antoine for a song or two.

Soon, the album side was repeating itself and it looked like each woman had paired off for the evening. The drinks continued to go down and a couple joints were smoked. A couple hours later, Malcolm was with Marion in one bedroom and Leah and Antoine were in the other. The Ohio Players album played side one over and over. The kids and neighbors on the stoop had gone home long ago. It didn't look like Malcolm would be going to the carnival after all.

"Hey, baby. Wake up." Marion rolled over on her stomach and caressed Malcolm's chest. "Your skin is so fine." He opened his eyes and they made love again. It was late the next morning and the sun was filtering through the blinds. Little beads of sweat glistened on their bodies. His body told him to go back to sleep but he felt like he should get up and find that little sucker Jeremy. Marion put her head under the sheets and kissed his navel. She ran her fingers through his hair.

"Just like a lamb's," she said.

Malcolm gently moved her head away and sat up. He stretched his arms and got out of bed. Marion sat up and leaned back on a couple pillows while watching Malcolm get dressed.

"Can I see you tonight, Malcolm?" Malcolm looked over at this fine woman. She was almost perfect. He couldn't believe his luck.

"I gotta work 'til 11."

"I'll come and get you in my car as long as Leah don't mind staying here with Antoine."

What else can I do but say okay, thought Malcolm. I'd be a fool to do anything else.

"All right. Maybe you can stay at my place if you don't feel like driving back here that late." Malcolm finished dressing and sat back down on the bed. Marion leaned over and kissed him. Malcolm ran his hands down her breasts, stomach and thighs. Then he got up to go and find Antoine, who was supposed to come with him back to Snowdon and then take Malcolm's car to the shop for new brakes.

"See ya later, Marion."

Antoine was already up and waiting to leave. After a cup of coffee, he and Malcolm got in the car and headed out. After they were out of the city and on Route 1, Malcolm found a roach in the ashtray and lit it. He passed it to Antoine, who declined.

"Antoine, I need your help today," began Malcolm. "I gotta get some weed or my money back from this little white guy. He's had my cash for over two weeks and keeps hiding whenever I'm around. I think he spent it."

"So what do you want me to do? Kick his ass? You know that ain't my thing."

Antoine was about the most non-violent person Malcolm had ever known. He'd even convinced his draft board to give him conscientious objector status—something they hardly ever did for black folks.

"No, man. Just stand next to me when we go to his house. It's not no problem really. He's a skinny little guy and his girlfriend is really cool."

"I can do that." Antoine turned on the radio. It was a hard rock station. He was the only brother Malcolm ever met who liked that kind of music. If Malcolm was right, this band was Deep Purple. "Smoke On the Water" was the name of the song. Shit, that was scary, thought Malcolm, I'm learning the white boys' music. Antoine was singing loud as he could…"Fire in the sky…" That's one crazy ass brother. He definitely had his own agenda and screw everyone else if they couldn't dig that. He worked as a delivery guy for some bakery and played bass in a rock band on the weekends. The band usually played in some little dive near Towson State College a little north of Baltimore. Antoine was often the only black face in the joint. The college kids were pretty cool, though. In fact, Antoine probably got more tail than the rest of the band combined. They played a gig at a bar in Snowdon once, but the redneck kids just weren't ready for a black rocker unless his name was Jimi Hendrix. The whole night was one long fuckin' fight for the band. They ended up splittin' without getting their money from the door. Every time Antoine went to the bar some fat redneck punk would call him nigger. Antoine, being mellow, just ignored them—let 'em wallow in their own ignorance was his take on it—but his band mates got tired of it and started throwin' glasses of beer at the fools. That's when the fighting began. An hour later the show was over and Snowdon proved its backward-ness once again. He could play the bass, though.

They were passing the Howard Johnson's in Snowdon. That meant Malcolm would be home in about ten minutes. He looked at his watch. It was right around 1:30 in the afternoon. Cool, that meant he had another hour before he had to go to work. Antoine stopped at the light at the intersection of Montgomery and Route 1. He turned down the radio.

"Hey Malcolm. How did you like my cousin? She's a hot one, huh?" Antoine loved to tease Malcolm about women. He always said that if black folk could get red, Malcolm would be the color of a fire engine when you talked about his girls.

"Man, did she take me away," said Malcolm. That's the best I ever had I think. "Don't tell her I said that, though."

"Gotta be cool. That's my Malcolm."

"Shit, yeah. She wants to hang out again tonight. Hell, she even offered to come and get me after work. I told her she should stay at my crib if you and Leah can get along."

"Oh yeah, we can get along." Antoine pulled into the parking lot of Malcolm's apartment complex. He found a spot and parked. "Should I come up while you get ready. Then we can go see that white boy?"

"Yeah. Sure. He's probably at work so we can just go there once I get cleaned up some."

"Cool." They got out of the car and went to Malcolm's apartment. Auntie Grace was sitting on the couch reading *Jet*.

"Hi Malcolm. How was your night?"

"Really good, Auntie. Where's Art?"

"He's with that boy Peter. They said they would see you at work."

Malcolm went to the bathroom to wash up. Antoine sat down in the kitchen. Five minutes later, Malcolm came out with a clean set of clothes.

"Let's go Antoine. See you Auntie."

"Good bye, Miss Grace," said Antoine.

"Bye, boys."

Antoine and Malcolm left the apartment and went out to the car. They got in and Antoine started up the engine.

"Where we goin'?" he asked.

"To my job. Jeremy should still be there."

"Oh. So the white boy got a name."

"As long as he got my weed or my money he got one," answered Malcolm.

It wasn't but a two minute drive to the pancake house. Antoine pulled in to a parking space and stopped the car. Both men got out and went in the rear door of the restaurant, where Jeremy was finishing up sweeping the floor. He looked up and held up his hand, as if to say don't worry. Malcolm stood there with Antoine behind him.

"What's up, Jeremy? You got something for me?" asked Malcolm, as menacingly as he knew how.

"Yeah. Hold on." Jeremy put down the broom and walked quickly back to the staff locker room. Malcolm and Antoine followed him. Jeremy reached in his locker and pulled out a brown shopping bag. He handed it to Malcolm. Malcolm opened up the top and looked in. He was immediately struck by the sweet smell of the contents. Inside were four baggies, each with four or five fingers of very red weed in them. He smiled and Jeremy sat down on the bench at one end of the room. Malcolm closed the door to the locker room, set the shopping bag down on the bench, reached in and opened one of the baggies. He pulled a bud out of the baggies and held it to his nose, pinching it all the while. This shit smelled really good.

"Thanks, Jeremy. Maybe it was worth the wait," said Malcolm. He stuck out his hand and Jeremy shook it. Malcolm gave him a bud and Jeremy left after sticking it in his pocket. After Jeremy was gone, Malcolm took two baggies for himself and gave Antoine the shopping bag with the remainder of the weed. Malcolm stuffed the baggies in his pants pockets.

"That was easy," said Antoine, relieved that nothing physical had gone down. "I gotta get your car to the shop man. See ya this evenin'?"

"I don't know. I tol' you Marion might come on down here to stay. If I ain't there by midnight, I ain't gonna be there 'til tomorrow. Make sure you give her real good directions to get here. All right? You gonna be able to sell that herb?"

"Shit. No problem. I could smell it as soon as I entered this room."

"Yeah. It's good," agreed Malcolm. Antoine left out the back door. Malcolm put on his apron and cook's hat and went into the kitchen, stopping by the soda machine on the way.

Lucy was putting in an order when Malcolm reached the galley. She smiled and said hi. Peter was already cooking. It seemed to Malcolm that there was a little electricity between Peter and Lucy that hadn't been there before. He took his spot next to the grill.

"Hey Malcolm. How you doin'?" asked Peter.

"Good. Man. Good."

"I want to buy some of that weed you got from Jeremy," whispered Lucy from where she stood preparing salads for her current customers. "It smells like God grew it Herself."

"No problem, babe. Talk to me before you get out of here."

Lucy took the salads to the table she was waiting on. Malcolm flipped the steak on the grill as Peter passed him the platter it would be going on. He read the next order and threw another steak on the flame. Then he moved a couple of steps to the right, dipped the basting brush in the can of melted butter, painted the inside of the egg pan and quickly cracked three eggs into it. Then he set the pan on the electric range. He grabbed the tongs, and took both steaks off the grill—one was rare and the other medium well. As soon as the eggs were done he slid them onto the plate with the rare steak and set both plates up on the ledge. He rang the bell, called Lucy's number and began cooking the next order.

"When's Art coming in?" asked Malcolm.

""'Round five or so. He was pretty hung over. I told him I had some desoxyn but he wasn't interested so I told him to sleep in. I'm here until 5:00 today, anyhow," answered Peter.

"Why's that? Don't you usually leave at 3:00?"

"Yeah, but I told the bossman I would work some extra hours until he trained that new cook. I need the overtime anyhow." Peter reached for the glass of ice water he kept under the frying grill and took a long swallow. He offered the glass to Malcolm.

"Nah, thanks. I'll just get one of the girls to get me one of my own. Hey Lucy, can you get me some ice water, please?" Lucy took a glass, filled it with ice and water and handed it to Malcolm.

"Thanks, babe," smiled Malcolm. "Why you so happy girl? Somebody take care of you last night?"

Peter blushed. Malcolm noticed. "Oh I see," he said. "Good for y'all. It's about time. Shit."

Jeremy walked into the galley to tell the two cooks he was leaving. Rock was supposed to show up soon. In the meantime, Peter would wash the dishes unless Malcolm really needed his help in the kitchen.

"See ya, Jeremy," said Peter.

"Yeah, later," said Malcolm.

Art arrived at the pancake house around 4:30

that afternoon. He went up to the office to do some bookkeeping and came down dressed in his cook's whites. He was supposed to interview a high school girl for a waitress position and was waiting for her in the section nearest the galley, which was currently closed to customers. While he waited, he joked with Lucy and Peter, who were taking a quick break from washing dishes. Both he and Lucy were scheduled to leave at 5:00. Art cooked with Malcolm until 10:30 or so, when Malcolm finished up his prep work in time to clock out at 11:00. Julie was scheduled to replace Lucy at 5:00. Usually there was another waitress to help during the dinner hour, but she had recently quit to move to California. That was why Art hoped to hire the girl he was interviewing, if she showed up.

"Where's Rock?" asked Art. "Wasn't he supposed to be here at 3:00?"

"Yeah. Jeremy said he was comin' in," answered Peter. "But he ain't shown up yet."

"Punkass son of a bitch." Just as he said this, Rock showed up. He apologized for being late and went to work immediately after putting on an apron. Peter relaxed, knowing that he was through for the day. Lucy went out on the floor to take care of her last couple of tables.

"So you gonna keep your thing goin' with her?" asked Art.

"We'll see what happens. It has its merits," said Peter, his blood rising as he remembered their recent lovemaking.

"She's a good lady, but you know that," Art confided. Shit, he thought, if he had someone like her, he'd hold on no matter where the ride took him. But he was 45, not 25. Things looked different to him than they did to Peter and the rest of these young bucks around here. He stood up. It was almost time to go to work.

Peter reached in his pocket and pulled out a small vial. He opened it, reached in and handed a small white pill to Art.

"Just in case you feel like you need it," he said. "It's a Desoxyn. It'll keep you going all night and let you sleep in the morning." Art had to work until 5:00 AM.

"Thanks." Art put the pill in his pants pocket.

Peter went upstairs to the employee locker room to change. While he was doing so, Malcolm came up. He was taking a break. After lighting a Kool, he reached in his pocket and handed Peter one of the baggies of pot.

"This is for Lucy," he said. "She owes me fifty bucks. Art said you could give it to her."

"Cool. Let me pay you now and I'll get her money later." Peter put the weed in his pocket. He gave Malcolm the money. Malcolm left the room. As he left, Lucy entered. She walked over to Peter and kissed him.

"What you doin' after work, Peter?" She stuck her hands in his back pockets.

"Nothin' in particular."

"You want to come over to my place and take a shower?" she asked. "Then we can smoke some of that weed and see what happens."

Peter knew he wasn't going to say no. He finished dressing, grabbed her hand and the two of them left the restaurant. They got in Lucy's Datsun and drove to her place.

Malcolm finished his cigarette and returned to the galley. Art was working on an order of pancakes and eggs. He nodded to Malcolm as he slid the eggs onto a plate.

"How were the cousins, little brother?" Art loved calling Malcolm this, even though they weren't related in that way.

"Only one of 'em came, but she brought a friend," answered Malcolm. "They were both fine. Real fine. Maybe I'll introduce you to the one who's comin' to pick me up from work tonight. Her name's Marion."

"Like the lady in Robin Hood?"

"I guess," said Malcolm, remembering something about a Lady Marion from a cartoon he saw once. Art was always comin' up with comparisons like that. Where he picked up all that literary shit was anybody's guess, especially since he quit school in eighth grade. He did read a hell of a lot. "How was the carnival?"

"Same ol' honky shit. But it was fun," said Art. "Lucy and Peter succumbed to their desire."

"You mean they finally jumped each other?"

"That's what I mean," said Art. "Couldn't you tell?"

"I thought Peter was looking pretty happy, but wasn't sure why. Good for them."

"That's what everyone been sayin'," said Art. "So you got a lady comin' to pick you up tonight? You goin' back to Baltimore? Auntie Grace wanted to see you."

"I seen her earlier today. I might stay here tonight," answered Malcolm. "My car's in the shop, anyhow. I'm supposed to pick it up Saturday morning. What's today?"

"Wednesday." Art took three pancakes from the grill and placed them on a plate. "Auntie wants us to cook for the church picnic on Saturday. I told her I could help out during the afternoon."

"Oh shit. Hanging out with a bunch of holy rollers. Just how I want to spend my first Saturday off in a month. She didn't already tell that preacher that I'd be there, did she?"

"Nah. She just gon' lay a guilt trip on you is all. That's worse."

Malcolm knew exactly what Art meant. The fact that he was twenty years younger than Art only meant that she had perfected her guilt trip routine on him. Perfected it so damn well that Malcolm knew he'd be cookin' some chicken on Saturday afternoon for the church folk. He might as well put a positive spin on it and hope he could get out of there in time to do some serious partying with Antoine and the girls. He threw two more steaks on the charbroiler and thought about Marion coming at 11:00.

4

It's hard to believe that it's Friday, thought Malcolm as he took off his apron and cook's whites. The weekend was finally here. He splashed some cologne under his arms and began dressing in his street clothes. Marion was supposed to be here any minute. They had spent every night together since they met. The Tuesday over at Antoine's and the next two at Art and Malcolm's crib. Art was his usual crazy but charming self around Marion and made her feel right at home. Auntie Grace was pretty cool, too. She even invited her to the church picnic which, just like he figured, he was gonna be cookin' at. Marion hadn't accepted Auntie's invitation but she hadn't turned it down, neither. Her and Leah were supposed to go back home to Camden on Sunday. Something 'bout Marion havin' to testify in court for her daddy on Monday. Guess he hit the landlord upside the head when he refused to fix the gas heater and the fumes nearly killed Leah's niece. So Malcolm wanted to get as much of Marion as he could these next couple nights.

Things had mellowed out between Jeremy, Rock

and Malcolm since the weed had been delivered. They weren't friends or nothin', they never were. Still, it made work easier when any combination of the three were working the same shift. And that weed sure was good. Peter called it two-toke. He meant that it only took two hits to get you high and three to get you wasted. He was right. Peter, Marion, Lucy, Art and Malcolm had partied over at Peter's on Thursday after work. Peter had this four-foot bong that just kicked your ass with regular Mexican weed. With this red shit, it was like a rocketship to your head. Peter was playing some Pink Floyd on his turntable and it was tripping everyone out. Finally, Art asked him to change to something less spacey. Malcolm figured Art was losing it or something. The weed kicked ass.

Malcolm was finished changing. He made sure he had his wallet and keys and went downstairs to wait for Marion. She was already there talking with Art in the section of the restaurant closed off to patrons. Marion pulled a pint of vodka out of her purse and handed it to Art. He twisted off the cap and poured a good portion of the bottle into his glass of Sprite and winked at Marion. Malcolm leaned over and kissed her. She squeezed his thigh.

"Hi baby," she said. "You ready?" She stood up and took his hand.

Malcolm grinned and said goodbye to Art. The two of them went out the door to Marion's car. The got inside and began kissing and grabbing each other's bodies. Malcolm reached under her shirt and Marion unbuttoned his Levis. They pulled away from their kissing to look in each other's eyes. Then they started to kiss again. Suddenly, the passenger door opened. Malcolm turned around, thinking it was Art being a smart ass. It wasn't. It was a big mean looking white guy with long black hair, a beard and a knife in his right hand.

"Hey fucker," said the white guy, low and menacing. "Let me have some of the nigger bitch."

"Fuck you." Malcolm bristled. Marion began to fumble with her car key, trying to find the ignition switch. The white guy looked at her and shook his head.

"Don't do that beautiful. I'll kill you if you do." He held up the knife. The blade was a good six inches. "I just want to ask your boyfriend a couple questions. If he gives me the right answers, you all can go."

Malcolm tried to slam the car door on the white guy's legs but they were too big and too much of them were in the way. He wondered if he should yell and if this fucker had any backup.

"What you want, motherfucker?" asked Malcolm.

"I heard you sellin' some killer red weed. Is that true?"

"What's it to you if I am?" Challenged Malcolm.

"I done got ripped off some red weed on Tuesday

night. Do you know anything about that?

"Shit, man. I don't even know who the fuck you are. I bought it from somebody, in case you want to know. Does that mean you gon' get the fuck out of my face now?"

"My name is Samson. Don't forget it black boy."

Malcolm jumped as if to punch Samson. As he did so, Samson slashed the upholstery on the seat directly behind Malcolm's head. Marion gasped.

"What you want, you white motherfucker?" she yelled. "My man ain't the one who ripped you off. He was fuckin' me in Baltimore on Tuesday night. Get the hell away from my car and us'n, you hear?"

"Who sold that weed to you then, cookie?" Samson asked Malcolm as he backed off a little. Marion had found the ignition and turned the key. "Was it that skinny little white boy whose stepdaddy fucked him in the ass? Who was it? I'm gonna find out and when I do I'm gonna kill the fuckin' thief. You tell him that. And if it was you, you one dead nigger!" Malcolm said nothing. He shrugged his shoulders and looked away. Marion pulled away and screeched out of the parking lot. She pulled on to Route 1 and headed north towards Baltimore.

"Slow down, baby." Malcolm said. "Samson ain't the only racist in this town. The police right there with him." So that's Samson, thought Malcolm. He is one mean and ugly son of a bitch, for sure. I feel bad for Jeremy if he did steal from that dumbfuck. And that fucker is Rock's hero. That adds some perspective. He nodded his head, thinking of some of the shit Rock said around him and Art when he thought they weren't listening. The car was out of Snowdon now. Marion, who had been gripping the wheel tightly, relaxed a little. Malcolm reached over and stroked her thigh. She smiled.

When they got to Baltimore, Marion stopped at a liquor store. The two of them went in and bought a bottle of wine, a fifth of rum and some RC. With their party materials in hand they got back in the car and finished the drive to Antoine's. He and Leah were already feeling good when Marion and Malcolm entered. As soon as the door was closed, Malcolm took the bottles from the bag, went to the kitchen for some glasses and came back into the living room. He poured a rum and RC for himself and a glass of wine for Marion. Then he sat on the floor next to Marion. She was already relating the run-in with Samson to their friends.

"...Then the fucker stabbed my passenger seat right behind Malcolm. I was ready to kill him right there. Malcolm got ready to jump in his face again. Then I jumped in his shit. Fortunately, just about then I found the ignition and put the key in. Then we tore out of that place."

"Didn't look back 'til we got to Baltimore," agreed Malcolm. He took a long drink.

"I know what you all need," said Antoine. He walked over to his record collection, shuffled through the first twenty or so albums and found the one he was looking for. He removed it from its sleeve and put it on the turntable. Within seconds the sound of Brother Jack McDuff's Hammond organ came through the speakers.

"All right. Perfect!" shouted Malcolm, making Marion jump a little. "Brother Jack McDuff doing some Down Home Style. I love this fuckin' music."

Marion smiled and settled into the grooves. Malcolm reached into his shirt pocket and pulled out a joint. He lit it and passed it on to Antoine. Marion lay her head on Malcolm's lap. Leah took the joint from Antoine. He ran his hand through her fro.

"This weed does kick some ass." Antoine exhaled the smoke slowly and tried not to cough. "I wonder if that white kid did steal it."

"It makes sense," said Malcolm. "But how the hell did that motherfucker know? Unless Lucy smoked some with someone who knows that Samson asshole."

"Didn't you say Jeremy—wasn't that that skinny boy's name—hung out with some guy named Rock?" asked Marion. "Maybe he snitched Jeremy out to Samson."

"But they bros, man," said Malcolm.

"Yeah, but that Samson dude is a mean mother. He scares me."

"Good point." The joint was back to Malcolm. He took another toke. Things were pretty mellow again. "I used to listen to this album in the army every Goddamn night. This older brother with a shaved head turned me on to it. It's about the only good thing that happened to me while I was wearing that baggy green suit. When I seen it in Antoine's record collection I knew we was meant to be tight."

"Do you think he'll kill Jeremy if he finds out he did rip him off?" asked Antoine, bringing the conversation back to Samson.

"Shit. I wouldn't put it past him. I wonder if I should tell Jeremy."

"It ain't your business, baby," said Marion.

"But Jeremy don't deserve to die just 'cause he's stupid. He may be an asshole but his lady friend is cool. She's a good friend of Art and Lucy's. Guess I'll mention it to her when I go back to work. Meanwhile, Jeremy must know he's gotta lay low."

"You know…" said Antoine, thoughtfully. "I think that Rock was tryin' to set you up. Listen to me. He must know that Jeremy ripped off this Samson asshole and he's tryin' to cover for him since they brothers, you know. So he told Samson that you done a B & E at his place and stole the weed. That way he's hopin' Samson don't look any further and find out it was Jeremy who stole some of his stash. Does that make sense?"

"And that Samson is dumb enough and racist

enough to believe it was me, even if the evidence showed otherwise," Malcolm thought aloud. "He'd much rather kill a black man than anybody white." Malcolm leaned back against the wall.

The party continued until the rum and wine were gone.

5

The sun was beating down on his face when Malcolm woke up Saturday morning. He looked at his watch. 10:30. Not bad. Where was Marion? Funny how it only took a few days of waking up with her there to miss her when she wasn't there. Just as he was becoming completely aware of his surroundings, she walked in the room. She was carrying a cup of coffee and a Baltimore Sun newspaper. She took off her robe and gave Malcolm the paper and coffee. He set them both on the floor beside the bed and reached out for her waist. She moved toward him without hesitation and sat down on top of him. They pulled the covers away.

"Forget the newspaper," said Malcolm. "And the coffee. You my wakeup, Marion." They ran their hands over each other's flesh and began kissing.

Half an hour later, the coffee was cold. Malcolm picked up the cup and drank it anyhow. He took the first section of the paper and began to read it when he remembered his Auntie Grace.

"Oh shit. I gotta go cook for Auntie's picnic, baby. You wanna come? You don't gotta. It won't hurt my feelins' none." Malcolm was up and dressing. He was supposed to be at the church yard by 1:30 and he had to pick up his car from the shop. He could just make it if he left now.

"I think I'll stay here Malcolm. Me and Leah gotta get ready to go back home tomorrow. When you gon' be back here?" She reached over and caressed his thigh.

"I be back aroun' 6:00 or so. I'll bring some chicken and potato salad for us all. Tell Antoine I'll bring some for his mom and sister too. I gotta go."

Malcolm bent over and kissed her breasts and lips. Then he left. The auto shop was three bus stops away. He got there in fifteen minutes. His car was ready to go, so he paid the mechanic and headed towards Snowdon. He should make it there with time to spare as long as traffic wasn't too bad. He reached for a tape and put it in the player. MFSB again. That's okay. They mellow. He thought about tokin' up some herb but then remembered he was gonna be with Auntie Grace's church folk all afternoon. They didn't mind the cook takin' a nip or two but the weed scared the shit outta them folks. He decided against the smoke.

As he drove down Route 1 towards Snowdon he tried to put together this whole mess with Jeremy and the weed. Maybe Jeremy had ripped off that Samson mofo. But if he had, how? He never talked about going over to the cat's house, like Rock did all the time.

With Rock it was always, Samson got this or Samson done this. It was like Samson was the greatest person on the planet. Course that proved what Malcolm thought all along. Rock was a stupid kid who was potentially dangerous mostly because he was so stupid. Art had told him when Malcolm first moved to Maryland that Rock couldn't be trusted. Shit, said Art, he'd steal his Mom's last fin if he wanted some whiskey. Plus, he was so fuckin' prejudiced. Like he was better than black folk just cause he was white. Out in KC we called them type of white folks peckerwoods. When we was being nice, that is, thought Malcolm. So maybe Antoine is right. Maybe he did try and lay the rip-off at my feet to cover for Jeremy. But, still, how would Jeremy know where Samson kept his stash? Or any of that kind of shit? Unless someone who knew Samson better told him. He knew it wasn't really his problem, but Samson had made it his problem by threatening him last night. The tape was starting to play over again. Malcolm was in Snowdon and on his way to 8th Street. Auntie Grace's church was five blocks away. He looked for a place to park when he got within a block. There were a lot of cars in the street and the church parking lot. Once he parked, he got out of the car and locked it. Then he headed towards the church. Grace saw him and waved a big hello. He walked over to where she stood with the minister and three other men. He kissed her cheek and said hello.

"This is my nephew Malcolm," she began. "Malcolm, this is Reverend Moore, Mr. Mathias, Mr. Jefferson, and Mr. Smith."

Malcolm shook the men's hands.

"My son used to work with you down there at the pancake house," said Mr. Smith. "Levon? By the way, you can call me Anthony."

"I remember Levon. What's he doing now?"

"He workin' construction in DC. My uncle got him a job with one of them companies building the Metro." The Metro was the subway system that was supposed to come to the DC area some day. It was already years behind schedule.

"That must be some good money he's makin'," said Malcolm.

"I hope so. They got him working fifty to sixty hours a week. Keep Levon out of trouble anyhow."

"Don't give him no time for the ladies, though," joked the man called Jefferson.

"With all due respect to Malcolm's aunt," said Anthony Smith. "He better off given his track record." Levon had fathered two kids before he graduated from high school.

"These men are goin' to set you up at the grill, Malcolm. Whyn't you go with them?"

Malcolm left with the men. They walked towards the back of the lot that the church was situated on. The whole piece of property was around three acres, including the church and the minister's house. There were six barbecue grills lined up end to end at the back of the lot. Each grill was actually an oil drum cut in half lengthwise and then some kind of thick chicken wire was laid across the top. The fires were burning down and would be perfect for barbecuing chicken in about fifteen more minutes. There were two large top-opening coolers set back about six feet behind the grills. These coolers measured maybe eight feet long, three feet wide and three feet deep. They were painted red and were covered with Coca Cola decals. Mr. Mathias walked Malcolm back to one of the coolers and opened the top. Inside were hundreds of chicken legs on ice. There were also several small buckets of some kind of red sauce that Malcolm guessed was the barbecue. Mr. Mathias told the minister, who had come up to the grills with the others, that he would explain everything to Malcolm. With that, the minister returned to where Auntie Grace was still standing, only now she was joined by a half dozen other women around her age.

"Between you and me Malcolm," began Mr. Mathias. "I had to send the minister off to welcome his flock. This chicken is ready to go. This here sauce in the buckets is the barbecue. It ain't too hot 'cause some of the folks don't like it hot. For those who do we got Tabasco sauce on the condiment tables. Usually we keep one of these buckets full of chicken legs so's they can just soak in the sauce then when we need to throw some more on the grill they all ready. There's some brushes for the sauce too if you wanna use them. The main thing is make sure it's cooked so it's fallin' off the bone and just keep it comin'. You work in a restaurant so you know how people eat in waves. We expectin' about 200 people today so you gon' be workin'. Since that's the case, let me show you somethin' else." The other men gathered around conspiratorially. "Reach on down in the ice below the chicken. Your hand gonna freeze but what you find down there make it worth your while."

Malcolm fished around in the ice until he felt something familiar. He pulled his find up out of the ice and smiled. It was a bottle of Ballantine Ale. These old guys were funny. Funny and alright.

"Don't let the minister or the holy roller ladies find you out," warned Mr. Jefferson. "Everyone else here pretty much brings their own bottle, but them folks don't drink a drop. We got some big paper cups that say RC on the side to pour them ales in. Help yourself 'cause we appreciate your help. You let your uncle know about the drinks, too. All right?"

Malcolm nodded. He put on an apron one of the men handed him and began to place the chicken legs on the grill. Soon the air was full of barbecue smoke and the yard was filling up with people. Sometime after the first wave of chicken was eaten, somebody brought over a transistor radio. Malcolm turned the dial looking for some music. The radio was AM only, so he knew he wouldn't find much. Hey wait that was Marvin Gaye. Malcolm tuned in the station and sung along. "Make me wanna holler, throw up both my hands...." He was so involved in singing and cooking the chicken he didn't notice Art coming up behind him.

"Hey Malcolm. Wassup?" Malcolm jumped. The song ended and Art picked up the radio. "Let's find the Orioles' game. I got a bet with Peter on this one. They playing the Red Sox."

"When I left work Baltimore was up 3—0 in the first. I can taste the rum already."

"What rum?" asked Malcolm.

"The rum ol' Pete's gonna buy me after Boston loses this game."

Art was wide awake. He had already worked the morning shift at the pancake house and gone home for some drinks and smoke. Which meant he was in fine form. The rollers would be entertained. Art had a way with those types for some reason. Even though his life was the life of sin, most of them fell for his charm. Malcolm looked forward to the remaining couple of hours at the grill.

The game was in the fourth inning and Yazstremski was up with two outs. Art grabbed a bucket of sauce and a brush and began painting the chicken legs. Malcolm told him about the beer in the coolers.

"What happened to you last night after you left?" whispered Art. He didn't want the church folks to hear the conversation.

"Some crazy white boy named Samson tried to kill me is what happened," said Malcolm. "He thinks I ripped him off for that herb."

"What did you tell him?"

"I told him I didn't and to leave me the fuck alone," answered Malcolm. "Then Marion squealed outta there."

"Yeah, we heard that." Art turned up the radio, mostly to keep eavesdroppers from listening in. "Ya know, I don't think that white sucker thinks you ripped him off anymore. Jeremy was pretty fuckin' scared at work this morning. I think he did the heist and I think that's what Samson or whatever his name is thinks, too."

"We was talkin' about it last night," said Malcolm. "And came up with the theory that Rock and Jeremy did the B&E and Rock tried to lay it on me to cover Jeremy's tracks. Jeremy didn't know the guy really and Rock is over there all the time coppin' dope and cookin' up trouble with the jerk."

"And probably buildin' crosses to burn," laughed Art. Uneasily. Malcolm went into the cooler for a couple Ballantine's.

"So what you up to tonight after this gig?" asked Art. "Goin' back to Baltimore to get some more Marion?"

"Yeah. She's goin' back to Camden tomorrow. She gotta be in court next week to testify for her daddy." He took a swig from his beer. "I'm gonna leave in a half hour, Art. I gotta stop by the house and grab some clean clothes, plus I wanna get a gift for Marion."

"She comin' back?"

"I ain't asked her. I hope so."

6

Malcolm lay in bed. It was Sunday morning. He and Marion had been out dancing until 5 that morning. Then they went to Antoine's and made love like two cats in heat. Shit, he didn't even know if Antoine was home. It was gonna be hard to take time away from each other. Neither one of them was in any hurry to get up this morning even though Marion and Leah were supposed to be in Jersey by dinner-time. They could hear someone in the front room. To be honest, though, it didn't sound like Leah or Antoine. The footsteps were much smaller. Must be Antoine's little sister, Karin, thought Malcolm.

"Hey Karin!" shouted Malcolm. "Get your pretty lil tail in here, girl!"

Karin came running into the bedroom. Marion pulled the covers up over her and Malcolm. Karin sat at the end of the bed.

"Hey Malcolm! When you gonna get up? Mama gone to work and y'all sposed to be watchin' me!" She started jumping on the bed. Malcolm reached over to the floor and found his shirt. He pulled it over his head and felt around for his pants.

"I'm gettin' dressed girl. You go wake up your brother." Karin left the room. Malcolm stood up and pulled on his pants. He leaned over and kissed Marion.

"I be back with some coffee, baby," he whispered. She sat up and pulled on a robe. Malcolm left the room. He went into the kitchen and set up the percolator for coffee. While it brewed, he read the Sunday Baltimore Sun. Antoine's mom must have left it there.

"Holy shit!" he yelled. "Look at this!" Malcolm ran into the bedroom and showed Marion the newspaper. He pointed to a story beneath the fold on the front page.

Baltimore Sun

Two Brutally Murdered in Snowdon
Police Say Drugs Involved

Snowdon, Md. – A young couple were apparently murdered in their apartment Saturday night, a Prince George's County police spokesman said. The couple, both of whom were employed at the Snowdon Pancake House on Route 1 in Snowdon, were discovered by the woman's sister around 3 a.m. Sunday. The sister, Roxanne Epstein, had gone to the apartment when the woman victim failed to show up for a midnight party at their parents' house. The party was to celebrate the deceased's birthday.

The two, Jeremy Prehausen (20) and Julie Epstein (21), had been living at the apartment for eight months, according to the property manager on the complex's premises. The apartment complex is a relatively quiet development of 150 units that is located near State Highway 198 in central Snowdon. Police say that this is the first murder in the complex since it opened in 1968. Other police calls usually involve domestic quarrels.

"The bloodied bodies of the two indicate that there was an intense struggle," said the police spokes-man. "That is all the information we can release at this point. The families of the victims and the residents of Snowdon can be assured we will find the perpetrators of this crime." Off the record, police said they believed there were drugs involved. One officer said it looked like a drug deal that went terribly wrong.

Snowdon has seen an upsurge in drug-related activity in recent months. In January, a 27 year old man who belonged to the Pagans motorcycle gang was arrested for manufacturing "angel dust" or pcp on a rented farm on Contee Road in Snowdon. He was convicted and sentenced to ten years in Jessup. Two other members of the same gang were arrested in March for possession and sale of methamphetamine.

Malcolm sat down on the bed. He was stunned. Yeah, that was the word. Stunned. Should he feel responsible? Or guilty? Should he have let Jeremy know that guy was after him? Poor fuckin' Julie. Malcolm put his face in his hands and took a deep breath. Marion sat a few feet away, trying to think of something positive to say. This was truly fucked, she thought. I wonder if Samson killed them. But who else would it be? She got dressed quietly. Malcolm left the bedroom. He went into the living room and found the phone. Then he dialed Art's number. He probably knew by now and could tell Malcolm what the scene was like at the pancake house. The phone rang. Malcolm hoped Art was home. Someone at the other end picked up their phone.

"Hey, this is Art."

"Hey. What's up, Art. This is Malcolm."

"Holy shit, man. You musta heard what happened." Art was a little breathless. Malcolm could tell he was dealing with some heavy emotions.

"Yeah, man. I just read it in the paper. What's going on at the restaurant?"

"Fuckin' cops and media people all over the place. You should stay away since you ain't scheduled to work. Mr. Lewin opened up. But he shortened the hours. We only open until 6 tonight."

"It's some fucked up shit, huh?"

"Yeah. You think it was that white fucker you was tellin' me about?"

"Hell, yeah."

"You know the police gonna wanna talk to you.

When you comin' back to Snowdon?"

"Later this afternoon."

"Cool. Call before you come home. If the cops are around, you can go to the bossman's house. He said that would be okay with him." Malcolm could hear Art lighting a cigarette. He took a Kool out of his pocket and did the same.

"All right, see ya later." Malcolm hung up the phone and sat down on the living room couch. There wasn't much he could do. Just hang tight and tell the cops what happened to him and Marion was all. Marion came out of the bedroom and sat next to him. She had her suitcase with her.

"Hey, Leah girl!" she hollered into Antoine's bedroom. "Get your ass out of bed. We gotta go soon." Marion threw her legs over Malcolm's and stroked his hair.

"You gonna be all right?" she asked. Malcolm could feel that she really cared. That was cool. "I can call my daddy and tell him I can't make it."

"No, no baby," said Malcolm. "You gotta help keep your daddy outta jail. You and Leah should go on home. When you gonna come back?" He hoped it was gonna be soon.

"If I can, by the weekend. Let me give you my number." She wrote down her number on a piece of newspaper, tore it off and handed it to Malcolm. He put it in his shirt pocket. "I'll call you when I know for sure."

"Cool. I'm looking forward to it."

"Me too, baby. Me too." They sat on the couch kissing. Leah got dressed and came out into the living room. She had her bag. Antoine followed. Malcolm looked up.

"Check this out," he said, as he tossed the paper to Antoine. Antoine looked at the paper, wondering what Malcolm might be referring to. He scanned the headlines and saw the one about Snowdon. He skimmed the article and looked at Malcolm.

"That's that white boy, ain't it?"

"Yeah. Pretty fucked up, huh?"

"Holy shit. Whatcha gonna do?"

"Art told me to just hang low until tomorrow. So I'm gonna go home later on. Like after dark. I gotta work tomorrow. The pigs gonna wanna talk to me." He wasn't looking forward to the interrogation.

Marion took her legs from Malcolm's lap and stood up. Malcolm followed. He took her bag and gently pushed her and Leah towards the door. Leah gave Antoine a kiss. Malcolm followed Marion out to her car. He put her bag in the rear seat once the car was unlocked. Karin, who had been playing outside, came over. Marion gave Malcolm one more long wet kiss and got in the car. Leah threw her bag in the back seat and got in the passenger side. They pulled away. Malcolm waved goodbye for a few seconds and then went back inside. Karin skipped into the house behind him. Antoine was sitting at the kitchen table eating a bowl of Wheaties.

"Hey girl," he asked his little sister. "You hungry?"
Karin nodded.

"Malcolm can fix you somethin'. Right Malcolm?"

"What you want sweetie?" asked Malcolm. "Grilled cheese?"

"Yeah," said Karin. "With lots of pickles."

"Comin' up."

While Malcolm cooked lunch, Antoine continued reading the paper.

"Baltimore beat Boston yesterday. 3-0. Palmer did it again, man. Nothin' but zeros in the scoring column. That guy can pitch." Jim Palmer was the Orioles' star pitcher.

"Yeah, Art was listenin' to that game yesterday when we was barbecuin' the chicken. Baltimore scored all its runs in the first, right?"

"Yeah. Then nothing but pitching from both teams. I love them kind of games." Antoine poured himself another cup of coffee from the pot on the table. The coffee was pretty cold. He drank it anyway. Karin's sandwich was cooked. Malcolm put it in a small plate and gave it to her. She opened it up to see if there were enough pickles.

"Lot of pickles! Just the way I like it!" she jumped up and hugged Malcolm. "You the best, Malcolm!"

While she ate, Malcolm made himself a fried egg sandwich. When it was done, he sat down at the table to eat it. Karin finished her sandwich and stood up.

"I'm goin' back outside, Antoine," she said as she placed her empty plate in the sink.

"Don't go far, girl."

"Okay. I'll be right out front." Karin left the townhouse to play.

"Man," began Antoine. "That's some heavy shit with that Jeremy kid. I wonder what's gonna happen next."

"I ain't lookin' forward to goin' back to that restaurant, that's for sure. I don't dig the thought of talkin' to the police."

"Do you have to?" asked Antoine.

"Probably," said Malcolm. "'Cause of what happened to me and Marion on Friday night. They gonna ask me all these questions about weed and shit. Hopefully Art done cleaned up the apartment."

"Art's smart, man."

"Yeah. Good thing," agreed Malcolm. "Plus Auntie Grace ain't gonna let no pig in the house without a warrant. She learned that the hard way with Art."

"What you gonna tell the pigs?"

"I guess about that Samson trying to stab me and then threatening Jeremy. The thing is they gonna want to know what the connection is between me and them white boys. It ain't a regular practice in Snowdon for white boys to be hangin' out with brothers except when dope is involved. I'm afraid they might try to bust me on some dealin' charge or something." Malcolm finished his sandwich and began washing the frying pan. When he was done he went into the living room. Before he sat down on the couch again, he found the Brother Jack McDuff album and put it on the stereo. Antoine joined him.

"Having them ladies around sure was nice," he said.

"I wish they was still here," Malcolm added.

Rock was in a confused state. His oldest and best friend was dead and he had no real idea who killed him. Plus, he had this bad feeling that the cops were going to be hauling him in. For questioning, if nothing else. He had already decided that the only thing he would tell the cops was that Jeremy owed Malcolm money. If the cops busted Malcolm, too fuckin' bad. He hated that nigger anyhow. Sleeping with white girls and shit. Plus the first day that fucker worked at the pancake house he made Rock feel like a jerk, by making him wash the floor twice 'cause the first time Rock didn't change the water in the bucket. The worst part about it was this other kid who was working then made fun of him the rest of the week. If there was one thing Rock hated, it was being embarrassed. Especially by a nigger.

Right now, he was going to the liquor store in the shopping center. He needed a beer or two to clear his head. He really wanted to go over to Samson's but knew that he shouldn't. He had heard yesterday that Samson was looking for Jeremy after his showdown with Malcolm on Friday. When Rock told Samson on the phone that Malcolm was selling Samson's weed, he had hoped that that would end everything right there. To be honest, he didn't think Samson would even know he was ripped off, especially after Jeremy found the cabinet unlocked. Then, when Samson did discover the theft and called Rock to see if he had heard anything, Rock had to do some quick thinking. The best he could come up with when Samson told him about the rip-off was that he had heard that Malcolm had some red dope for sale. That was enough to keep Samson happy. After hearing about Samson's attack on Malcolm Friday night, though, he didn't know which way to turn, especially since he figured Malcolm told Samson about Jeremy selling Malcolm the herb. Now, Rock's primary goal was to keep Samson's suspicions away from Rock. Even if it meant Jeremy was dead because of that. That sounded cold, but survival was his goal now.

Rock saw a police car up ahead. He took a quick left onto 5th Street off of Greenhill and continued walking. Fast. He reached Montrose Avenue and took a right. Maybe he would go to Camelot Liquors instead. That way he could cross over Montrose and walk in the culvert under Route 1. That should lose the police if they were following him. He looked behind him and did not see the cruiser. He walked quickly across Montrose in between the traffic and then down 5th Street until he reached the concrete drainage ditch that turned into a culvert when it ran under 4th Street and then Route 1. He walked quickly down the concrete side and into the culvert. There hadn't been much rain in the past month or two, so the culvert itself was dry. A few tadpole skeletons were stuck to the cement. As he walked, Rock could hear the traffic on the street above him. Ten minutes later he emerged a block away from the liquor store. He walked the half block and entered the store. The clerk asked him for ID when he brought the six pack to the counter. Rock produced his license and made the purchase. The clerk bagged the beer and Rock left.

He went back into the culvert to drink. It was unlikely that the cops would find him there. That is if they were looking for him at all. He opened the first bottle and drank the beer in two long swallows. He felt better already. He repeated the same pattern with the second beer. Then he leaned back against the curved concrete pipe and watched the spiders in their webs. Three beers and an hour and a half later, he stood up and walked to the end of the culvert to piss. As he pissed, he could hear the cars and trucks driving on the road above him.

One stopped. Rock pulled his zipper up quick and walked toward the center of the culvert, hoping against hope that the car that stopped was not the police. He squatted down and hid in the shadows. A flashlight shown from the end of the culvert he had just left. He looked in that direction and saw a cop.

"Come on out of there, please," said the officer. "Slowly."

Rock stood up and began to go towards the cop. It wasn't more than two minutes and he was outside. The cop turned off his flashlight. He was from the county.

"What were you doing in there? Can I see some identification, please?" He held out his left hand and kept the other near his pistol. Rock reached into his pocket and fumbled for his license.

"Have you been drinking?" asked the cop. He took Rock's license and looked at the picture and the birthdate. "You'll have to come with me while I call you in."

Rock followed the cop up the side of the drainage ditch to the cruiser. The cop opened the rear door and told Rock to get in. Rock climbed in the car. The cop climbed in the driver's seat and began to talk on the radio. Rock listened.

"I have a white male. DOB 2-13-57. Six feet, 2 inches, 220 pounds. Dark hair and brown eyes. Name is Garazio, Roman. That's G-A-R-A-Z-I-O, R-O-M-A-N. Need a warrant check."

The radio crackled and stuttered. Rock grew apprehensive, wondering if the cop and the dispatcher would put two and two together. Finally, the dispatcher spoke. It was all in cop talk. The only thing Rock recognized was the code 10-4. When the dispatcher was finished, the cop looked back at Rock.

"I'm bringing you in for public drunkenness. If you know someone who might bail you out, you'll only have to stay for a couple of hours for processing. If not, you're in jail for the night. Are you going to behave or should I handcuff you?"

"I'll behave." Rock wondered if his parents would bail him out. He didn't know another person who he could call, anyhow. Shit, he might as well call his parents. He didn't want to sit in jail overnight in fear that the cops might figure out his connection to Jeremy and Julie. The cruiser was heading towards Main Street. Good, that meant they were going to put him in the Snowdon Jail instead of Hyattsville or Upper Marlboro, which is where county cases usually went.

Rock had been in the holding cell for two hours now. He hadn't been allowed to call anyone. He wasn't drunk anymore either. The jailer was ignoring him. The whole scenario was making Rock nervous. Two cops came into the room. They were wearing jeans and polo shirts. Rock knew them from earlier run-ins. Their names were Mulhaney and Smith. They were undercover and everyone called them Starsky and Hutch after the cop show. Basically, they were assholes who solved most of their cases by kicking the shit out of suspects. The only good thing about them, thought Rock, was they hated niggers as much as Samson did. Still, he wasn't too happy to see them. He had a feeling he wasn't going home tonight.

They finished talking with the jailer and looked over at Rock. Mulhaney. the big one, known as Starsky, flashed Rock the finger. Smith, who was younger, muscular and considerably mellower than his partner, laughed. "Take him out of the cell, Barney," commanded Mulhaney. The jailer unlocked the holding cell. Mulhaney grabbed Rock and twisted his right arm behind his back. They pulled him towards a room set up for interrogation. Rock had been there before. Once inside, he sat down on a chair. The cops sat directly opposite.

"So," began Mulhaney. "What happened to your friend Prehausen, big man? Did you kill him over some snatch?"

Rock looked at the cop. He wanted to punch him, but knew that would be pointless. He had tried that the first time they brought him in this room and Smith broke his arm. Smith might have been mellow compared to Mulhaney, but he was still a cop. Rock just looked at Mulhaney full of hate.

"Fuck you, man," said Rock. "I was as surprised as you to hear what happened. Shit, he was my best friend."

"Hutch here thinks you were asshole buddies," taunted Mulhaney. "Jeremy was kind of cute like a little girl."

"I tol' you. I don't know nothin'." Rock looked around the room. He did not want to make eye contact with either of the cops. He was tryin' to think of a good enough story so they would let him go. The Malcolm angle seemed like it would work. Plus it had the bonus of screwing that nigger good.

"How long you wanna stay this time, Mr. Garazio?" asked Smith. "Me and my partner work here so we can stay forever. Shit, we even got ladies who will bring in food and drinks. You're gonna get real hungry and thirsty if you don't help us out here." He leaned toward Rock. "What do you know about the fuckin' murders?"

"I really don't know nothin'," began Rock. He cleared his throat. "Nothin' except that Jeremy owed that new nigger cook at the Pancake House a bunch of money."

"Oh yeah?" asked Mulhaney. "Now, why would he owe the cookie money?"

"Dope," said Rock. "Lots of it."

The cops looked interested. Maybe this would work, thought Rock. He continued, "Jeremy got Malcolm, the cook, to front him a bunch of money to buy some weed. Then Malcolm was gonna sell it, but Jeremy spent the money and Malcolm found out. He told Jeremy he better get his money by Friday or else he and his boys was gonna kick his ass…."

"Were you present when this threat was made?" asked Smith.

"Yeah," said Rock. "I was standin' right next to Jeremy."

"What's the cookie's last name, Rock? You must know."

"McRice," answered Rock.

The cops told Rock to stay right where he was. They gave him a pack of Winstons and a lighter and left the room. Rock hoped against hope that his story worked, at least enough to take the suspicion off of him. He lit a cigarette. And waited. Two cigarettes later, the cops returned.

"I'll tell you what, Garazio," said Smith. "We're gonna check out your story tonight. We're gonna let you stay at our little hotel here overnight while we do. If it checks out, you can go in the morning. Anybody you want to call?"

Rock shook his head no.

The two detectives left the jail area of the police station and went upstairs to their offices. They had to design some kind of strategy. Rock's story seemed plausible in some regards, and they didn't really know anything about the cook other than he was the nephew of the Pancake House's manager and that he was recently discharged from the Army. Besides, the whole double murder was pretty bizarre. At least

this was something of a lead. If they could make a
case for an arrest, then the county boys would give
them jurisdiction, something the Snowdon chief
really wanted bad. Mulhaney sat on his desk. Smith
pulled up a chair and they began to brainstorm.

"What do we got?" asked Mulhaney. "A possible
motive with the drug angle. No weapon and no
prints according to the Hyattsville lab boys. A punk
in jail who knows the deceased and the man with the
motive. And two corpses. Did we find any drugs at
the crime scene?"

"Just a small bag of weed and some valiums,"
answered Smith, reading from the county police report. "Nothing that smells of big time dealing. Why
don't we call the Army and see if this cook guy has
any priors. What's his last name, again?"

"McRice. I'll make the calls. I still have some
friends over there from my days as an MP. They can
speed up the process," offered Mulhaney. "Remember, it's the Army and everything takes twice as long
as it does in civilian life."

"Why do you suppose that is?"

"Because the taxpayers are paying for it," answered Mulhaney.

"Should we go talk to the Pancake House crew
again?" asked Smith.

"Nah. We should wait until we got something
solid. That punk in jail is not too reputable."

"I'll go pump the county boys for whatever other

info they might have come up with. I'll mention the angle we're working on and see if that helps them tie some loose ends together. Give me a call if you get any positive stuff on that cook that makes him a likely candidate for our crime." Smith left the room and headed for his car. He was on his way to Upper Marlboro.

Peter had slept Sunday away. Lucy stayed over Saturday night, but had left around noon. Once she went out the door, he went back to sleep. He was kind of pissed, because he was thinking about going to the Red Sox - Orioles doubleheader, but he had been up all night. Lucy had procured some coke from somebody and the two of them spent the night doing lines, listening to music and drinking. The sleep had done him good. He felt rested for the first time since he began sleeping with Lucy. The whole week was a bit of a haze. He and Lucy had spent four of the last five nights together and they still enjoyed each other as much as the first foray on Tuesday. She must feel the same, since she was planning on coming back tonight after she got back from her parents over in Cheverly. He decided to take a shower.

The phone rang. He answered. It was Art.

"Where you been, man. I been trying to get a hold of you all fuckin' day!" yelled Art.

"Sorry about the game, man. I been sleeping like

a rock. I never even heard the phone once."

"Fuck the game, man. Some heavy shit done gone down. Serious." Art sounded excited in a way Peter had never heard.

"What you mean, man?" asked Peter.

"Shit. You ain't heard? Jeremy and Julie was killed."

"You're shittin' me!" exclaimed Peter, alarmed. "How?"

"Details are real sketchy, man. The cops ain't saying much. What I can put together is that they were beaten with a baseball bat or a crowbar or something. One of Julie's sisters found 'em around three o'clock this morning. The cops been all over the pancake house. Bossman closin' early tonight. He said it's the first time ever. The cops are gonna want to talk to all of us soon. They wanna use his office upstairs tomorrow. That way they figure they can catch us all what with tomorrow being payday and all. Clean up your place, man. I don't expect them to visit us at home but you never know."

"Shit. Does Lucy know?" Julie and Lucy had been pretty tight.

"Yeah. I called her at her parents. She said she was gonna see you tonight."

"Yeah. That's the plan," said Peter. He was still assimilating the information Art had given him.

"Be gentle, brother. Be gentle."

"I hear ya, man," said Peter softly.

"Later," said Art. "I gotta go talk to Lewin about keepin' the restaurant goin' and out of the news."

"Later." Peter hung up the phone. He found a towel in his bedroom, took off his clothes and headed to the bathroom to shower. This was some fucked up shit was all he could come up with when he tried to comprehend what had happened.

Mulhaney was back in his office. He had done some investigative work after placing a call to his army contact. It was after midnight. His contact at the Army's Criminal Investigation Division (or CID as they called it) had come through with the info on McRice. Three priors. One for possession of hashish with intent to distribute and two assaults. The first assault was on a commanding officer and the second was on another GI. The second was connected to the dealing charge. The army must have screwed up the prosecution or cut a deal, because the only conviction was on the first assault. His discharge was six months early. General discharge. Like his contact said, it looked like they wanted to get rid of him so they let him slide on the charges. McRice did six months hard time on the assault charge. So, he did have a record for violence. In fact, the weapon in both assaults had been a piece of steel pipe. And drug dealing. No information on the actual amount of hashish in the drug bust, but the bust was part of a base-wide sting operation to bust a ring that dealt to GIs and dependents. In Mulhaney's mind, they could get an arrest warrant unless his partner found that the lab in Upper Marlboro or Hyattsville had uncovered some positive evidence that linked another individual to the crime. Still, it would be nice to connect a few more dots. Where was McRice between the time of his discharge and his employment at the Pancake House? His uncle's history was well known at the station house, but his jacket was so old that it served no purpose. As far as the law went, Art had been clean for more than fifteen years. Nobody on the force liked his familiarity with the white girls who worked at the Pancake House, but unfortunately those days when the law could do anything about that were long gone. Emmett Till wouldn't get killed today. Not even down in Mississippi. And if he did, the jury would find his killers guilty. And McRice was just a younger, more uppity version of his uncle. Too dumb to know his place. Or maybe too smart.

Rock couldn't sleep. He guessed that he had been in this particular cell for four hours, which meant it was probably around 1:30 in the morning. There were five cells in the station and it sounded like only one other was inhabited this Sunday evening. Or Monday morning, as it were. Rock kept on seeing Jeremy dead. Even though he hadn't seen the corpse, he could imagine it. I mean, he knew Jeremy almost as well as he knew himself. What the fuck was that asshole cop talking about asshole buddies? He and Jeremy were bros, not faggots. They were just trying to get him to slip up and say something to keep his ass here.

It was hard to believe it had come to this. He really thought that Samson wouldn't miss the little bit of weed they stole. The man sold pounds every week. What was four measly ounces? Jeremy and him used to play kickball down at the park on Montrose with the Watson kids. That was only ten or fifteen years ago. Then they'd go home and mom would have Popsicles. Or dad would give them a couple quarters when the Mr. Softee truck drove through the neighborhood. Jeremy was so easygoing. Even in junior high after his mom hooked up with that asshole who raped Jeremy. Why she stayed with him Jeremy never could figure out. That's when he started to change. Rock's mom never knew what happened, but she noticed the change in Jeremy. She just put it down to the age. You know, teenager shit. Our first rock concert was Grand Funk. That was fun. We musta smoked a fuckin' bag of weed that day. Jeremy was so damn high and that girl kept on grabbing his ass and saying she loved his hair. Platinum was the color she called it. Jeremy didn't know what to make of her so he kept moving away from her in the crowd and she kept finding him. It's the hair, she told him. I can find you anywhere 'cause it shines like a light. Finally, we lost her.

Our first acid trip. Little purple pills. That nigger Levon sold it to us. Microdot, he called it. We went to school and never made it past the parking lot 'cause we was trippin' so hard. So we went into the woods and drank from the booze we kept stashed there. It was fall and the leaves looked really cool. Jeremy climbed some fuckin' high tree and then refused to come down, like he was some scared kitten. I just laughed and laughed. So did Jeremy. It was an oak tree so he started dropping acorns on me. Isaac Newton he was calling me. Finally he came down. That was probably the best acid trip I ever took.

Rock's lament for his lost innocence made him feel sleepy. He lay down on the metal rack they called a bed in this jail and put the hard pillow under his head. Slowly, he drifted off to sleep.

Smith was not finding anything new. The county lab had some blood samples, but they were contaminated with some kind of liquid that rendered them unusable. The photos of the bodies showed nothing beyond the usual gore. No sign of unusual activity in the days preceding the murders. Neighbors say they didn't notice anybody other than the usual couple of young people visiting the victims. The poor girl. How do such young and beautiful things get mixed up with these types? You have to wonder. Even his partner's youngest went out with coloreds and hippies. Of course, Smith thought she did it partly to get back at her dad for cheating on her mom. That was a messy time. The Mulhaney divorce and its aftermath hadn't been much less so, especially for Mulhaney's daughters. Could be worse, thought Smith. Could be him. So far his wife was dealing pretty well being married to a cop.

He wished he had something solid. A weapon or even a partial fingerprint. The crime scene had been gone over three times though since early Sunday morning. If there wasn't anything concrete, he would support his partner's request to charge the McRice fellow, even if it was based solely on circumstantial stuff. It would be worse to let him leave the state if he was the perpetrator. They could always ask for murder one and convince McRice to plead to manslaughter. Then they could avoid a trial. Nowadays, every time a colored got charged without being positively linked to the crime you always ran the risk of getting one of them NAACP lawyers. Once that happened, the DA said his chances of getting a conviction in court dropped by a third. Course, usually them coloreds was so scared or dumb that they pleaded to a lesser charge. Even when they didn't commit the crime. Stuff like that used to bother him. No more though. This work made you see most people, especially coloreds, hippies, and white trash, as less than human, anyhow. He never thought it would happen to him back in '65 when he first joined the force, but it did. You live with it, that's all.

Lucy was shaken. Poor Julie. She thought she was doing the right thing by sticking with Jeremy despite all his emotional problems. She had decided that she really did love him, even though she wandered every once in a while. What the hell, thought Lucy, everyone does these days. Julie said that Jeremy was her guy and that he turned her on to no end. Plus he was such a little boy sometimes. Lucy wasn't sure that was the best scenario for a long-term relationship, but who thought long-term anyhow? She knew she didn't. Hell, her and Peter might be over in a week. Thinking of Peter made her horny. She interrupted her reverie to put the paintbrush she had been cleaning away. She was glad that she had decided to come up and help her parents paint their new house. Especially in light of the tragic news of the day. Now she needed to go back to Snowdon. She washed her hands and turned off the hose. Her parents were already in the house having a drink. She went in.

"I'm headin' back to Snowdon."

"Have a glass of wine first, honey," said her mom. She poured some Chablis into a wine glass and handed it to Lucy.

"All right, but just one, then I have to go."

"Will you be okay, dear?" asked her mom. "You can stay here. I'm sure your boss would understand if you called in sick."

The offer sounded tempting. She really wanted to see Peter, though. Julie's family might want her help, too. She had to face the bullshit sooner or later, anyhow. Her dad put his arm around her.

"If you need to get away, Lucy," he consoled, "you can stay here. Hell, so can your boyfriend. Just give us a call."

"Thanks dad," said Lucy. "And mom."

She finished her wine, grabbed her purse and went out to her car. Her parents waved as she drove away. She pushed the Grateful Dead From the Mars Hotel cassette into the player. "Scarlet Begonias" came through the speakers. It was nice to hear the Dead. They had a way of transcending the fuckedupness of the world. What was that line Peter quoted to her last night while they were partying? "In the land of the night, the ship of the sun is pulled by the Grateful Dead." God knows they were in the land of the night now. Fuckin' killed. It was just plain hard to comprehend. Only three days ago they had been joking about how Peter was in bed. Lucy rated him higher than Julie did, but then her memory of the event was fresher. Julie joked that Lucy was falling in love with him. Lucy laughed then. Part of her had been in love with him since she was twelve. Speaking of Peter, she wondered if he went to the ballgame like he planned. If she remembered right, it was a doubleheader. She couldn't see him doing so in light of what had happened.

She was right. Peter was listening to the second game of the doubleheader. Luis Tiant was putting on a show. The Sox were winning. The O's had taken the last two from the Sox, but the front of the Sox' rotation was coming back around, so the Sox had a good chance of winning the next three. Listening to the game and drinking Miller High Life helped Peter forget his friends' fate. For a couple minutes, anyway. Then he recalled the one time he and Art took Jeremy and Julie to Memorial Stadium. Art had brought in a pint of moonshine Peter purchased at a bluegrass festival the week before. They were buying sodas and mixing the moonshine in. Jeremy felt it more than all the rest of them and was getting pretty damned crazy. Around the seventh inning he stood up in his seat about seven rows up from the visitors' dugout and mooned them. I think it was the Twins that night. Within a minute, the security guys had him on their shoulders and the others were running after them. Julie convinced them not to arrest Jeremy, and Peter drove the two of them home. The funniest part of the whole thing was that the next time Jeremy saw Julie's mom, she asked him if it was his ass she saw on the television the other night. He was embarrassed, to say the least.

Julie was just a sweetheart. Blonde, smart and com-passionate, her beauty was enhanced by her vivaciousness. Her family has got to be wondering why they didn't protest more about her romance with Jeremy. His friends always made her sisters uneasy. Her mom, on the other hand, was a lot like Julie and figured that Jeremy being with Julie might help him move away from his past. Maybe if they had moved out of Snowdon that would have happened. Snowdon was like a lot of towns, though. Your past was always there, kind of like your shadow.

Boston just scored another run. They were up 4 to 1. Peter would have loved to be at the game. He had yet to see Tiant this year. Maybe he would get up to Fenway this year. If he decided to see some of the Springsteen tour up that way and the Sox were in Boston at the same time he could mix the two. See what happens. Lucy should be here soon. She's probably some shook up. Her and Julie were pretty tight.

Malcolm and Art sat at the kitchen table in their apartment. Auntie Grace was at some church event. They talked about the murders. Art explained the scenario he thought would unfold at the pancake house the next day.

"The cops gonna set up in the boss's office," explained Art. "Then they gonna bring each of us one at a time and ask their questions."

"What we gonna tell them?"

"What we know," answered Art. "They don't suspect us any more than they suspect anybody else far as I know."

"What about the dope?" asked Malcolm. He was afraid that the cops would find out about the dope deal he had made with Jeremy.

"If they don't ask," said Art. "Don't tell." He lit a cigarette.

"Yeah, you right." Malcolm put his hands behind his head and leaned back on the chair.

"How's that Marion girl?"

"She finer than the best weed I ever smoked," answered Malcolm. "I wish I was with her right now. Far away from here." He thought of her warm brown skin and her deep eyes and wondered what the hell he was doing here with his fuckin' uncle talkin' about what to say to some cracker pigs. Pigs who didn't like him or Art or any other blood who didn't walk in fear of them. He hoped things went pretty smooth.

It was now seven in the morning. The two detectives had both been up until two. Nonetheless, they were ready for the day. This kind of case got a cop's adrenalin flowing and enabled him to go on little more than coffee, burgers, and adrenalin. They were at a diner in Burtonsville, maybe five miles from the Pancake House. The chief had given them complete control of the case now that the county boys had dropped it. This was their chance to shine. The meeting was to determine exactly how they would run the questioning today. There was a news conference scheduled for five in the afternoon. They hoped to have an arrest by then.

"The lab boys in Marlboro had no prints. Indeed, they only found blood on the walls and carpet. After looking at their reports and talking with a guy in the lab, we concluded that the perp was wearing gloves of some kind. The only thing they found was some red pot and some pills, like we already knew."

"Any thoughts on the weapon?" asked Mulhaney.

"The lab seems to think it was a pipe or cut-off

baseball bat," answered Smith. "The shape of a fungo bat if it was the latter."

Mulhaney shook his head affirmatively. He was taking notes and trying to figure out a plan of attack.

"I went back over to the Snowdon Gardens apartment complex last night," he began. "Nothing too unusual for this kind of crime. Some bushes trampled in the front of their entrance. If you remember, these are more like townhouses than apartments, so everyone has an entrance on the ground level. It's an end apartment and the only neighbors with an adjoining wall were gone all weekend. They said the two youngsters were quiet, except for their rock music, which they always turned down when asked."

"What about the McRice fellow?"

"Drugs, assault, general discharge." Mulhaney explained what he had learned about Malcolm's arrest record.

"Is that enough?"

"I talked to the chief and the DA," answered Mulhaney. "They said it was a beginning. We need to confirm his whereabouts Saturday night, search his car for blood, weapons, hair, even weed. Anything that might tie him to the scene, no matter how remotely. When we question him we should try to piss him off or trip him up. If he doesn't have an alibi and we can link him to the drug deal, that could be enough."

"What about the threat he made to Prehausen

that Garazio talked about?"

"If we can get McRice to admit that, that can only help." The waitress finally brought their breakfasts. Ham and cheese omelets with home fries and toast. She refilled their cups with coffee. They begin to eat in earnest. "The DA wants to get this wrapped up before the media make too much of it."

"They gonna be at the restaurant?" asked Smith.

"I hope not. If they are, try and ignore them. Otherwise, no comment them to death."

The two cops finished their meal. After leaving a tip on the table, they headed to their car. A quick ride down Route 198 and they were at the Pancake House. Art and that hippie guy Peter were in the galley, Lucy was waiting tables, and the news media were out front. The owner was waiting for the two officers. After they parked the cruiser, he walked over to them and led them to the rear of the restaurant. That way they could avoid the media that swarmed towards them.

Mulhaney waved them away. "No comment. Wait until the press conference."

The three men went upstairs. Peter and Art continued to cook and Lucy tried not to cry. The media came into the restaurant and began to fill the tables. If they couldn't get a story, at least they would get breakfast. The police officers prepared the owner's office for questioning, putting away his papers and locking up his files. When they were ready, they sent him down to send up either Art or Peter. Peter went first. His visit was short, since he really had not been around over the weekend and whatever he knew was only from hearsay. He thought it interesting that they didn't ask him anything about Malcolm's run-in with that Samson fellow. Not that he knew anything about it, but it was interesting that they didn't ask.

Art was next. Peter took over the cooking. Art headed upstairs.

"Hi Art," began Smith.

"Hey."

"Where was your nephew Saturday night?" asked Mulhaney.

"Why?"

"Just answer the question."

"He went to Baltimore in the early evening."

"When did he come back?"

"Last night."

"At what time?"

"I don't know. Around 7, maybe. Why you askin' about my nephew?" Art didn't like the way the questioning was going.

"Does he smoke pot?"

"You have to ask him that. That's his business."

"Do you smoke pot?"

"None of your fuckin' business." What the hell did this have to do with the fuckin' murders? These fuckin' pigs really thought they were somethin'. He knew he had to be cool. He lit a cigarette.

"Anything else you can tell us?"

"About what?" asked Art. "What kind of alcohol I drink?" He said nothing more.

"Go on," said Smith. "We might talk to you some more later."

Art left the room. He was pissed. Why the hell were they asking him so much about Malcolm? What about that mean ass white sonofabitch that attacked Malcolm? How come they didn't ask about him? It was curious, that's for sure. When he returned to the galley, Lucy rook off her apron and headed up the stairs. Art took over waiting on tables. Lewin had already left for the day. He had to tend to his horses. Besides owning three restaurants, he also owned some racehorses and ran a stud farm in the Maryland countryside.

While Lucy was upstairs with the cops, Malcolm came in the restaurant front door. He wasn't supposed to come on until 11:00, but wanted some breakfast. He was already dressed in his cook's whites. Art motioned for him to join Peter in the galley. Malcolm did so and started cooking. Once Art was finished taking orders, he headed back there himself. The three of them divided the cooking chores.

"Malcolm, watch out with them cops," whispered Art. "They was askin' me all these questions about where you were on Saturday night and shit."

"Why?" asked Malcolm. He flipped the omelet

he was cooking and sprinkled some chopped ham into the runny part of the egg and water mixture. "Shit, I was in Baltimore."

"Just don't let them make you say something you don't mean to, little brother," counseled Art.

Lucy was back on the floor. Her entire interview didn't take more than five minutes. She motioned to Malcolm that it was his turn. Malcolm said shit under his breath and went up the stairs to the office. As soon as he did, two uniformed officers who had been in a cruiser in the pancake house parking lot, began to search his car. Nobody in the restaurant noticed because they were all busy working. Malcolm hated these types of situations. When he had to go through this in the service, the fuckin' MPs had got him to admit to something that he didn't do. What was really a matter of him being in the wrong place at the wrong time turned into a possession with intent to distribute charge. Pigs, man did he hate them.

He walked into the office. The two cops they called Starsky and Hutch were speaking in low voices. They stopped and motioned to Malcolm to take a seat.

"Malcolm McRice, correct?" asked Mulhaney.

"Yeah."

"Where were you Saturday night?" Mulhaney was sitting on the edge of the owner's desk. He was drumming his fingers on the oak wood top.

"Baltimore."

"Where?"

"Me and a lady friend was out dancin'. We went to a few places," answered Malcolm. He was trying to keep his answers short. Less chance of making a mistake that way.

"What was her name? Can she verify your whereabouts?" asked Smith. Malcolm didn't respond. Mulhaney got up off the desk and leaned into his face. His breath smelled like coffee and cigarettes. Malcolm turned his face away.

"Her name is Marion," he answered slowly. "I don't know where she lives so I can't contact her."

"What, is she a hooker?" taunted Mulhaney.

"Fuck you." These fuckin' cracker cops. "No, she ain't no hooker. I just don't know where she lives. She ain't from this cracker state."

"What, you didn't get her phone number?"

Malcolm really wanted to leave Marion and them out of this shit. Besides, he didn't kill nobody, so he didn't see any reason to tell the cops about his friends. It would just give them an excuse to fuck with them. He kept quiet. The cops began another line of questioning.

"Do you smoke weed?" asked Smith.

"I have." Malcolm saw no harm in telling the cops that. Shit, they already knew the answer.

"Have you ever dealt?"

"No."

"That's not what the Army told us, McRice,"

said Mulhaney. "The CID—you know what that is, I'm sure—said you were busted for dealing hash while you were in the service. Let me ask you again. Have you ever dealt drugs?"

"That bust never held up," said Malcolm. "It was a false arrest."

"Answer the question."

"I done answered it. It was my friend's dope. I just happened to be in the room when the MPs came in." Malcolm didn't like the way this was going.

"That's a standard tale," said Mulhaney. "Gee, how many times have I heard that?'

The room was quiet for a couple of minutes except for the sound of the three men breathing. Malcolm shifted his feet. Mulhaney motioned for Smith to leave the room. Once Smith was gone, Mulhaney leaned into Malcolm's face.

"You better come up with a positive identification of your whereabouts all night Saturday, especially the hours after midnight, boy. As far as I'm concerned, you are our number one suspect. You have two assaults on your record, both with a pipe. You use and deal drugs. You don't have anyone who can prove where you were during the time span that the crime was committed. We have a witness who says you threatened the male victim. You only been in this town for a few months and don't know what the rules are. I've been given orders to solve this crime quickly. You're making it real easy, boy. Real easy."

Malcolm jumped up. He saw what was happening. They were trying to set him up. He yelled, "Fuck you, you fuckin' pig. I didn't kill nobody. You ever hear of some cracker named Samson? What about him? He tried to stab me!" Smith ran back in the room. Malcolm sat back down, still pissed but under control.

"I don't know anything about that," said Mulhaney. "That sounds like a completely different situation to me."

"No, man," insisted Malcolm. "It ain't!"

"You can go, Mr. McRice," said Smith. "Just don't go far."

Malcolm left the room. He was freaked. These pigs were gonna try and pin this on him. He needed to figure out how he could prove he wasn't even near Snowdon on Saturday night There were lots of obstacles to that, though. First, every place that him and Marion went that night was an illegal club so that meant they wouldn't appreciate him telling the pigs about them. Second, they were out all night and that meant Antoine and Leah couldn't vouch for him, either. Neither could Art or Auntie Grace since the last they seen of him was when he left the church picnic. And Marion—hell, he had her phone number but that was it. Plus, he didn't see no purpose in getting her or Leah or Antoine involved since the answers they gave the police wouldn't really prove anything anyhow. That is, if the pigs even believed them in the first place. Besides, he didn't do this fuckin' crime. He was innocent. So fuck them.

He returned to the galley. Art knew it had not gone well, just by looking at Malcolm's face. He told Malcolm to go sit down. Malcolm didn't want to see the cops again, so he ignored Art and began cooking an order.

Auntie Grace was watching one of her soaps when she heard the knock. It didn't sound friendly. She got up from the couch and went to the door. When she opened it, the person on the other side tried to push his way in. She had left the little chain on, though, so he couldn't. He stuck an identification card in front of her face. She read the words "Snowdon Police Department."

"Can we talk, Ma'am?" asked the detective on the other side of the chain.

"We can talk through the door, sir," she answered. She wasn't gonna let this big ofay in.

"Okay. That will work." It was Mulhaney.

"Yes," said Grace. "It will."

"I only have a couple questions," continued Mulhaney. "Do you know where your nephew, Malcolm McRice was on Saturday night and Sunday morning?"

"Yes. He was in Baltimore with his new girlfriend."

"Can you prove that?"

"He said that's where he was goin'," answered

Grace. "That's proof enough for me."

"One more question—" said Mulhaney. "Does he sell marijuana?"

"No." Grace began to close the door. The detective turned and walked away. Grace didn't like the feeling she had. Mulhaney went back to his car and called Smith on the radio.

"No positive ID of McRice's whereabouts on Saturday," he reported.

"The search of his vehicle found a blond hair and about a half gram of the red marijuana Garazia spoke of. The hair matches the color of the female victim."

"I'll meet you at the station in fifteen."

It was three in the afternoon. The two detectives had compiled their report, submitted it to the chief, who read it and passed it on to the DA with a rec- ommendation to charge Malcolm. They were wait- ing on his response. By three-thirty they had the warrant they wanted. They decided to drive Smith's car to the restaurant. When they arrived, the media were gone except for a stringer who wrote a lot for the Sun. He walked up to the cruiser.

"You got a suspect?" he asked.

Mulhaney joked with the reporter. "Yeah, it's your exclusive. Come on in."

The cops walked into the pancake house. They headed directly to the door that led to the galley.

Malcolm was washing dishes and had his back to the door when the two men entered. He turned around and knew what was gonna happen next. He made a move towards the rear door. Mulhaney jumped and tackled him. Smith pulled out his handcuffs.

"You are under arrest," he read. "You have the right to remain silent. Anything you say can and will be used against you in a court of law. You have the right to speak to an attorney, and to have an attorney present during any questioning. If you cannot afford a lawyer, one will be provided for you at government expense." Smith slipped the cuffs on Malcolm and tightened them.

Art and Peter ran out of the galley. Lucy looked over the ledge to see what was happening. Art began pounding on Mulhaney's back.

"Leave my fuckin' nephew alone!" he shouted. "Go out and do your homework, you idiot cracker! He didn't kill nobody. Look in your own backyard!" Art was distraught and angry. It's not because he couldn't believe the cops were arresting the wrong man. It was because he knew that Malcolm didn't have a chance once he got into the court system. He didn't have no money and since he was new to the area, neither did he have friends with any pull. Especially in this town, where the fuckin' Klan still held sway. Peter had told him some stories. He knew. Peter put his arm around Art's shoulder.

"Hey Art," he said, softly. "Don't give 'em an excuse to bust you, too. We'll get Malcolm out of their racist paws." Art backed off. The cops took Malcolm out the back door to the waiting cruiser. While Malcolm was being arrested, Rock had been let go, with instructions to stay in the area. The DA was gonna need him to testify. After all, the case partially rested on his contention that Malcolm had threatened Jeremy. Rock celebrated by going to the bar at the end of Main Street and drinking a double shot of Old Crow. He recognized some of Samson's buddies in the bar shooting pool. Rock did not know that Malcolm was being arrested while he drank shots, so he stayed out of sight of Samson's friends.

Art called the owner and asked if he could close the restaurant. He consented after Art related what had gone down in the last hour. Mr. Lewin, the owner, was surprised. He believed himself to be a pretty good judge of character and couldn't believe that he was that wrong about Malcolm. Sure, the young man had some growing up to do, but he didn't seem like a killer to Lewin. He said as much to Art and hung up the phone. Art took the keys and locked the entrance. There were only four tables still occupied, which meant he would be here another half hour at least. He sent Lucy and Peter home with the request that they stop by his crib and let his mom know what had happened. She was gonna be some upset.

8

Baltimore Sun

Snowdon Police Make Arrest in Double Murder

Snowdon, Md. – The Snowdon Police Department announced an arrest in the June 21, 1975 murders of Jeremy Prehausen and Julie Epstein. Malcolm McRice was apprehended at his workplace Monday afternoon by detectives Richard Mulhaney and James Smith. Smith told reporters that McRice had been involved in a drug deal with Prehausen that had gone wrong.
"Prehausen owed McRice a lot of money and McRice got tired of waiting for it," said Smith. "So he decided to beat it out of him."
The District Attorney told the press that there was enough circumstantial evidence to link McRice to the crime. "It's only a matter of time before our fine officers find the smoking gun. However, our office is convinced that it has enough evidence to prosecute and convict the suspect."
McRice is being held on $100,000 bond at the Patuxent Correctional Center near Snowdon. A date for the arraignment has not been set.

Art set the paper down. He still couldn't believe it. Those crackers had busted Malcolm and planned to put him away. Forever. Talk about a star-crossed life. His daddy in prison before he knew him. His time in the army a waste. Now the police charging him with something unspeakable. Art didn't know which way to turn. His mom was at the church praying with the minister. She knew that Malcolm was innocent, but she didn't know what else to do but pray. Peter said she collapsed on the floor when him and Lucy came by the night before. They had to revive her with smelling salts. Art lit a cigarette and sighed.

Peter was talking crazy last night about his radical friends. Something about getting them to picket the courthouse and demand that Malcolm be freed. In Peter's mind it was a racist conspiracy, plain and simple. He was convinced that the cops were Klansmen and so was Samson and they planned the whole frame-up. Art couldn't go that far. These cops were crackers and all, but they did have to cover their tracks. Shit, they might even be Klansmen. Definitely overzealous when it came to locking up black men, but they did have to follow the rules to some extent. Lucy was just shell-shocked. First the murders, now the bust. She couldn't even talk she was in such shock. Peter had his hands full, but he was also on a crusade. Art had seen him like that one other time while he was still going to college and there was antiwar stuff going on out in College Park. Politics was trouble as far as Art was concerned. Peter had to convince him that they could get his nephew out of this shit. In Art's mind, prayer was just as effective, which meant neither of them was worth a good

Goddamn. Of course, he would tell Peter his thoughts before he told his mom his opinions on prayer.

It was Monday night. Peter didn't know what to do. Lucy was drinking herself into a stupor in his bedroom and refused to stop. She still had her waitress uniform on, coffee and syrup stains and all. Her words slurred between threats of violence toward the police and to herself. While Peter shared her desire to harm the pigs he knew it would only put them all in jail for life. As for danger to herself, he was not going to let that happen to anyone he cared about. Especially Lucy. He wondered how Malcolm was holding up and how much the cops were beating him in an attempt to get him to confess to something he didn't do. He knew his fears were not unfounded. Charles X, the Muslim brother Lewin hired on work-release had related the story of a brother in the Jessup Correctional Facility who was convicted of a murder even though he was twenty miles away from the crime scene. The brother, said Charles, was beaten with rubber hoses filled with sand and his testicles were squeezed with one of those giant pipe wrenches until one busted. Finally the brother broke and confessed to the murder he didn't commit. His lawyer was a public defender who was an ex-prosecutor who had lost his prosecutor job for being a drunk. This wasn't something that happened back in the fifties either. The brother was convicted in 1970.

Peter was stymied. He didn't want to ignore Lucy since it was obvious she needed some comfort and understanding, but he wanted to get on the phone with his buddies in the Maryland Coalition Against Racism and Police Brutality. If he did that, though, he knew he would probably have to leave Lucy here by herself. That was something he didn't want to do. After putting Leon Russell's album Stranger In a Strange Land on the turntable, he grabbed a beer from the fridge and went into the bedroom. Lucy was still sobbing. He sat next to her and she grabbed on to him like she was never going to let go. Peter let her squeeze him. She stopped crying and pushed her hair out of her eyes. Her makeup that she wore for work was running all over her face. Peter took the pillowcase and wiped it away. Her eyes were a fiery red from all the crying. He kissed her forehead.

"Make me forget this ever happened, Peter," she sobbed. "Make me forget." She removed her uniform and underwear and snuggled up next to Peter. She sang along with Leon—"Stranger in a strange land...." Peter began to kiss her legs and up her thighs. Lucy directed his head to her crotch. She pulled off his pants. Then she pulled him up to her face. They kissed long. After making love, she fell asleep. Peter lay back and tried to think up a strategy, but was too tired. He fell asleep on his back.

When they awoke Tuesday, Peter called Art to ask about the work schedule. Lewin was back to his regular hours and needed Peter to put in even more overtime. It was okay if Lucy didn't come in. The place would be closed on Thursday for the funeral. Two different churches and closed caskets. Jeremy's mom had been on television that morning and was quoted: "I hope they put that nigger away for life." As if she gave a shit about Jeremy when he was alive. Peter hung up the phone and went to the kitchen to make coffee. While it brewed he showered.

He brought Lucy a cup of coffee and sat down next to her on the bed. She was holding her head.

"Oh man, do I feel like shit," she whispered. "Thanks for being there last night, Peter."

"Sure." Peter took a long drink from his coffee mug. Lucy lay back down. "Lewin said you don't have to go to work if you don't feel like it."

"Good," said Lucy. "What about you?" She buried her face in her pillow.

"I gotta go in," he stood up and dressed. "I'll call you around 11. There's more coffee and whatever else you want. You gonna be all right?"

"Sure, babe," answered Lucy. "I'm gonna sleep. Love ya."

Peter kissed her and left. She never said that before. He was gonna try and convince Art to let him mount a campaign to free Malcolm. Art wasn't real big on the idea, but Peter was gonna ask him what did he have to lose. Shit, they got Malcolm for as long as they want him unless somebody shows that they care. If Art refused, Peter was gonna talk to Miss Grace. She might let him go for it. He had put in a call to Raymond, who was the main cat on the coalition, but asked him to wait until he got the family's approval. Raymond said he'd wait a couple days, otherwise he was gonna start organizing. Peter knew he would have to do some convincing to get Art to agree. He wondered about Malcolm's friends up in Baltimore, too. Would they help out? Or were they too involved in illicit activities and unwilling to draw attention to themselves? That's another reason he needed Art, 'cause they respected him as an older brother who been there before. Peter knew he was just a white boy to them.

9

Malcolm had been up all night reliving his nightmare. He was having a hard time believing it was real. This shit only happened in stories, right? Where the big bad cracker takes off his sheet and puts on his police uniform and then he goes off to kill some black boy for screwing his daughter or, even worse, his wife. This shit was crazy. He kept on going over and over in his mind what had happened in the last twenty-four hours and no matter what it was just unbelievable. What was worse, he thought, was he didn't know how the hell he was gonna get out of it. He had not been allowed to make a phone call yet and had not been fed. The only good thing that had happened to him was that he wasn't in the Snowdon jail, although he had heard plenty about the Klansmen that worked here in the facility he was in. So far, though, all he had seen was a couple black guards who just did their job. The sun was shining full blast now. When was he gonna get some food?

He knew the Snowdon pigs weren't finished with him. They knew they had to beat a confession out of him or do something—make him plea to a lesser charge or something—'cause their case was too fuckin' weak. Unless they were fuckin' with the evidence. Malcolm knew absolutely nothing about what they were up to. He needed a lawyer but had no idea how he could get one that he could trust. The public defenders around here were notorious for being drunks or in cahoots with the prosecutors. They didn't want justice, just a quick resolution. That meant copping a plea to something you didn't even do. That way they kept the brothers in jail and the honkies could control the streets. Emancipation, my ass.

"Hey. You want some breakfast?" It was one of the guards.

"Yeah," replied Malcolm.

"Coming in the slot, then," said the guard. "Grab it from your end."

"Thanks." Malcolm took the tray and began to eat. It was like Army food. In other words, starchy, fatty and overcooked. He was hungry and ate it quick. He thought about Art and his aunt.

Art was probably pissed off as hell. Auntie probably praying her ass off. I wonder what ol' Lewin said about the whole thing. He can't be happy as far as his business is concerned. I wonder if those fuckin' pigs had the nerve to show up there for breakfast. If they did, Art liable to put rat poison in their food. Man, I wish I could get some news or something. I wonder why I'm all alone in this cell.

Maybe 'cause I'm so dangerous. Yeah, right. Or maybe so they can beat me until I say I did something I would never do. Wonder what they try and make me confess to? Manslaughter? Deadly Assault? Shit. Don't matter 'cause it ain't gonna happen. They gonna have to do their police work and find the motherfucker who killed Jeremy and Julie. I could point them in the right direction if they wanted to look there, but them Snowdon pigs already got their mind made up. Fuck, thought Malcolm, do I need a lawyer.

Here come the guard to take his tray back. I'm gonna ask about my phone call.

The guard rapped the cell door with his nightstick. "Give me back the tray now." Malcolm handed the tray through the slot.

"When can I get my phone call?" he asked.

"When your lawyer comes," answered the guard. He continued to the next cell.

"I ain't got a lawyer," shouted Malcolm.

"The court's gonna send one around until you get your own," said the guard. "Just be patient. You ain't going anywhere."

Malcolm sat back down on the metal slab they called a bed and put his head in his hands. He hoped he could get contact with somebody soon. Like today soon. This was bullshit. Even in the army they woulda sent some flunky 'round by now. Even if he only was gonna tell you that you wasn't goin' nowhere. Malcolm was thinkin' about that. Those two assaults while he was in the service. One against that Alabama cracker who was the CO. None of the brothers and half the white boys couldn't deal with him. He was always makin' 'em get up in the middle of the night and standin' for inspections. If you were slow at gettin' out of bed or anything else he didn't like, he wrote you up. Malcolm and this white hippie guy had the most write-ups. One day they just said fuck it and when he told them to come to attention they started walkin' away. The CO yelled and ran over in front of them. The white guy told the CO to go fuck himself and got punched. Malcolm grabbed a piece of rebar that was laying on the ground—it wasn't more than five inches long—and smacked the cracker fucker on the right shoulder. It didn't do much to the mean ol' sonofabitch, but the next thing Malcolm knew he was down on the ground. It was just his luck that some redneck MPs were comin' around the corner at the time. They tried to charge the white guy with the assault, too, but Malcolm wouldn't let 'em. He did the time. It was worth it. The other shit those cops pulled off his sheet were jive things. Once the Army got him on the CO rap, he was marked. The dope thing was a lie and the other assault charge was really self-defense. The sonofabitch he knocked over with a piece of wood that turned into a steel pipe when they wrote up the report pulled a fuckin' piece on

Malcolm. Malcolm whupped him upside the head with the chunk of wood and ran like a motherfucker. The pigs found him at the NCO club later. They made up most of the fuckin' story that was wrote in the report. So Malcolm copped to a lesser charge. He looked out the small window at the back of his cell. It was a sunny day.

Antoine couldn't believe it when he read the article in the paper on Tuesday. They busted Malcolm for that murder! How could that be, he wondered? Malcolm was in fuckin' Baltimore with Marion. Couldn't Malcolm prove that? And what about that Samson guy? What the hell kind of police work was that? Because of his personal experience, Antoine never believed Malcolm or anyone else when they swore the cops were that racist but he might have to reconsider. He had tried to get a hold of Art or Malcolm's aunt but kept getting either a busy signal or no answer. Today he was heading down to their place right after work. He wondered if anyone had talked to Malcolm since he got busted. It was Wednesday already. He hoped to be at Art and Malcolm's crib by three this afternoon. Maybe between the bunch of them they could figure out some way to get the man out of jail. He had tried callin' Marion yesterday, but she wasn't around. Her daddy's court date must have taken longer than she had hoped. He would try again today.

Auntie Grace had finally settled down. She prayed all night with the minister and a couple fellow church members. Although it had not provided any answers to how to get her baby out of jail, it had given her some peace of mind. The reverend had insisted that she go home to sleep and said he would call Tuesday evening to check in on her. Art was at work. She did sleep about five hours and was waiting for one of Art's friends to bring a turkey sandwich and some chips by for her lunch. She figured it would be that white boy with the long hair. Peter was his name, she thought. Art mentioned that he might know some people who could help Malcolm get a lawyer, at least. Once that happened, they might be able to get some of this mess straightened out.

Peter knocked on the door to Art and Malcolm's apartment. He had promised Art that he would deliver some lunch to Art's mom. Art had agreed to his plea to let the politicos get involved in Malcolm's case on one condition. That condition was that Malcolm and Grace also agreed. He hoped to convince Gracie this afternoon. The biggest difficulty in convincing Malcolm would be getting in to talk with him. Shit, Art wasn't even sure they would let him in. Grace might be the only visitor the cops would allow, since she was, for all purposes, his mom. He heard her moving towards the door. Art asked him to be sensitive to the fact that she hadn't slept much and had been crying her eyes out since Monday evening. Peter figured he would let her eat the sandwich first, and then he would let her bring up the topic of Malcolm. From what he knew of her, she was one tough lady. Peter liked that and knew her strength would be a bonus in the battle that lay ahead.

As for that battle, who knew what the hell shape it was gonna take. There was so little known about the evidence that the cops had or how they conducted their investigation. The only thing Peter knew was his gut feeling the Malcolm was gonna get screwed bad unless they got him a good lawyer who knew how to get beyond the police. This was a Jeremy Mason kind of case. The real culprit was gonna have to be found out by somebody besides the cops. From Peter's view, the whole thing looked like a fucking setup. Art's mom opened the door and let Peter in. He stepped inside so she could close the door.

"Hello. Miss Grace," began Peter. He handed her the Styrofoam container that held the sandwich. "Here's a turkey sandwich. Art said it was your favorite."

"Have a seat, Peter." She gestured towards the kitchen table. "That your name, right?"

"Yes, ma'am." Peter sat down in one of the chairs. Grace sat in another.

"Would you like somethin' to drink? There's stuff in the fridge."

Peter opened the fridge, found a beer and popped

the top. Gracie asked him for a soda and he handed her an RC. She ate hungrily. The only sound was her chewing and the hum of the refrigerator. While she ate, Peter thought of a way to broach the subject of the political action he hoped to generate around Malcolm's situation. Grace wondered how she was going to get in to see her nephew.

"Have you been able to talk to the jail people yet, Miss Grace?" asked Peter.

She finished her sandwich and shook her head. "No. They keep tellin' me I gotta call back later after they verify my relationship to the prisoner, as they say." She sounded a little pissed off. "I'm hoping Reverend Moore can help me out. Malcolm don't have no other relatives 'cept me and Art. His daddy got out of the army, got a girl pregnant, got in a fight, got convicted and died in prison. Art been like his daddy and his brother even though he a lot older. I got legal guardianship of him when his daddy went into prison."

"Who's Reverend Moore, ma'am?" Peter figured he must be the pastor at the Zion Baptist Church that Art and Malcolm made fun of.

"He's the pastor at the church I been attendin' since I come up here," she replied. "He a good Christian man. He studied under and worked with Dr. King and Reverend Abernathy. Malcolm and Art make fun of him 'cause he don't drink or womanize, but that's their shortcomings, not his."

Peter was intrigued by the civil rights connection. Maybe this minister would understand what he hoped to do with the Coalition Against Racism and Police Brutality. He probably wasn't no radical, but he could mobilize the church people. That might be very important. He finished his beer and threw the can in the trash.

"I just talked with Art about this," he began. "And he agreed on the condition that both you and Malcolm agreed to it, too. I belong to a group called The Maryland Coalition Against Racism and Police Brutality. We probably have fifty regular members all around the state, from Baltimore to St. Mary's City and we're of all different colors and backgrounds. Some of us are students, some of us are workers, and some of us are schoolteachers. We got started in 1973 after two police in this county beat the crap out of a black man over at the 7-Eleven near Strawberry Hill projects because he left his engine running in his car while he ran in to get a cup of coffee. It was a real cold day and he didn't want his beater car to not start, which probably would have happened if he turned it off. I guess in Maryland there's a law that makes it illegal to leave a car motor running in a store parking lot. Anyhow, when he came out with his coffee there were four policemen standing around his car. One of them was writing up the violation and, when he was done, he asked the man to sign it. He refused and the other three cops jumped him. Soon, two more cruisers rolled up and their occupants jumped out. All told, a total of eight cops beat on this guy for twenty minutes in the sub-freezing weather. All because he didn't want to turn off his car's motor while he bought a cup of coffee at the 7-Eleven. The cops left him in the parking lot with two broken arms, a bloodied face, and damage to his ribs and lungs. They were cleared of any criminal wrongdoing by the unit within the department that investigates brutality charges. At first, the man's family didn't want anybody to make it a political thing, even though a bunch of us from the University of Maryland and Howard University had wanted to get involved as soon as we heard about the incident. After the cops were cleared, though, they got really pissed—excuse my language—and told us to do whatever it took to get justice for their father, son, and brother. We mounted a campaign of rallies and this got the NAACP to get him a good lawyer. The DA refused to file criminal charges so we sued the cops and the department. We eventually won and all of the cops got reassigned. Of course, it didn't change the basic racist nature of the force, but it put them on notice. This is what we would consider doing for Malcolm if it was okay with the folks involved. Sorry to go on like this, but I want you to know we are serious."

Grace never figured this hippie for this kind of stuff.

She coughed. "I have to talk to Reverend Moore before I give a final yes or no, Peter," she said calmly. "But I think it sounds like a good way to go if we keep hitting brick walls. I understand that you gotta put some pressure on these white folks sometime, no offense. Let's see what the minister says. I'm going to talk with him at four this afternoon about getting me in to see Malcolm. I believe he has some friends in the NAACP, also." She sat back in her chair. "I appreciate your concern a lot."

Peter thanked her for her time and left. He felt pretty good about the conversation. Now, he had to wait. He also had to go see how Lucy was doing. She was probably still at his place. Hopefully, she was staying away from the alcohol. She really needed to find something to do so she wouldn't go off the deep end. Losing a good friend to a murderer and then seeing another friend getting busted for the murder had to be totally fucked, even if you knew he wasn't guilty. It's just the nature of people to start questioning what they know to be true when your reality gets fucked with like that. Too bad she wasn't a political person. Or a religious one. At least when you had a belief system you could make some kind of sense out of tragedies like this. Of course, folks who don't have those kind of things are often able to see things more clearly precisely because they don't have whatever system to filter the reality they are viewing. Usually, though, those folks were just confused and doubted everything including themselves. That's probably what Lucy was dealing with. Peter knew what he would do. He stopped by the bank and withdrew fifty bucks. If she wasn't wasted he would take her out to dinner somewhere nice—just so she could pretend that it was only the two of them. He laughed. It was kind of scary how quickly he was falling in love with this chick. Of course, the enlightened observer might say that the two had been casually courting since they were both twelve years old. If you don't count the couple of years Peter was on the road doing his hitchhiking thing and the year in the army, that meant they'd been leading up to this blossoming romance for almost thirteen years.

He got home around 3:30. Lucy was up and around. She was playing a tape of the Grateful Dead's 1973 RFK Stadium show and eating a cheese sandwich when Peter walked in the door. She looked a hell of a lot better. No tears and a smile on her face. Peter waved as he sped toward the bathroom. The beer he drank at Art's was running through him.

"Hey, Lucy. How ya feelin'?" Peter shed his work clothes while he talked through the bathroom door. "You wanna go get something to eat at some nice place?"

"I'm feelin' much better," she answered. "I'd love to go out."

"Let me take a shower and get dressed. Go ahead and pick the place while I'm showerin'." The next thing Lucy heard was the sound of water rushing from the shower head. She knew exactly where she wanted to eat. The Italian Gardens in College Park. Good selection of food and drink, plus a band. Besides she knew that it was one of Peter's old hangouts. He'd dig the idea. She decided to go climb in the shower with him.

Reverend Moore was talking to someone else when Grace got to his place behind the church. She waited in the front room of the house while he finished up his business with the previous visitor. Five minutes later, he came out to greet Grace. She smiled and shook his hand. He responded in kind.

"Good afternoon, Miss Grace. I hope you are holding up all right."

"By the grace of God, I am, Reverend." They sat down in the front room and began to talk.

"I have been able to get in touch with the prison authorities in Patuxent prison," began Reverend Moore. "And they tell me your nephew is still in their facility. They will put you on his list of permitted visitors."

"When can I see him?"

"They wouldn't say." Reverend Moore tried to look hopeful. However, he knew of other men in the Patuxent facility who were not allowed to see their relatives for weeks. This usually happened because they were recovering from beatings given by the police and guards. He didn't want to get Grace's hopes up too high but neither did he want to scare her with horror stories. "I do know that they have visiting hours four days a week. If you need a ride I am sure we can provide one."

"What about a lawyer?" queried Grace. "He gonna need one to prove he didn't do this. Any suggestions? I can take a loan on my house in Kansas City if I have to." She hoped that she wouldn't have to sell it but was willing to make the sacrifice if it meant Malcolm would go free.

"Let's get in to talk with Malcolm, first," said the minister. "We should ask him what he would like. I will contact my friends in the NAACP and see what they can do. I don't know much about the law, but it does seem like the police have some questions to answer. Furthermore, we need to make some contact with your nephew for his own emotional state. And yours, too."

"I talked to a nice young white man who works with Malcolm," stated Grace. "He talked to me about some group in the area that he belongs to. The name has something to do with a coalition against racism? Have you heard of them?"

"Yes," answered Reverend Moore. "They are well-meaning, mostly young, and have worked with some of us Black churches and the NAACP on other cases involving community members and the police force. What did he want?" The minister was noncommittal. He did have some hesitation about aligning himself with this group, given their radical connections and reputation.

"He spoke about organizing a campaign to get Malcolm out and the charges dropped," she answered. "He told me a story of a man who was beat up by the police at a 7-Eleven a few years back."

"Oh yes," recalled the preacher. "Mr. Anthony." The preacher cleared his throat. "I would like to talk with this young man, Grace. What did you say his name is?"

"Peter," she answered. "Can I give him your number?"

"Yes. Or just let him know he can drop by almost any afternoon," answered Reverend Moore. He stood up to hold the door for Grace. "I need to go and minister to Sister Melody. She is very ill. You can go to the church to pray if you wish."

"Thank you. I will." Grace left the minister's house and walked over to the church.

Art was just leaving the pancake house when Antoine walked in the door. Art had been wondering when Malcolm's friends were gonna show up. They might have some info on his whereabouts on the night in question. From what he could figure, the cops didn't do much asking about proof. Of course, he didn't know how much Malcolm had told them, but hey, he isn't guilty so why should he have to prove where he was. None of their fuckin' business, no how. Art said hello and Antoine nodded his head.

"Hey Art," said Antoine. "You leavin'?"

"Yeah. My shift's over. I'm goin' home. You wanna come with?"

"I'll meet up with you in a few," answered Antoine. "I was gonna get some food."

"We got some food at the crib," offered Art.

"I'll get some beer, then."

Ten minutes later, Antoine knocked on the door to Art's apartment. He had a case of Miller in his arms. Art let him in. Once a dozen beers were in the fridge, they both grabbed one and popped the top. Art began to prepare dinner. Antoine turned on the TV. Cartoons were on the screen. Antoine leaned back on the chair next to the sofa and let his mind wander. He had never hung much with Art except when Malcolm was around. Malcolm's absence was certainly noticed. Art was grilling onions and potatoes. The meat was in the oven. The apartment smelled good.

"So, Art," began Antoine. "What the hell we gonna do about Malcolm? We know he wasn't nowhere near those people's house and we know he ain't a killer, but the police seem set on sending him up the river for life."

"I was wonderin' what you knew about his whereabouts on Saturday after he left the church barbecue?" asked Art.

"Shit. That's a problem. Me and this Leah girl was out dancin' and playing cards at a friend's. Malcolm and Marion was out dancin' 'til five or six the next morning. And all they was hittin' was the illegal dance clubs. Them brothers don't want to draw no attention to their operations. Too much goin' down in the back rooms."

"We gonna have to get them to change their minds," said Art. He took a couple more beers from the fridge and handed one to Antoine. The other one he opened for himself.

"That's gonna be tricky."

"If anyone gonna do it," joked Art. "It's gonna be us. Cause we bad."

Antoine chuckled. "Anybody been able to find out how Malcolm doin'?"

"My mom was gonna work on that today. She with her preacher friend now tryin' to figure that shit out."

"Cool."

"What's up with them ladies you and Malcolm was with last week? Where they at?"

"I tried to call Leah and she in New York lookin' at some college she thinkin' of attendin'. Marion was still in court 'bout her daddy up in Jersey."

"What'd her daddy do?"

"Jacked up a landlord who refused to fix a gas heater and the fumes nearly killed Leah's niece," answered Antoine.

"Good for her." Art began filling the plates with food. Antoine got up from the couch and sat at the kitchen table. After Art set the plates on the table, they began grittin' down. Neither of the men said a thing until they were done.

"I was talking to that guy Peter that I work with, you know…" said Art.

"That hippie cat?" asked Antoine.

"Yeah. He in some group called the Maryland Coalition Against Racism or somethin' like that and he tol' me they interested in helpin' Malcolm out," said Art. He leaned back on his chair, opened the fridge and retrieved two more beers.

"I heard of them. They helped out that brother who got his ass whupped by the county pigs at the 7-Eleven."

"I told him okay as long as Malcolm and Grace agree," said Art. "But I don't know when we gonna be able to talk with Malcolm. What you think about it?"

"I say do whatever it takes," answered Antoine. "Like Malcolm said, by any means necessary."

Art laughed. "I'll see what my mom says. I was always more of a Redd Foxx fan, but Malcolm did have a way." Foxx and Malcolm X had worked together in a restaurant when Malcolm was still Malcolm Little.

10

Wednesday afternoon. Mulhaney and Smith were back. Despite the fact that there were probably regulations against it, they were in Malcolm's cell. No guns were evident, although Malcolm figured they were packing something concealed. They had Malcolm cuffed to the bottom bunk in the cell. Smith was hanging back, his nightstick in its sheath. Mulhaney was not more than a foot away from Malcolm, his garlic, whiskey and cigarette breath hitting Malcolm's nose every few seconds. Every thirty seconds or so Mulhaney hit Malcolm on this thighs or arms with his nightstick. Or he jabbed it into his gut. There was not a guard in sight.

"Look, McRice," said Mulhaney. He jabbed Malcolm hard. "You're going to confess. You did it. We know it and you know it. We're just waiting on you to tell us how."

Malcolm said nothing. He looked at Mulhaney with a hatred he didn't even know he had. Mulhaney whacked him hard across the thighs with his stick. Malcolm winced in pain. Smith hung back. Malcolm looked at him. He shrugged his shoulders.

"Look here, boy," continued Mulhaney. He spoke quietly, yet menacingly. "Let me see if I can help you out. You were pissed at that little prick Prehausen. He owed you money and you were tired of his lame excuses. So you decided to go push him around a little. Things got out of hand when his girlfriend came home. Prehausen had a knife or something. You were drunk and just went crazy on them both. Ain't that how it happened?"

Mulhaney poked Malcolm again. Hard. Malcolm bent over and the cuffs pulled at his wrists. He could feel the warmth of his blood dripping down his wrists from where the cuffs cut in to his flesh. He lifted his head slowly, looked Mulhaney in the eyes and spit. The saliva hit Mulhaney right in his eyes. Mulhaney lost it.

"Listen you fuckin' nigger!" he shouted. He punched Malcolm in the face a half dozen times and kneed him in the balls. Malcolm crumpled as far as the cuffs allowed. "You're goin' down for this fuckin' crime! Unless I kill you first." He looked back at Smith, who had not moved. "Take me away from this nigger before I kill him."

Smith yelled down to the guard to open the cell door. The door slid back and Mulhaney left. Smith uncuffed Malcolm and shook his head. He closed the cell door behind him after putting the cuffs back in his belt and leaving the cell. Malcolm sat down on the bed. He was gonna be sore in the morning.

Raymond stood at the front of the room. People continued to come in through the doors of the Greenbelt community center. It was Friday night. Between him and Peter, every black liberation, civil rights, radical, and women's group to the left of the NAACP and Democratic Party had been contacted, plus several of their personal friends who weren't connected to any group but hated bullshit and injustice. It was a good turnout. Over fifty people. There hadn't been much to organize around for most of these folks. Only the commie groups cared enough to commemorate the recent victory of the Vietnamese and the student groups hadn't done much except riot for a couple days over police raids in the dorms at the University of Maryland. The energy in the room was good. Raymond decided to open the meeting.

"Hey all," he began. "Good to see so many faces. As you know, this meeting is about a brother who's setting down in Patuxent right now for a murder he didn't commit. Our job tonight is to start strategizing how we gonna get him out. If it's okay with folks, I'll chair this meeting and then we can choose someone else for the next one and so on. Is that all right?"

Nobody objected. Peter was pleasantly surprised. That was a good sign. He'd been to meetings that had ended before they began because the idiots in attendance couldn't agree on who was gonna chair the thing. Peter pretty much figured that no matter who was in charge, you could always make the points you wanted to make and achieve whatever you hoped to achieve. Who cared about all the procedural bullshit, anyhow? He hoped Lucy was okay. She was gonna hang out with Julie's sisters until ten or so. The funerals were yesterday. She went to Julie's and Peter went to Jeremy's. It was a funeral. The minister tried to say something nice about Jeremy, even though he never met the kid, and his mom cried like she had lost someone she actually loved. The only interesting aspect to the whole fuckin' ceremony was that Rock wasn't there. Peter was still thinking on that one. Anyway, Lucy had invited Julie's sisters out to dinner and drinks. Just to help them ease the stress and pain. It was a nice gesture even though she didn't really know them.

"Let's set up a couple ground rules for discussion, okay?" Raymond was doing the chair thing. Peter listened. "Before you speak, please say your name and, if you're with a group, what group that is. The other rule is we have to end this meeting at 9:30 'cause we gotta be outta here by 9:45. Is that all right with everybody?"

A murmur of agreement went around the room. People settled into their seats while Raymond took a drink of soda from the can he had set in front of him. Peter knew he was going to speak first, since he was closest to the situation and knew the most about it. Raymond nodded toward him.

"Go ahead, bro."

"Hi. My name is Peter and I'm not with any particular group at this time except the Coalition. Used to be with the Revolutionary Student Group out in College Park, but the university asked me to leave so now I ain't a student." Some folks laughed. Peter continued: "I'm gonna talk first so I can introduce the situation so far. I work with Malcolm and am pretty good friends with his roommate. Plus, I grew up in Snowdon and know its racist legacy in a personal way. Here goes." Peter turned his chair around to face the crowd and sat up on its back. He coughed and began. "I been workin' with Malcolm—that's the accused—for close to seven months. He came to Snowdon a couple days after he was discharged from the Army, where he spent a few months in the stockade for attacking his CO. His uncle got him a job at the Pancake House there on Route 1 in Snowdon and he's just a regular guy. Likes to party, hates work, and tries to enjoy life as much as us working folks can.

"There was some shit between him and a couple of the white kids who work at the restaurant. It was mostly over petty shit like who was supposed to do what at work and girls. Stuff like that. The white kids who work there are usually working class kids who need money and this place hires anybody 'cause they pay shit wages. Like a lot of white Marylanders, they use the n-word too much, but for the most part I don't think that they are really wicked racists. Some of y'all might have a different take on it and I have to admit that I'm so used to the shit I might be a little desensitized to it. I apologize. Anyhow, there's a lot of petty dealing that goes on between the employees at the pancake house and that's how this shit got started. Malcolm apparently fronted Jeremy—that's one of the dead victims—a couple hundred bucks to pick up some pot. Jeremy spent the money and kept giving Malcolm excuses. Malcolm wanted his weed and started puttin' some pressure on Jeremy. Still there wasn't no threat of violence, just some vague nonsense about Malcolm gettin' some of his bros from Baltimore together to pay Jeremy a visit.

"As it turned out, Jeremy had the weed for Malcolm on Wednesday night before last. Malcolm was happy and was headin' for Baltimore on the following Friday when some dope dealer who calls himself Samson tried to stab him in his car. The word is that this cat Samson got ripped off and the weed he had been selling was the same as the stuff Malcolm had. The way dealing works in Snowdon is that if someone has really good shit, he or she is the only one who has it. This Samson cat is a Pagan biker and pretty racist. Rumor has it he's in the Klan. Anyhow, the next thing Malcolm knows is that he's being charged with murder 'cause he can't prove where he was when the murders occurred and that he supposedly threatened

Jeremy over the money he was owed. Plus, according to his uncle, his priors in the Army include another assault charge and a dealing charge. And, one of the cops conducting the investigation is a well known drunk and racist. Black folk in Snowdon don't even challenge his ass."

Peter sat down. The rest of the folks at the meeting began to talk amongst themselves. He didn't know how militant he had sounded. Or if he had overplayed Malcolm's police record. Hopefully, this group was still radical enough to overlook the white man's bullshit and get to the core. The first person to speak was a brother from Hyattsville.

"My name's Angel." he began. "I got a couple questions for Peter. First, what does this man's family think of us? Why ain't they here? Second, how we know this Malcolm cat didn't do this?"

Peter answered. "His family consists of his uncle and his great-aunt, who raised him since Malcolm was a couple weeks old. They ready to go along with us. At the same time, his aunt is talking to her preacher in Snowdon. Some of you might remember the church—it got burned a few years back by some klan initiates and raised a lot of ruckus." Some people nodded. "They aren't here because his uncle had to work so I could attend and his aunt was socializing at the church. She was hoping to talk to a brother who's a lawyer. As to your second question. Malcolm was in Baltimore on Saturday, the night of the murder. His lady friend can attest to that. Why she hasn't is anybody's guess. His uncle thinks it's because Malcolm don't want to get her involved since he knows he's innocent. His friend in Baltimore has tried to contact her but has been unable to. Oh yeah, she lives up in Jersey. Plus Malcolm ain't a murderer."

"How we know that?" asked a woman with short, curly hair. "Oh yeah, my name is Joan."

"You gotta trust me on it," said Peter.

Raymond cleared his throat. Most of the folks in the room looked towards him. He began to talk.

"So that's the story. I think the coalition should take up this man's case and see what we can do. If nothin' else, we'll bring some attention to it and hopefully raise some questions in the minds of the judge and potential jurors. What y'all think?"

The floor was open. An older man stood up in the back of the room.

"Roger Lipschutz, Socialist Worker's Party. I just want to know how we're supposed to support this guy when the main person talking here so far used to be in the RSG. Everybody knows that they've aligned themselves with racist elements in Boston."

Peter hadn't expected this. Lipschutz was referring to the Revolutionary Student Group's parent organization that had, thanks to their interpretation of Lenin, decided that the real issue was class, not race. This meant that they saw the busing of working class white students into a working class neighborhood that was primarily black in Boston or anywhere as a means of dividing the working class. Of course, the real issue was not just race or class—it was both. In America, the two were inseparable. The Socialist Workers saw RSG's parent organization's position as tantamount to being in the Klan, even though it was based on Marxist analysis, not racist hatred. It had been a point of contention around the left for months and had caused fist fights locally between various activists. Peter wanted to nip this nonsense in the bud. He hated internecine battles over what seemed like meaningless and miniscule points of theory. Of course, the anti-busing position was almost impossible to defend, mostly because of the racist fuckers who were at its forefront. Louise Day Hicks and that bunch.

Raymond spoke up. "This meeting is to discuss action around Malcolm McRice's case, not to rehash the left's debate over busing. By merely calling for this meeting, it's clear to me that Peter's intentions are genuine. RSG had different opinions from its parent organization, anyhow." He pointed to another individual in the room who had his arm raised. It was Gabriel Lewis, a Black man who had helped found the coalition a couple years back when he saw the NAACP doing nothing around his younger brother's beating from the Sheriff's department.

"Look people," he began. His voice sounded like

he was a little pissed at how the meeting was going. "We ain't here to battle over y'all's political position. I for one don't give a flying fuck about the positions of different little remnants of the sixties on any issue. The question here is, how can we help this brother sitting out there in Patuxent and looking at life in prison for something that him, his family and his friends swear he didn't do. We ain't gon' make no progress on that question if we spend our time fighting about shit that ain't relevant to the current question. I came here to formulate some ideas for action around getting this brother out and gettin' him a fair trial if'n it goes to that. I hope that's what we all here for. I wanna know when his arraignment is so we can be there and I wanna know how we gon' get him a lawyer who gonna fight for him. Can anybody answer those questions?" Gabriel sat down to a burst of applause from other folks in the room with the same intentions.

Peter waited for the clapping to end. He asked Raymond for permission to speak. Raymond assented.

"I'll be brief here," he said. "We don't know exactly when the arraignment is, but Malcolm's family members have been told to come to court in Hyattsville on Monday morning. Also, his aunt went to the prison today for visiting hours. I assume she got in because she hadn't returned home by the time I left Snowdon. She was hoping to get a good look at her nephew to see if he had been beaten and was gonna try to ask him if he thought our organizing around his case was a good idea. Also, she has been working with a relatively progressive minister at the Zion Baptist Church who might be able to get him a real lawyer, not some public defender who doesn't give a damn."

A woman Peter knew from the Women's Alliance at the University of Maryland raised her hand. Raymond acknowl-edged her and she began to speak.

"My name is Leanne. I suggest we picket the courthouse on Monday and that we work with this minister in whatever way we can to mobilize as many people. While it might not be possible for more folks than us to be there on Monday, if we can start packing the courtroom whenever this man is in there, we can make a difference. Especially if a lot of the folks are just regular churchgoers and citizens, not fringe like some of us."

"Is that a motion?" asked Raymond. Leanne shrugged yes. "All in favor?"

The entire room assented. The discussion continued over logistics and other matters, such as building a phone tree to alert people of changes in the schedule or anything else. The time was getting close to 8:30. Peter was ready to go home and relax. He hoped things were going okay with Lucy and Julie's sisters. All three of them women definitely needed some down time, although Lucy seemed more at peace with the reality of Julie's death after the funeral yesterday.

While Peter was daydreaming, the meeting had ended. People were getting up to go. Some gathered in small groups to decide when and where they would meet to carpool on Monday or to exchange phone numbers for the phone tree. Others just left. Peter hung around to talk with Raymond for a minute or two, then headed to his car. He could taste the beer waiting for him at home.

Grace sat in the passenger seat. Reverend Moore was driving. Two other women around Grace's age sat in the back. The four of them were going to the Patuxent Correctional Facility. Grace hoped she would be able to see her nephew. The other women were making their regular weekly visit to see their sons. They worked the rest of the week and Friday was the best day for them to visit the prison. Grace prayed silently to herself. She prayed that Malcolm was in good shape mentally and physically. It seemed like only minutes and Reverend Moore was parking his car in the prison's lot.

The four of them walked toward the entrance gate. They had left most of their belongings locked in the car. The guards weren't going to let them take much inside anyway. Grace waited while the other two women went on ahead. Since it was her first time, she was going to have to do some extra registration. The minister was there to help her negotiate the bureaucracy since he did this visit quite often. It was this facet of his ministry that depressed him the most. Even deaths were not like this. To see and feel so much hopelessness. And wasted lives. And why? In his opinion, it was all primarily because of the legacy of slavery. The chains of the slave ships and the whips of the masters left scars that would take generations to heal. As long as the laws and those who enforced those laws perpetuated the legacy of slavery's evil those scars would only be rubbed raw. Reverend Moore knew this. His mama had seen two of her sons killed by a white man in Calvert County. His older brothers were sitting on the side of a river fishing when a white man shot them with a rifle. He told the court that he thought they were deer. It wasn't deer season and deer aren't black. He never did a lick of time. Reverend Moore was only two at the time and didn't remember his brothers very well. He remembered his mama crying and watched her become a drunk unable to keep even the most simple job. They lived on a few bucks the state gave them. She got pregnant three more times and had the midwife give her tea that aborted the fetuses each time. She swore she wasn't gonna make no more young men for the white people to kill.

Grace went through the process. She showed her identification and her papers that proved her guardianship of Malcolm when he was a juvenile. She emptied her purse and the pockets of her jacket. She let the female guard pat her down for weapons and so on. Then she waited. Eventually, she was allowed into the waiting room. Only then did the prison guard go to get Malcolm. There was another forty-five minutes left of the visiting hours. Ten minutes later she saw her nephew. From a distance, he looked to be in good shape. He wasn't smiling, but why should he be? There was an open cubicle and the guard told Grace to go sit over there.

On the opposite side of the vertical piece of glass that divided the cubicle in two was Malcolm. On closer inspection, Grace could see that he was un-shaven and his eyes were red. His face was also thinner. His beard wasn't very heavy, though, since Malcolm had baby skin and probably only needed to shave once a week at the most. His daddy said that Malcolm's mama was part Sioux or Ojibwa—some kind of Indian and they just didn't have much body hair. She kissed her hand and put it against the glass. Malcolm did the same and smiled. He spoke through the little hole in the glass like one of those openings you talk through when you buy tickets at a movie theatre.

"Hi, Auntie," he whispered. "I'm so sorry you had to come visit me here."

"We gonna get you out of here, Malcolm," said Grace. "And we gon' put the man who killed them young folks in here. We workin' on it hard." She held back her tears. She didn't want Malcolm to see how afraid she was that no matter what they did they were going to fail.

"Thanks, Auntie." Malcolm smiled. "How's Art and them?"

"They doin' okay, considerin' everything. Your friend Peter done got some folks working on your case. I'm talkin' to Reverend Moore and he workin' on gettin' the NAACP to help us out. Between the bunch of us we'll get you a good lawyer."

"I got a lawyer, Auntie," said Malcolm. "He talked to me yesterday. He seemed okay."

"We gon' get you one who can take his time with your case," she said patiently. "How they treatin' you in here?"

"The guards and other prison people are decent," answered Malcolm. "They get me cigarettes and stuff. But the other day those two cops from Snowdon come into my cell and beat on me. They tryin' to get me to confess to them killings."

"What day was that?" asked Grace. She wanted to get the details right so she could let Peter and the preacher know. That would be something for the lawyer to address. "Don't let them make you sign anything."

"I know," said Malcolm. "I won't." He looked at the clock. Shit, only five more minutes.

"What's your lawyer's name?" asked Grace. "When's your arraignment?"

"His name is James Brian. I think my arraignment is on Monday." The guard came up behind

Malcolm. It was time for him to go back to his cell. "Bye Auntie. I love you."

Grace blew him a kiss. "I love you too, Malcolm. My church is all prayin' for you. I'll see you Monday in court." She turned and walked towards the exit. The minister was waiting there with the two other women. They left the building. Grace was relieved. She had been able to visit and he didn't look too bad, all things considered. But he needed to get out of this place.

11

Art got out of the shower and started dressing. Red pants, pink shirt and a leather vest. Platform shoes and nylon socks. He sipped on his pint of Smirnoff Silver. The radio was playing "I Can't Get Next to You" by the Temptations. Whenever he heard the Temps he tried to sound like Eddie Kendricks—"I can fly like a bird in the sky…" but never succeeded. The plan was for him and Antoine to check out some of the clubs Malcolm and Marion hit the week before and see if they might be willing to testify or somethin'. Marion was in jail up in Camden for jumping on the bailiff's back when they took her daddy away for beating that landlord. They got her for contempt—two weeks. Gotta like that girl's spirit. Goddamn fireball. He hoped his mom would get back before he left. He wanted to know how Malcolm was doing.

Just as he thought this he heard the key turning. It was his mom. She entered the apartment with a peaceful look on her face. Things must have gone okay.

"Hi Mom," said Art.

"Hi Art." She sat down at the kitchen table. Art took her dinner out of the oven and set it in front of her. He reached in the fridge and took out the iced tea. She poured herself a glass and began to eat the meat loaf and potatoes Art had saved.

"He seems to be holdin' up in there. He said the guards are decent to him. I guess he's in a cell by hisself."

"Them cracker cops been around?" asked Art. He knew they couldn't stay away. They needed to cover their asses.

"Yes," said Grace. "He said they beat on him some. You know they tryin' to get him to sign a confession they done already wrote up."

"He didn't, did he?"

"Malcolm stupid some times, Art, but he ain't no fool." Grace smiled. "Neither of y'all is. This here food's good."

"Thanks. I'm gonna go to Baltimore with Antoine like I tol' you. We gonna try and get some of them boys to talk that run those clubs. You gon' be all right?"

"Sure, honey," she said. "I know my boy is okay even if he is in their jail for no good reason. You comin' back tonight?"

"I hope so," answered Art. "I gotta work at 11 in the mornin'. Plus I'm borrowin' Malcolm's ride."

He left. Grace took her plate and moved over to the couch. She needed to rest her bones. This would be the first night that she could truly rest now that she had visited her nephew and seen that he was okay. Reverend Moore said he would ask folks who could make it to attend the arraignment on Monday morning. That reminded her. She needed to let Art know about that so he could take time off of work. She figured Peter was already planning on being there along with his group of folks. The radio was playing that song by the Staples Singers. "I'll Take You There." She set down her food on the floor next to the couch and lay back on the pillows. Soon she was dozing off. In the landscape of her mind she saw Malcolm as a young boy. His eternal smile, like little Michael Jackson's. No matter how you felt about something he did, once he smiled all your anger or frustration melted away. Too bad his mama never got to see that. He came home from kindergarten every day of the first week with tear stains running through the dust from the playground on his cheeks. Auntie, he said, there's a little boy named Timmy who I want to play with but he say he don't like me. When I ask him why, he say 'cause his daddy told him not to. I tol' him no matter. His daddy wasn't at the school. He didn't have to know. But he still say no.

That hurt so bad, remembered Grace. Poor little fellow just wanted to play. Turned out the boy was a white boy whose daddy had led the fight against integrating the school district. Grace found this out at Malcolm's first conference. The teacher called Malcolm's persistence endearing. She was a small cute white woman who couldn't have been more than twenty-five. Not long after that conference Malcolm came home just a-smilin' as happy as a pig in manure. Auntie, he shouted, Timmy played ball with me today. We gonna be friends! She hugged him near to death just to get some of that happiness and hope in that little boy's smile for herself. He never meant no harm to nobody. It's just this world that brung him down.

It was Saturday morning. Grace was awake and resting on the couch. Art was already at work. He hadn't said much about the night before with Antoine. The phone rang. Grace jumped up, startled. She picked the receiver up.

"Hello?"

"Hi, Miss Grace." It was Peter. "Sorry to disturb you but I thought you might want to know what happened at our meeting last night. I can call back another time, if you want."

"No, go ahead, son." Grace found a pencil and paper just in case she needed to write anything down.

"Well, there were over fifty people present, which was great," began Peter. "We decided to hold a picket outside the courthouse on Monday and to get people to pack the courtroom every time Malcolm is there. That way the judge will know he has friends and supporters in the community who are watching this process. Also, we would like to meet with the minister from your church and talk about our plans and about a lawyer and whatever else we need to prove that Malcolm didn't do this."

Grace spoke softly. "He said he would like to meet with you and perhaps a couple other folks in your group. He did talk to some lawyer friends and they may be in court on Monday."

"Do you have Reverend Moore's number, Miss Grace?"

"Yeah. 498-7896. He said you can drop by his house pretty much any weekday before five if you can't schedule somethin'."

The conversation continued for a few more minutes. Grace updated Peter on Malcolm and her visit and told him about Mulhaney and Smith's visit to Malcolm at Patuxent. She asked him to keep in touch and hung up. Peter was at home. Lucy was working. When she left she complained of a headache from drinking too much the night before. Peter guessed that meant the dinner with Julie's sisters had gone all right. He put some Quicksilver Messenger Service on the turntable. The second side of the Happy Trails album. The whole side was one long jam. He took a bong hit. What the hell, it was Saturday. He took another one. Cippolina's guitar really sounded good now. He lay back on the sofa and closed his eyes. Lucy said she was gonna go back to her place after work. That meant he could just lie around and do nothing if that's what he felt like doing. It was. He picked up the Saturday Sun from the floor and turned to the box scores. Boston was doing okay. They were playing the Yankees. Beat 'em 9 to 1 on Friday and lost yesterday. They were playing each other again today. Catfish pitching for the Yanks against Moret. It was then that he realized he hadn't listened to or watched a ball game in almost a week. That hadn't happened since he was on the road. Between this budding romance and the situation with Malcolm, he just didn't seem to have the time. He would try and remedy that today. The Orioles were probably playing an afternoon game. Even better, maybe Boston was on the game of the week.

Antoine was drinking coffee and listening to Karin ramble on. She was all dressed and ready to go to his other sister's house up in Towson for the day. Antoine was supposed to get her there by noon. It was ten. He gulped the coffee and thought of the night out with Art. It was a lot of fun to watch an older brother at work. He hustled all those young brothers into thinking he was doing them a favor when it was the exact opposite. They were helping Art out. Big time. He walked into the first place over off of West Lombard poppin' his fingers and drinking on his Smirnoff Silver. The cat at the door asked him if he was a member and Art told him not only was he a member, but so was his daddy. The bouncer looked at Art like he was wearing a dress or somethin' and then just said come on in, pops. Art bowed and walked in. Within five minutes he was playing cards, talking shit, drinking Smirnoff, and smoking on a stick. He had a couple ladies sitting on both sides of him and he was talking his shit like he did so well. Doing the dozens. Yo' mama this and yo' sister that and the white man got a boll of cotton up his ass and on and on. The folks in the place ate it up. After they was there an hour or so, the owner of the place come up and asked Art if he wanted to deal cards for him. Art said he'd consider it. On his way out, he broke out a photo of Malcolm and asked the bouncer if he recognized him. The cat said yeah, why. Art explained the situation and asked the brother if he could help out.

"I don't know man," said the bouncer. "I don't wanna bring no heat down on this place. My boss have my ass if I do."

"Look here, brother," said Art. "How 'bout we don't say nothin' unless there's no other way to get my man out of jail? Then I'll explain the situation to your boss and convince him to help out? I just wanna know if you with us on this if we need your help?"

"I is. I is," said the bouncer. Art shook his hand.

"You all right, my man." They repeated the scenario at three other places. Two of the other three recognized Malcolm's photo, especially when Art or

Antoine mentioned he had been with a beautiful woman. Marion is definitely a looker. Malcolm was no fool on that, anyhow.

"Hey Antoine!" Karin interrupted his thoughts. "Let's go! Wake up!"

Antoine laughed and got up. He found his car keys and the two of them headed toward the car. He planned on hooking up with Art and Peter over at Peter's later on as long as his sister could watch Karin overnight. She usually said yes.

Antoine and Art arrived at Peter's around five that evening. Peter had slept away most of the day and was trying to catch up on the afternoon baseball scores. Art carried in a case of Michelob and Antoine had a bucket of chicken and some oysters from the sandwich shop on Main Street. Each of the men took a beer and found a seat. Antoine set the food down on the floor and they began eating and talking.

"How did it go with y'all last night?" asked Peter.

"We did all right," answered Antoine. "Your man here is one smooth-talkin' motherfucker."

"Ain't he?" asked Peter. Art sat there grinnin' and eatin'. He knew he was smooth and loved it when people acknowledged this particular skill of his.

"Yeah," he said. "We got every single one of them bouncers to say they recognized Malcolm as being in their club last Saturday. They all promised to testify if it came to that."

"Cool," said Peter. "What's up with Marion?"

"She in jail," said Art. "Jumped on the bailiff when the judge sent her daddy to prison for jumpin' a landlord who almost killed Leah's niece by not fixing the gas heater."

"Good for her, 'cept she's in jail and we got no witness. Gotta admire her fire, though."

"Shit. Lot of them brothers in Baltimore was admirin' somethin' else of hers, seems like," joked Antoine.

"Yeah," laughed Art. "Every single one of 'em remembered Malcolm being in their club when Antoine described Marion."

"She is damn nice, that's for sure," agreed Peter.

"Shit," said Art. "You got you a woman now. Where Lucy at?"

"She went home after work," said Peter. "Been a week since she was there."

"Cool."

"At the meeting I went to, we agreed to work with that preacher on getting a lawyer and also in getting people to attend all of Malcolm's court dates," said Peter. He looked at Antoine. "Did Art tell you about that?"

"The coalition stuff?" asked Antoine. "Yeah, he did."

Peter told the others about the picket on Monday. Then he filled Art and Antoine in on Grace's visit with Malcolm. He went over to the turntable and put some Dylan on. "The Lonesome Death of Hattie Carrol." Art and Antoine listened, since that was about all you could do with Dylan.

"Shit," said Art as he listened to Dylan tell the story of a black cleaning woman who was killed by some rich white guy in Maryland and got away with it. "Did this really happen?"

"Yeah," said Peter. "Some things don't change. Some things don't change."

"So them punk cops still beatin' on him," stated Antoine, turning the conversation back to Malcolm's situation. "They think he gonna crack and sign their bullshit confession. Man I thought that shit only happened on TV." He shook his head. The three men drank until the beer was gone. Antoine and Art ended up staying at Peter's. His mom walked to church the next morning.

12

Monday morning. June 30, 1975. Eight o'clock and already 90 degrees in the shade. Out on the lot in front of the courthouse it was closer to 100. A typical summer day in Maryland. There were close to forty people walking slowly in a circle in front of the courthouse building. Most of them carried signs demanding Malcolm's release and a re-opening of the investigation. Some of the signs were more rhetorical, attacking the judicial system as racist and a legacy of the slaveholders. For the most part, the picketers talked amongst themselves and refrained from chanting slogans. In one corner of the lot, about fifty feet away from the steps and the marchers, stood another thirty or forty folks. These were the church people, except for Art, who was there with his mom. Reverend Moore had done well. Most of the people now gathered around him were from the church in Snowdon, but there were also a dozen or so who came from allied churches in Beltsville and Bowie. These were two neighboring towns that had their own shameful legacy of race relations. Indeed, it was only a year ago that the klan had held several meetings on a farm less than a mile from Route 1 in Beltsville. Bowie was still segregated into two parts, both by race and economics. The old part of the town was primarily black and was still without running water in some of the houses. Just across the highway was the newer section of the town. This part was composed of newly-built suburban houses inhabited by white people with considerably more money than their neighbors across the road.

Peter and Raymond walked over to the church group, mostly to introduce themselves to Reverend Moore. He must be hot in his suit, thought Peter. He extended his hand to the minister when he reached their assembly. Reverend Moore smiled.

"You must be Peter," he said as he shook his hand. "Nate Moore. Thanks for caring."

"My pleasure," said Peter. "This is Raymond. He's the chair of the coalition for now." Raymond and the preacher shook hands. "What is your plan for today?"

"We plan on going into the courtroom and staying through Malcolm's arraignment," answered Reverend Moore. "What about y'all?"

"We figured we would do more good if we stayed outside," answered Raymond. "We have a bit of a reputation here that probably wouldn't help Malcolm at this point in the process."

"Sounds good." Moore looked at Peter, "Miss

Grace tells me you want to meet with me. You're welcome to come by my house if you get there before dinnertime. If you want dinner you'll have to call so the cook can make sure there's enough food." He looked at both men. "We should probably try to coordinate our campaigns as much as we can while still keeping their own identity, if only for the sake of those in each group who might have problems working too closely with one or the other of the groups."

Peter was impressed. This guy knew his shit. He seemed genuine. Time would tell. He asked Raymond the time. Nine o'clock. The three men agreed to talk some more and the minister went to gather his group. Once they gathered, they headed into the courthouse. Peter and Raymond joined the picket line. The temperature was deadly. A couple policemen sat inside their air conditioned cars watching the marchers.

Inside the courtroom, Malcolm sat with his lawyer. He looked back and waved at his aunt and Art. His lawyer was a public defender who was known to be a dealmaker. It was rare that one of his appointed clients ever went to trial. He prided himself on the swiftness with which he moved his cases through the system. How many of those who copped a plea were actually innocent was unknown. That was no concern of his, however. He wasn't in it for justice, just efficiency. The bailiff entered: Oyez, Oyez, the Honorable so-and-so presiding, all rise. and the people in the courtroom stood. The judge came in and took his seat on the pedestal. Everybody sat back down. Malcolm and his lawyer were having an animated discussion. From the way that Malcolm kept shaking his head, Art guessed that the prosecutor had offered Malcolm a deal and the lawyer wanted Malcolm to take it. Naturally, Malcolm was refusing.

The judge turned his attention to the defendant's bench. Malcolm and his lawyer stopped talking. He called Malcolm up. Malcolm was handcuffed and was wearing shackles. Two cops left their positions behind the judge's bench and stood next to him while the judge spoke. After asking Malcolm his name and reading him his charges, he looked up at him.

"Do you understand the charges against you Malcolm McRice?"

"Yes, sir."

"How do you plead to the charges?"

Malcolm got ready to answer. Suddenly the prosecutor stood up and asked for a moment to speak with the judge and defense attorney. The judge called the two lawyers to his desk. The three men talked amongst themselves. Every once in a while those members of the audience nearest the bench could hear the prosecutor say something about a deal and the defense lawyer saying something about Malcolm refusing any deal. The judge ended the conversation with a wave of his hand. The two law-yers returned to their respective places. The public defender tried one more time to get Malcolm to agree to something. Malcolm shook his head no.

The defense attorney cleared his throat and said, "My client pleads not guilty, your honor."

"Okay." He pounded his gavel. "Pretrial hearing set for August 4th, 1975." Malcolm turned and smiled at his aunt. She had her best churchgoing clothes on. Holding back tears, she blew him a kiss. Art smiled at Malcolm and gave him a subdued clenched fist salute. Malcolm nodded in acknowledgement, then the cops took him from the courtroom. Art and the church people left the courtroom. As soon as they were out of the building they began talking amongst themselves. The picketers put down their signs and walked over.

"What happened inside?" asked Raymond. "How did he look?"

Art and the minister gave a brief rundown of the arraignment and answered a couple questions. Then Reverend Moore asked everyone to put their name and phone number on a piece of paper. He planned on calling a meeting to discuss Malcolm's case and how they were going to get him out of jail. Art asked Peter if he needed a ride to work. Peter reminded him that he was working nights this week and had his car with him. Art said he had to go and wondered if Peter could give Grace a ride home. Peter said yes and Art headed off to work.

Friday noon. Fourth of July. Art had finally been able to take a day off to go visit Malcolm. He and his mother were on the way. Peter had mentioned the irony of him going to visit Malcolm in prison on the day the rest of the country was celebrating its freedom. The temperature had not dipped below 90 degrees the entire week. Art had broken down and bought a window air conditioner for the apartment. His mom was near seventy and having a little bit of difficulty breathing and getting around in this extended heat. Plus, it sure as hell made it easier to sleep at night or whenever Art got the chance. Without Malcolm, he and Peter had been pulling extra shifts at the Pancake House. The overtime was starting to wear on the both of them. But they were better off than Malcolm, no matter how hot it was. Even Lewin had been doing some hours behind the grill. Make that man earn his money for a change.

After parking the car, Art and his mom entered the visitors' area and began the process of getting in. Since Grace had visited before she sailed through pretty quickly. It took a little longer for Art to get approval. Once in, they sat and waited. They had to see Malcolm one at a time, so Grace went first. He had a total of thirty minutes to visit. Grace kept her visit short.

"You looked good in court, Malcolm," she whispered.

"That lawyer was trying to make me plead," he

said.

"I know he was," she answered. "Don't let them men make you say somethin' you don't mean, ya hear?"

"Sheesh, Auntie," said Malcolm. "I ain't gonna cop to their lies. I know I didn't do nothin'. Heck, I loved that Julie girl." He pushed away a tear.

"I know honey," comforted Grace. "I know."

Malcolm looked at his aunt and smiled. She kissed her fingers and put them on the glass and waved goodbye. As she walked away, Malcolm mouthed the words "I love you." It was Art's turn next.

Art sat down on his side of the glass. He nodded.

"Hey, l'il bro'," he said. "How you feelin'? The guards being decent?"

"Yeah, they okay," said Malcolm. "How's everybody outside? How's Antoine?"

"We okay," laughed Art. "Shit, we doin' better than you. Peter and Lucy sent their love and all that shit."

"Cool." Malcolm looked over at the guard and then moved his face closer to the little hole in the glass. "How Marion doin'? I ain't heard shit."

"She went to jail for two weeks."

"What the hell for?" asked Malcolm, surprised. Just what he needed, his new lady in jail.

"She jumped on the bailiff after the judge gave her daddy six months."

"She one feisty female," said Malcolm to himself. He looked at Art. "How long she got?"

"She should be out tomorrow." Art looked at the clock on the wall. "Them cracker cops been back?"

"Once," answered Malcolm. "This time the guard stayed around so they couldn't fuck with me. They had their little piece of paper they want me to sign, though. That lawyer I got is a dumb fuck."

"Gracie's preacher workin' on gettin' you a real one. Once that happens, we gotta get the police report and all the evidence. The preacher say the other lawyer never even looked at your police report. We gon' take care of you, my man. Peter and his crazy political friends I told you about are on the warpath. They crazy, but they get shit done." The guards came up behind Malcolm. It was time to go back to the cell. Art nodded goodbye. Malcolm responded in kind. They both left the room in opposite directions.

Lucy was driving. Peter and her were returning from a cookout on a farm near Gaithersburg. The place was owned by some hippie friends of Peter's. There had been a band, lots of beer, chicken, salads, and pot. Most of the people were pretty cool and seemed to dig Lucy. Peter had wanted to stay but Lucy had to work the next morning at six. As they rode home, they were listening to Bruce Springsteen's album The Wild, the Innocent, and the E Street Shuffle. Peter kept rewinding the tape deck to the song called "4th of July, Asbury Park." It was a cool song about the Jersey boardwalk, but Lucy was wondering when he would get tired of hearing that particular song and let the tape proceed. She actually liked the last song on the tape the best. It was cool, she thought, how it began with autoharp. As far as she knew, it was the only rock song ever that featured an autoharp.

The car was on Route 198 now just past Bond Mill Road. They were almost home. Peter turned the music up. At the same time Lucy thought she saw a flashing red light in her rear-view mirror. She looked back. Shit, the fucking cops. She pulled the car over to the side of the highway and hoped the cruiser would drive by. No such luck. She and Peter waited.

"Oh shit," said Peter, as the driver got out of the cruiser. "It's Starsky and Hutch." He sat very still. One false move and these jerks were likely to shoot. He noticed Mulhaney had his holster unfastened and his hand on his gun. He hoped Lucy was sober. They were certain to make her walk the line and all the rest of that shit. Mulhaney walked up to Lucy's window. She rolled it down.

"Yes?" she asked. She noticed that Mulhaney smelled like whiskey.

"License and registration, please." Mulhaney took the pieces of paper and headed back to this car to call them in. Peter noticed that Smith now stood at the rear of Lucy's vehicle. Neither Peter or Lucy moved. After four or five minutes, Mulhaney came back and gave Lucy her license and registration. He leaned down and looked in the car. He had a flashlight and shone it around the car and in Peter's face.

"Please step out of the car, ma'am," said Mulhaney. Lucy did as she was instructed. Mulhaney ran her through the field sobriety routine. She passed and got back in the driver's seat. Mulhaney shone the light in the car again.

"We're watching you two," he began. "Especially you, hippie boy." He looked at Peter. "The County boys told us about your actions in College Park before you got kicked out of school. Don't think you can start your equal rights shit in Snowdon. It won't play here. You understand?"

Peter didn't say anything. He felt like telling the pig to go fuck himself, but knew that such an act would be stupid. Mulhaney continued to talk.

"You hear me, boy?" He shone the light back on Peter's face. "I can hurt you or your little floozy girlfriend and nobody can do a thing about it. Remember that. You're lucky she ain't drunk. Otherwise I'd kick your ass all over this highway and say you attacked me. This is a warning, in case you're too dumb to figure that out. Now go home." Mulhaney walked back to his car. Smith was already back in the passenger seat. They drove away. As they passed Peter, he noticed Mulhaney pointing his index finger like a gun at him through the window.

"Fuckin' asshole," said Peter. He and Lucy went to her place for the night.

13

"Brothers and Sisters"—Reverend Moore was in the pulpit.

It was the Sunday after Malcolm's arraignment. He had wrestled with this sermon the entire week. Not its content or its righteousness, but whether he should give it at all.

His meeting with that young man Peter convinced him he had no choice but to speak out.

He hoped he didn't lose his ministry, since he loved this church and these people. On the other hand, it didn't matter because he had to do what was right.

He continued, "Last Monday I stood in the heat of the summer with a hundred of the Lord's children. We were there to seek justice for a child of God who has suffered the wrath of the evilness of today's centurions. Those of you who were with me know of what I speak. There is a lamb from God's flock right here in our town—his great-aunt who has cared for him all his life is in our flock—who has suffered the wrath of injustice. He has been falsely accused by those who have an interest in maintaining the injustice and oppression that the yoke of slavery has cast upon this land. These men who do this wrong will tell the newspapers and the television that they are the purveyors and arbiters of justice. They will tell you and me that it is they who will decide whether this man, this child of the Lord, is guilty. They will decide his sentence. I say they have no right to decide these things, even though they be the children of God, too. I say this with a sadness that weeps because we of the darker skin and the poorer classes can still not trust those who would dole out justice. But, I also say this with a righteous anger that we will change this dynamic. We will make the world a place where those of us who are darker in skin and poorer in terms of cash can walk this world with the knowledge that justice—even earthly justice—is for all of God's children, not just those who have by the grace of God, been born into a different set of circumstances.

"You look at me now with a surprised look on your faces. Reverend Moore, you're thinkin', done got militant on us. He goin' the way of Brother Martin or even Malcolm X. I respond to your looks of surprise with this response: I have not changed my mind or my thoughts. I was sent here to do the Lord's work. Sometimes that work is not so pretty. Let us recall the Lord Jesus in the temple when he threw out the moneychangers and those who would profit wrongly in the name of the Lord. Sometimes it demands that we shake things up a little. Sometimes it demands that we shake things up a lot. Either way, it demands that we shake things up. It look like that's what we gonna have to do to get our son and brother some justice.

"I was in that courtroom on Monday and I saw that lawyer man demanding that Malcolm McRice plead guilty to a crime—a very heinous crime—that he insists he did not commit. Justice was not in that courtroom, only the trading of men's lives for the sake of expediency and the evils of racism.

"Once again, I say those men do not deserve to do the Lord's work and dispense justice for they have perverted justice into something a just man or woman could not identify no matter how they tried. Does the Lord call this justice? NO! Brother Job asked once, and I repeat: 'Does God pervert justice? Does the Almighty pervert what is right?' The answer is: No, he doesn't.

"If the Lord doesn't do this to justice, why should these men be allowed to do so? Psalm 64 tells us: 'They plot injustice and say, "We have devised a perfect plan!" Surely the mind and heart of man are cunning.' Why do they do this? The answer is simple, too simple. What is that answer? Because we allow them to. We give our desire for justice away to small-minded men who have venal and earthly interests in the front of their minds, not the interests of justice, not the interests of the Lord, not the interests of society. Just the interests of humanity's basest reasons for existence—money, power, greed, and lust.

"It is not only the fault of those who sit in these courthouses and trade daily in human freedom and lives. No, it is our fault, too, for letting them get away with these evil actions. Every one of us in this church have said to ourselves, 'That doesn't affect me. None of my children committin' crimes. I don't care about that neighbor boy goin' to jail for somethin' he did. Or for somethin' he didn't do.'

"Every single one of us have done this. When we do this we allow the venal men to take our lives away from us.

"When we do this, we are giving the freedom we done fought for so hard right back to the powers of Satan that want us back in chains! The powers of Satan who will lie and cheat to put our young men in prison. It could be a prison with steel bars or it could be a prison that comes out of a needle. It could be a prison that turn you into a slave of lust and gambling or it could be a prison that make you act like a shufflin' house boy who say yassuh. The venal men done put up a lot of prisons for us poor and colored folk. It's up to us to stay away from them and to keep our children out of them.

"So, I'm askin' each and every one of y'all to say a prayer that our son and brother Malcolm—he's the man who grilled up that chicken a couple weeks ago—get some justice and his freedom. I'm askin' those of you who have the time to contribute that and I'm askin' those of you who got the money to contribute that. Just as Jesus wandered into the wilderness, we have wandered into the wilderness that is injustice and we will wander out, our brother's freedom restored. I say AMEN!"

"AMEN!" The church crowd was surprised. The minister never sounded like this before. Grace was ecstatic. He had made her nephew's freedom a mission of the Lord. Some of the other church members were less happy. This sermon and the campaign it seemed to be beginning marked a new phase for the Reverend and the Snowdon Grove Zion Baptist Church.

The elders knew they had always survived in Snowdon by keeping their anger to themselves. If they needed to protest segregation back in the Fifties and Sixties, they went to another town. The further away the better. Even when the klan initiates tried to burn down their church back in 1967, they opposed the protests called by the young people and the NAACP. Then, when the klan marched down the middle of 8th Street and stopped in front of the church so they could throw rocks and eggs at it, the elders said nothing.

This was different. Back then the pastor supported their conservatism. Now, it was the pastor riling up the assembly. Needless to say, they had their apprehensions.

Grace could hardly wait to tell Art and Peter. She knew Peter had been disappointed with the lack of commitment from Reverend Moore after their meeting Wednesday. He had told her he thought the preacher was chickenshit, with all due respect. She tried to defend him, but found it hard when she was told he wasn't so sure Malcolm wasn't involved. The only thing she could figure was that some new information had come up or Reverend Moore had had some kind of revelation.

What she didn't know was that Art had called the preacher after Peter's dismaying report about the preacher's response and told him the details of Malcolm's encounter with that Samson fellow.

The preacher, not being no dummy, asked Art if he thought Samson was the murderer. Art told him yeah, that's what he thought, but there was no way to prove it and it didn't look like the cops had even looked in that direction. The preacher thanked Art and called up a lawyer friend, who, upon a small investigation of his own, counseled that it really looked like something was fishy in the whole investigation.

This had raised enough doubts in Moore's mind about the whole scenario that he re-examined his whole perception of the case. He prayed all night and came to the conclusion that he could not live with himself or stand in front of his flock or his God unless he did everything to get Malcolm out. Since

Friday morning, he had been on the phone to the NAACP and the SCLC trying to get the names of some good lawyers whose help he could implore in this endeavor. The only commitment he had received was from an Irish-American fellow with the name Jerry McCaffrey. He hailed from Virginia and knew how rednecks worked. That was how he put it to Moore on the phone. He, Moore and Grace were scheduled to meet over dinner that Sunday night. If all went well, he would go visit Malcolm on Monday. He had already notified the court of the potential change.

Reverend Moore stood outside the church after spending time with the congregation after the service. Most of the members had congratulated him on his sermon. A few of the older members of the flock had left right away. He would call them later. Hopefully, they could be stirred to the cause. If not, he hoped they wouldn't try to tip the ship. He knew the risk he was taking.

Peter woke up. It was Sunday afternoon. He had worked all night and was happy as a pig in shit to find Lucy in his bed when he got home around five that morning.

They hadn't been spending much time together this past week. Work schedules were screwing things up, as were the meetings Peter had been attending. He wished Lucy would come to a couple but she was pretty adamant about staying away. She did say she would sit in court to support Malcolm whenever she could. He could hear Lucy in the living room. She had some Coltrane playing on the stereo and sounded like she was cleaning up or something. Her footsteps were quiet but continuous. Peter went into the other room. Lucy looked over at him and laughed.

"Hey," she giggled. "Where's your clothes?" Peter realized he was naked.

He took Lucy's hand and led her back to the bedroom. They had some catching up to do. He thought about checking the radio for a baseball game, but gave in to his more immediate desires.

Baltimore Sun

Drugs, Lack of Direction
Story of Murder in Snowdon

Joan Epstein said her daughter Julie was always bringing home orphan puppies and kittens. "It seemed like every week there would be another little furry animal sharing the kibbles with those animals that already lived here." She reminisced with this reporter the day after her daughter's funeral in Burtonsville last week. The family home sits on a half-acre lot set back from Route 29 and is accessible only by a dirt road. The parents were given the lot by a relative when they married in 1952. They built their home there and raised three children—all girls. Julie was the middle one. She was barely 21 when she died.

The circumstances of the murder are these. Two young people were found in their apartment before dawn on June 22, 1975 when one of Julie's sisters went to the apartment to see if they could find out why Julie failed to show up for a surprise midnight birthday party the family had planned for her. What the sister found is still impossible for her to talk about. Epstein and her boyfriend Jeremy Prehausen were dead. Both had been brutally beaten by what police say was either a steel pipe or a baseball bat. The two had lived together for almost eight months. They had been seeing each other for twice that long. Both youths worked at the Pancake House on Washington Boulevard in Snowdon. Miss Epstein was a sophomore at the University of Maryland.

The puppy analogy works for Mrs. Epstein because that was how she perceived Prehausen. Where Julie's childhood was a story of love and family, Prehausen's was a tale of an absentee father, abuse, time in juvenile detention, a mother in and out of jail herself for drugs and alcohol, and an incomplete education. The two met at the pancake house and fell in love almost immediately. "Jeremy was a tormented soul when Julie met him," said her sister Roxanne. "Julie made him a happy kid again. When he first started coming over to get Julie and eat with a real family he was kind of sourpussed. Soon, he was Mr. Sunshine." There was never any apparent drug abuse by the two, although everyone in the family agrees that the two smoked pot. "Nothing big or anything," insisted Joan. "Just what most kids do today." The father, who has been divorced for a year and since remarried, declined to be interviewed. His wife told this reporter that her husband has been taking medication for severe depression since Julie's death. "He misses her terribly."

Police have arrested another young man for the murders. He is also an employee at the Pancake House. Malcolm McRice is a 25 year old Black man who recently moved to the area. After being discharged from the Army, he moved to Snowdon and took a cook's job at the restaurant, which his uncle manages. McRice is originally from Kansas City, Missouri and was raised by his great-aunt Grace McRice. Mrs. McRice was in town for a visit when her grand-nephew was arrested. "Malcolm got in his share of trouble growing up," said Grace McRice. "But never for nothing malicious. He didn't kill those people. Heck, he was friends with the girl." Her son,

Art McRice (Malcolm's uncle), agreed. "Malcolm is kind of a fool sometimes," said Art. "But he don't have a mean bone in his body. He would never think about killin' nobody. It's just not his nature."

Snowdon police and the District Attorney's office disagree with this assessment. "Malcolm McRice was convicted of assault on his commanding officer while he was in the service," said Detective Mulhaney, whom locals call Starsky, after the television character. "He spent six months in the stockade for that conviction. He also was arrested once for dealing drugs." Police claim that the murders occurred after Prehausen took some of Malcolm McRice's money to buy some marijuana. When Prehausen failed to come up with the drug, McRice threatened him to get the money or the drugs. According to police, when this did not happen, McRice paid a visit to the victims' apartment, where an argument ensued. The argument turned into a fight, which resulted in the deaths. Grace and Art McRice challenge this characterization of events. They tell of a threat on Malcolm McRice's life the night before by a large white man who attacked Malcolm McRice and his new girlfriend in the parking lot of the Pancake House after Malcolm had left work the evening of June 20, 1975. After the attack and threats, Malcolm McRice's relatives say he went to Baltimore to go dancing. Police say this story is not only unverifiable, it "plain just didn't happen" in the words of Mulhaney's partner, Detective Smith, who is known as Hutch, of course.

Local civil rights groups have become interested in the case, as have some churches in the Snowdon area with predominantly Black congregations. At McRice's arraignment on Monday, June 30th, over fifty members of The Maryland Coalition Against Racism and Police Brutality picketed quietly in front of the Courthouse in Hyattsville. Close to fifty members of the church congregations from the Zion Baptist Churches in Snowdon, Beltsville, and Bowie filled the courtroom itself. The Coalition was instrumental in seeking justice in the 1973 police brutality case against the Prince George's police officers who beat a black resident of Snowdon for leaving his motor running in a 7-Eleven parking lot in

Snowdon. When reached by phone, the chair of the group, Raymond Jackson, told the Sun, "We believe Malcolm McRice is innocent of these charges and we will not stop our campaign until the charges are dropped. We would hope that the police will do their work and find the real killer, but even if they don't we are gonna fight until Malcolm McRice is free and absolved." Reverend Nathan Moore, of the Snowdon Zion Baptist Church, echoed Mr. Jackson. Moore was reached at his home, where he ministers to the Grove community in Snowdon. "I believe that a very grave mistake has been made in this case," said Reverend Moore. "I have made it my endeavor to help Malcolm McRice back to his freedom and to bring real justice to the memories of Julie Epstein and Jeremy Prehausen."

This story is just beginning. McRice's pre-trial hearing is set for August 4th at the Hyattsville Courthouse. McRice's supporters are hoping to hire a lawyer soon. Julie's mother and sisters just want to see justice done. Prehausen's mother could not be reached, despite several attempts. She was quoted on WMAR-TV news on the day of McRice's arrest: "I hope they put away that nigger for life."

14

Rock was bumming. Heavy. No one was talking to him at work and he never talked to his parents. It was getting pretty Goddamn lonely. It's like everybody knew what had really happened. He knew he would miss Jeremy, but not this much. Lucy brought back another tray of dishes. Rock unloaded it and began to rinse them. Lucy felt bad for the guy, but was still pretty pissed at him so she said nothing. She went back out on the dining floor. Rock put the dishes in the rack and stuck them in the dishwasher. He gave them one more rinse and closed the dishwasher door. The jet sprays kicked in and did their job. He looked at the clock. Half an hour till he was out of here.

Malcolm looked at the wall across from his bed. He was still in a cell by himself. That got pretty fucking lonely, but the other side of it was he could have some freak in the cell with him. Then he would have to be wary all the time, not just when the guards or pigs came around. Mulhaney had been in earlier that day, poking and hitting him. He was pissed off about the newspaper article that questioned his and Smith's so-called detective work. In Malcolm's mind, the article was bullshit 'cause it took them liars at face value just because they wore a uniform. He counted the little dots in the concrete block across from him. He never expected to get an accurate count. It was just a way to pass the time and trip out a little when the holes floated around a little. Tomorrow he was supposed to meet his new lawyer that Auntie and the minister had got for him. Jerry McCaffrey was the cat's name. An Irish civil rights lawyer who knew the redneck mentality—that was how Auntie's preacher had described him. What the hell, thought Malcolm, at least he'll ask to see the police report and the evidence. Malcolm didn't even think the fuckin' deal should go to trial. They had no evidence.

Rock finished up his shift and left the restaurant. He was gonna go to Samson's and get high. Even if he had to walk there. He stopped at Camelot Liquors and bought himself a soda. Then he took side streets to Route 216. At Route 216 he stuck out his thumb and continued to walk, only backward. Five minutes after sticking out his thumb, he had a ride. The driver let him off near the dirt road that led to Samson's driveway. Rock hadn't been there since he and Jeremy rode their bikes out there that Tuesday night. Shit, he only talked to him once since then, when Samson called about the rip-off. The whole conversation probably only lasted a minute. He walked into the woods. By the time he arrived at Samson's driveway he was soaked with sweat. Mostly from the heat, but a little bit from the fear he felt. He hadn't called before he came out here and he had no idea where Samson's head was at in the wake of everything that had happened.

Samson let him in. He gave Rock a bit of a hard time about not calling beforehand, but let it drop. He seemed happy to see the kid.

"Where you been, Rock?" asked Samson. "I been expectin' you to come around. You must need some pot or something." Rock followed him into the front room of the house. They sat down on a couple chairs that were directly across from each other. Samson pulled a joint from behind his ear and lit it. He took a long toke and handed it to Rock, who did the same. While Rock was toking, Samson went into his kitchen and came back with a couple quart bottles of Miller High Life. He handed one to Rock. Rock unscrewed the top, raised the bottle and took a long drink. He was fuckin' thirsty. They smoked the first joint and Samson rolled another. When they had finished that one, Rock was wasted. He sat back in the chair and listened to Samson rattle on.

"See how that nigger's gonna go down for that killin' I did?" he bragged. "Stupid fucker. I bet that all he gotta do to get outta it is tell them that I almost killed his ass, too. Stabbed the seat right behind his head in his fuckin' whore's car. Then I told him I was gonna kill that little queer boy who done sold him the weed 'cause that weed was mine. That fucker stole it from me, plain and simple and nobody steals from the mighty Samson without paying dearly. You want some crank?" He looked at Rock, who had yet to say a word.

Rock shrugged his shoulders, quite stoned. "Sure." Samson left the room for a couple minutes and returned with a baggie filled with a white powder.

"A whole fuckin' ounce of crank," said Samson. "Made a week ago and cured. Ready for the streets. I just gotta cut it up some. It's wicked strong. Go ahead, have a snort, Rock." He handed Rock a straw. Rock stuck one end in the bag and the other in his nose. He snorted. The shit hit him like a fuckin' lit match up his nose. Then his blood began racing and his head cleared. This felt good, thought Rock. He handed the straw back to Samson. Samson set it down next to the baggie.

"Shit, yeah," said Samson, sitting down again and talking a mile a minute because of the amphetamine coursing through his veins. "I went over to that faggot's house and asked him where the hell my pot was. He looked at me all scared, seen I was wearing gloves, and started cryin'. Said he didn't know it was mine, like I was gonna believe that shit. Then I hit him once. Made his mouth bleed. He said he could get some money from his girlfriend to pay me back. Too fuckin' late I told him. You done ripped me off. You gonna have to give me your girlfriend. He really started bawling then. No, he says, no. I pulled the little piece of pipe I had with me out of my pants and smacked him good upside the head. It ain't your choice no more you faggot, I told him. Just then that pretty little blonde kike comes in the door. She seen me and tried to leave, but I got to the door and closed it. See, I knew her neighbors were all away. I was gonna fuck that bitch. Just as I got her pants off, that little faggot comes running at me with a knife. He got me once in the ass before I turned around and hit him even harder with my fist than I did with that pipe. That bitch had run into the bathroom by then so I went after her and locked the door. I made her take my dick in her mouth and told her she better not bite it. Just then that little fucker knocked the door off its hinges and on my back. I guess his fear made him stronger than he really was. She bit down as hard as she could. Shit I still can't fuck it hurts so bad. That was when I realized I was gonna have to kill that little faggot if I wanted to get inside the Jew girl's pants. So I turned around and pushed that sonofabitch on the floor. Then I just pounded his head with my fist 'til he was just flopping around like a Goddamn fish out of water. His girlfriend come at me with the top of the back of the toilet. That fuckin' porcelain shit hurts. I grabbed it from her and pummeled her little ass into the carpet. Then I took that porcelain and did the same to her faggot boy. I didn't know if they was dead. I just knew I had to get my ass out of there. I grabbed everything I could find that had blood on it that wasn't attached to nothing. I came back here to gather my thoughts and bury the evidence. Then I got the hell out of town. Went back to the Poconos until I heard they busted that nigger. Yee-fuckin-haw!" Samson was yelling. Rock was scared and the crank rushing through his bloodstream didn't help matters. He knew he didn't have any choice but to sit there and act dumb. So that's what he did. For four hours. Finally, Samson passed out in his chair. The two had consumed four or five quarts of beer, smoked several joints and done a couple snorts each of the crank. Still, Samson passed out. Rock knew he had to get out while he could, before Samson started putting things together. If Samson figured out that Jeremy couldn't have stolen the pot without some help it wouldn't be long before he suspected Rock. Once he was sure Samson was sleeping, Rock hightailed it back to his parents home. The crank made the five mile walk easy.

He was beginning to think his best bet was to tell Lucy or someone the truth. How he had helped Jeremy and set up Malcolm. Samson was slow but when he figured shit out he would kill Rock just as easily as he killed Jeremy and Julie. People were gonna hate him but, what the fuck, they already did. This was a matter of survival. If Samson got sent up for the murders he would be gone for a long fuckin' time and as long as Rock didn't end up in prison he could get his ass out of Snowdon and away from the Pagans. Maybe he could start over in Texas or somewhere. But he was gonna have to tell someone. Lucy, probably. Anyone else was likely to kick his ass.

Antoine had finally got in touch with Marion. She started crying when she heard what happened to Malcolm. Her first reaction was to go right to the police in Snowdon and tell them what she knew. Antoine counseled that that might not be a good idea given the statements and actions of the department.

"I think they want to railroad Malcolm, Marion," said Antoine. "They been going to his cell and beatin' on him and the public defender tried to force him to cop a plea to a lesser charge at his arraignment. They don't want to catch the real motherfucker. We gonna have to do that."

"Shit," said Marion. "How we gon' do that? We ain't got money to hire no Kojak or nothin'."

"We got a preacher on our side, sister," answered Antoine. "And a militant civil rights group that loves to fuck with the honky mofos. The preacher done found Malcolm a real lawyer. He some white man who worked for H. Rap Brown and some other brothers in the civil rights times."

"Who the hell is H. Rap Brown?" asked Marion.

"Oh sister," answered Antoine. "He was one of the baddest brothers in the black power scene until the man put him away. He was a Panther and a SNCC member. He done got blamed for startin' a riot over there in cracker land—the Eastern Shore of Maryland just 'cause he said nothin' had changed there since the civil war. The crackers knew he was tellin' the truth and tried to chase him out of town. By the time he was gone, the town was burnin' up."

"Thanks for the fuckin' history lesson, Antoine." Marion could feel her longing all over her body. She wanted to go to Snowdon and spring her man no matter what it took. Ain't that crazy, she thought, I only know this guy three weeks and he already my man. That never happened before. "As soon as I take care of some business up here I'm comin' down. You got room for me to stay?"

"Sure do," answered Antoine. "Bring that Leah girl wit' ya'."

"I'll try. She up in New York still lookin' at colleges." She hung up the phone. Antoine thought about the whole fuckin' crazy mess that was erupting around him. Shit, he was even gonna go to a political meeting with Peter Tuesday—tomorrow. The next place he'd be goin' to was church with Miss Grace if he didn't watch his ass.

Art and Peter were taking Grace and Lucy to

dinner. They had chosen an Italian place. Both men had even worn ties for the occasion. Lucy wore a dress and looked incredibly desirable. When Peter saw her he wanted to skip the dinner and go straight home. Of course, he couldn't. The plan was to meet Reverend Moore and the lawyer here. The maitre'd sat the four of them at a table. While waiting, they had a couple drinks. Grace had soda. The talk was mostly about the quality of the food. Midway through the second drink, the two men came in. Nate introduced Jerry McCaffrey to the others and everyone sat down. McCaffrey ordered a boiler-maker right off. Art and Peter looked at each other. This guy looked like he was gonna be okay.

"Reverend Moore has filled me in with what he knows," said Jerry. "What can you all tell me?"

"Have you heard the part about Samson attacking Malcolm?" asked Lucy.

"A little bit. Fill me in."

Art jumped in. "Malcolm had just left the restau-rant with Marion. They was sittin' in her car in the parking lot makin' out. Out of nowhere the door opens and this big white sonofabitch is yellin' at Malcolm about some weed he had. He was accusin' Malcolm of rippin' him off. Now Malcolm never seen this cat before in his life, but he big, white and ugly, no offense, and he had a knife. Marion tried to start the car but couldn't find the ignition she was so shook up. Next thing Malcolm knows there's a knife comin' at him. He ducks and the knife goes into the upholstery behind his head. Malcolm says he don't know nothing about no theft and that he bought the weed from somebody else. This white asshole asks him who and says he's gonna kill whoever it was. Finally Marion found the ignition and they squealed out of the lot and head north on Route 1 towards Baltimore. That's what Malcolm tol' me the next day while him and me was cookin' chicken at the church barbecue."

Jerry nodded. He was trying to figure out how Malcolm's name even got in the mix. It didn't make sense. It was quite possible that Malcolm was dealing stolen weed, but he had no idea that it was stolen, since he didn't know the source of the marijuana. It seemed that he just wanted something for the money he had given to the Prehausen kid. There had to be another person involved who knew Jeremy and Malcolm and perhaps the primary dealer—this Samson guy. He asked the three Pancake House workers about that. Peter and Art told them Antoine and Malcolm's theory about Rock pointing the police towards Malcolm by saying Malcolm was owed money by Jeremy and had threatened him. Jerry nodded. He needed to figure out a way to substantiate this theory. If they could get this fellow to tell his story to the DA, they might be able to get the charges dropped.

"Do any of you see this Rock fellow?" asked Jerry.

He ordered another boilermaker and a round for the rest of them. Grace thought about ordering wine but stuck to her soda.

"Shit. He still works with us," answered Art.

"Do you think he would talk about this?"

Art and Peter shook their heads. Lucy hesitated, then began. "You know, he seems really down lately. Maybe I can get him to express his emotions. I mean, Jeremy was the best friend he ever had. It's gotta be messin' with him somehow. Give me a couple days."

Jerry agreed to this idea. The waitress came and took their orders. Art ordered the veal scallopini and another drink. Grace stuck with spaghetti and meatballs. The reverend seconded her order, while Peter and Lucy decided to share a creamed salmon dish that came with fettucine verde.

The waitress came back soon with the salads.

"Did you guys see the Orioles' game last night?" asked Reverend Moore.

"I din't know you liked baseball, Reverend," said Grace.

"I used to play in high school. Then I got the fever for the Lord." Reverend Moore chuckled.

"What position?" asked McCaffrey.

"Third base," answered Moore. "I made All-State my sophomore year."

"Do you have a favorite team?" asked Art.

"No," answered Moore. "Just a couple favorite players."

Peter wondered who they could be. "Like who?"

"Bob Gibson and Cool Papa Bell."

"I hear ya." This man knew his baseball, thought Peter. He was more normal than he appeared. You never knew with these preachers.

The conversation during the rest of the dinner revolved around baseball, and when Peter discovered that the lawyer Jerry loved the Grateful Dead, Grace and Reverend Moore found themselves mostly listening. After dinner was through, Grace got in the car with Peter, Art and Lucy, and McCaffrey caught a ride with Reverend Moore. Despite his aversion to alcohol, Moore had been very tolerant of the dinner party's excessive consumption. Jerry was staying at a motel in College Park. The two men discussed the case while Moore drove McCaffrey back to his lodging.

"What is your immediate appraisal of the situation, Jerry?" asked Moore once they were on Route 1 heading south.

"At first glance, Reverend," answered McCaffrey. "It would seem the entire case rests on the testimony of this young man who was Jeremy's buddy. That can be good or bad. He seems, from the descriptions those three folks rendered, to be a shaky witness."

"But the police believe him," interjected Moore. "I mean, the police seemed to have used his story as the start of their investigation."

"The start and the finish," said McCaffrey sarcastically. He had seen this type of police work before. The detectives decide beforehand who the culprit is and then make the evidence fit their theory. This meant ignoring some very obvious evidence and suppressing other evidence. In some cases, it even meant altering the evidence to fit the suspect. From the information he had so far, McCaffrey was pretty sure this case was of this type.

"My point is that, if his story was good enough for the police," said Moore. "Wouldn't it be enough to convict before a Maryland court?"

"Not necessarily," answered McCaffrey. "But, we can't count on anything. We have to get this kid to tell us everything he knows and go from there. Even then, his reputation could either hurt us or help us."

"I see," said Moore. "You know, Jerry, I think the aspect of this entire situation that is most disturbing is the godlessness of it all. I don't mean the drugs or the underlying current of sexuality. I mean the pure hatred that resides so close to the surface of so many men and women. That the police would lie and send the wrong man to his fate just because they don't like his skin color or that a person's best friend would instigate the police action because of a similar hatred appalls me. Assuming this young man named Rock did point the police in Malcolm's direction because of his own fear and hatred, I just ask myself over and over, why? What happened to justice? Or even friendship? Is it all about saving one's own ass, to use the vernacular? If it is, then why do I bother?"

McCaffrey listened to Reverend Moore. He knew the despair of which he spoke. He remembered growing up as an Irish-American in South Boston and seeing everyday the reality of hatred based on nothing but ethnicity and class. Oppression was the name of the everyday reality in his neighborhood. When he was a kid it seemed that the WASP assholes owned everything in Boston except for a few apartment houses. Those were usually owned by an Irishman or a Jew who had forgotten his origins and treated the Irish poor even worse than the WASPs did. To top it off, the Irish treated the Blacks the way that they were treated by everyone else. In college, he learned that this was known as the hierarchy of oppression. That's why he headed south when the Freedom Rides began. He never looked back. Got his law degree in Virginia and started practicing law. Mostly routine stuff—helping people keep their homes, probate, the usual—every once in a while, though, a plum was dropped in his lap. H. Rap Brown was one of those plums. It wasn't the money that made it a plum. Hell, he barely covered his expenses. It was the feeling that he was fighting the good fight against the racist SOB's that run the world. He smiled when he heard Moore lament the godlessness of it all. He had despaired so greatly during the Freedom Rides after the Freedom School he had helped to build and organize got burned to the ground with his girlfriend sleeping inside that he had cursed God to eternal damnation. Only later while he was in law school did he realize that it was a faith in God or something greater than humanity that gave him hope. Shit, humanity sure as hell didn't. Not very often, anyway.

"Nathan, my friend," said Jerry to the minister. "Despite the godlessness of it all we must do what we believe to be right. Maybe some day in some little way we'll help someone find that bit of God in themselves. Humanity has always fallen but it still tries. Now this may be the alcohol I just consumed talking, but it seems to me that the fact that you have undertaken this young man's cause is testimony to your ultimate faith in the godliness of every human. Our trick—and this is between you and me—is to find the human involved in this tragedy who is willing to risk whatever he or she thinks they have to acknowledge their little bit of godliness and tell the truth. Of course, we might have to use a little strong-arm, too."

"I didn't know you were a believer, Jerry," said Moore.

"Don't really have a choice, now do I?" asked McCaffrey. "The life I have chosen has got to have some meaning and some reward, neither of which I've found in sufficient amount on earth to justify what I do."

Moore chuckled bemusedly.

"Besides," said McCaffrey. "I figure there's got to

be more than just earthly justice. I mean, some of these rich SOB's who profit from the misery of others on this earth have got to get their just rewards somewhere. Here on earth they eat well, live well, get the women they want and everything else. All because they steal, lie, cheat, and kill. I say let them enjoy themselves in this life, because they are gonna catch hell in the next one."

"Literally…" laughed Moore. "Literally." They were at the motel. The two men shook hands and agreed to meet the next day before McCaffrey went to visit Malcolm. A strategy was forming in McCaffrey's head.

15

The Pancake House. Tuesday afternoon, July 8, 1975.

The work routine had returned to the restaurant. Rock was finishing up his dishwashing shift, Lucy was waiting tables and Art was training Charles X in the galley. Lewin had decided to make him a cook to replace Malcolm. So, whenever Art or Peter had the time, they got some training in. Rock was still somewhat ostracized, but Peter and Lucy were trying to be friendlier in the hope that they could break down his defenses. They needed him to talk. Nobody at the restaurant but Rock knew about his visit with Samson and Rock was scared to tell anyone. He was convinced that if he mentioned it he would be a dead man. Samson seemed to delight in the fact that he had murdered Jeremy and Julie. That freaked Rock out. How could anybody be so fuckin' twisted.

Lucy came back to smoke a cigarette in the dish-washing area. Rock was taking off his apron and getting ready to leave.

"Hey Rock," said Lucy.

"Yeah?"

"Me and Peter was wondering if you wanted to

come over and party some?"

"When?" Rock was a bit suspicious. Why did they want to party with him? Wasn't he on their shit list?

"I don't know. Today or tomorrow? Peter and I both have off those nights."

"I guess so," said Rock. "How about tomorrow?" He wasn't sure that he wanted to do this, but he was really desiring some kind of human contact outside of work.

"Cool. Peter can give you a ride."

Art was explaining the trick to flipping eggs in a pan. "It's all in the wrist Brother Charles." He jerked his wrist and flipped the eggs in the pan over. "Now you let 'em cook for a couple—three minutes on that side and they over easy."

Charles attempted flipping the eggs in the pan he was in front of. Two flipped fine but the third folded over bursting the yolk. "Oh shit."

"That's all right," said Art. He picked up a platter and had Charles slide his pan of eggs onto the platter. Then Art hid the broken yolk with a side of pancakes. "They'll never know."

Rock came into the galley. "I'm leavin' now, Art. See ya tomorrow."

"See ya." Art nodded in Rock's direction.

Charles waited until Rock was gone and then said in his even, measured voice, "I think that boy got somethin' he's hidin'. I think he knows a lot about why Malcolm in jail."

"Shit," said Art. "I think he knows who killed them younguns."

"Me too," agreed Charles. "I known a lot of killers in my day. Malcolm ain't a killer. He ain't got the look. He ain't got the meanness. That Rock boy know somethin'."

"Peter and Lucy think so, too," said Art, "and they made it their business to find out what he know."

"Y'all need any help," said Charles. "You let me know. I got a couple brothers on the outside twice as big as me. They got experience at gettin' information from people who are reluctant to provide information."

Art whistled. "Bigger than you! Shit, they must be awful fuckin' big." Charles was easily 260 pounds and over six feet tall.

"They is, Art. They is." Charles went back to working on his egg-flipping skills.

Art went upstairs to talk to Lewin. He was hoping he could get a loan from the man so that he and his mom could pay that lawyer. He didn't want Grace to put up her house. The church operated on more or less of a shoestring and, even with the donations the preacher had received in response to his sermon, could only provide a couple thousand dollars. McCaffrey said he didn't care about the money, but Art figured that he probably worked more when he was getting paid. Hell, who didn't. Lewin was finishing some paperwork when Art entered his office.

"Hey, Art," invited Lewin. "Have a seat."

Art sat down. He lit a cigarette. Lewin pulled a bottle of Chivas out of his desk and poured a couple fingers into two glasses. He handed Art a glass. Art took a swallow. "I was wonderin'," he began. "If you could help me out with a small loan. It ain't for me—no new car or a vacation—it's to help pay for Malcolm's lawyer."

"I've been meaning to talk to you about this whole mess, Art," answered Lewin. "How is your nephew doing? What's the status of the case and his defense? The papers haven't said much."

"Malcolm's doin' okay, considerin' where he is and why," said Art. "As for the defense and that shit…we got a long way to go. Pretrial is on August 4th and his lawyer ain't even seen the police report yet. Goddamn county prosecutor is draggin' his ass. The good news is we got him a real lawyer and dropped that jive public defender—he hadn't even read the police report and tried to talk Malcolm into pleading to double manslaughter. But now that we got this lawyer we gotta at least cover his expenses. My mom is talkin' about sellin' her house out in KC to pay for everything. I don't want her to do that."

Lewin shifted in his seat. He pulled out a ledger and opened it.

"I have to be honest with you here, Art. I do not believe Malcolm killed them kids. That doesn't mean

I think he's going to go free, though. The word justice takes on a different meaning in this town. You probably know that, already. I can remember a young fellow who used to clean the stables out at the track—little colored guy who was kind of simple—folks say his daddy hit him on the head when he was little and that made him a retard. I don't know about that. He was the most honest and kindhearted person at the track, though. Anyhow, some white girl around fifteen who was something of a jockey slut—she liked them little men—got drunk after the first race of the season back in '60 or '61 and fell asleep in one of the stables. Four or five of the jockeys and trainers found her and pulled a chain on her. They were all white men. This little colored fellow found her the next morning when he came into work—he lived in that little town right next to the track. Odenton? He found her with no clothes on, her body bruised, and bleeding from her crotch. He ran to his aunt in Odenton who was some kind of healer and brought her back to the stable. His aunt gave her some herbal medicines and that kind of stuff, but couldn't revive her. By now, there were some other folks at the track, including some of the same assholes who raped the girl the night before. They called the police, who arrested this colored retard, despite his protests. Then the police and track people conspired to charge and convict that poor fellow with rape. When that girl died later in the hospital, they got him for murder. I was just starting out in the horse business back then and had a couple three-year-olds running at Snowdon, so I heard the real story just from being a white man at the track. But I didn't say anything because I wanted to be part of the scene so bad. That colored fellow killed himself in jail and the white guys who did the deed are living in fancy houses. I live with the fact that I might have been able to keep him from even going in."

Lewin shook his head. He knew Art didn't want to hear his story, but it had been on his mind since Malcolm was arrested.

"So," said Lewin. "To make a long story short and to spare you any more of my stories and guilt, I can help your family out. Would $5000 be enough to keep that lawyer around for a while?"

"Yeah. Thanks." Art extended his hand. Lewin shook it. "I'm still gonna whup your ass in poker this Thursday." Art, Peter, Lewin and some other local restaurant owners had been getting together for poker once a month for almost a year. Before Malcolm was busted he joined in, too. Art, Peter and Malcolm usually won. Not because they were individually all good card players, but because they had a system worked out between the three of them that ensured that whoever had the best hand of the three would take the pot. Peter called it redistributing the wealth. Art called it cheating. However, he had devised the system.

"Yeah. You probably will," agreed Lewin. He wrote the check and handed it to Art. Art went back downstairs to see how Charles X was doing with the eggs.

It was Thursday already. Art was finished working until Saturday. He and Peter had just smoked half a joint in the back of the Pancake House near the dumpster and the fifty gallon drum where they emptied the grease traps. He was feeling good. Tomorrow he was going to visit Malcolm. On his way home Art stopped at the liquor store in the shopping center. McCaffrey was coming for dinner and he liked bourbon. Must be from living in Virginia for so long, thought Art. After all, didn't most lawyers like scotch? Art went straight to the shelves that stocked the bourbon. He was looking for Maker's Mark. That was supposed to be the best. Art knew it was his favorite and he didn't like bourbon. He found what he was looking for and headed to the checkout. That Samson fucker was in line. Art wasn't sure if he knew who Art was, so he hung back and watched him. As he did so, he noticed a clerk opening up the other checkout. Art walked quickly to that counter, bought the whiskey and a pint of Smirnoff Silver and headed to Malcolm's car, which he was still driving. He waited until Samson got in his car and pulled out. Art followed the sonofabitch out of the shopping center parking lot. He felt like Shaft.

Samson's vehicle pulled into traffic on Fourth Street heading north. He was driving the speed limit despite the fact that the traffic was not very heavy. Art followed at a reasonable distance. He wasn't sure why he was following the asshole, other than to discover where he lived, just in case Charles X's information seekers needed to pay the guy a visit. They were crossing Montgomery Street now and heading towards Route 216. Samson's car crossed Main Street and gained speed as it hit the highway. Art followed suit. A few miles up the road, Samson put on his left blinker and waited. Art slowed down and got in the right lane. He passed by Samson's car and saw a dirt road off to this left. That must be where that cracker lives, thought Art. He took careful notice of his surroundings and continued on. Once he found a place to turn around, he did so and headed home.

McCaffrey was sitting at the kitchen table when Art walked in the door. The house smelled like fried chicken and biscuits, with a hint of greens thrown in the mix. Art's mom was entertaining Jerry with stories about living in Kansas City. She had been a bit of a party girl before she found Jesus. That's when she met Art and Malcolm's dad's father—when she was a party girl. She knew all the clubs and heard all the hot musicians. Charlie Bird and Benny Goodman. Louis Armstrong and Big Bill Broonzy. McCaffrey was eating it up. He loved blues and jazz and told Grace that his real goal in life was to play guitar half as good as Big Bill Broonzy. She laughed.

"I sure am glad to see that bottle of bourbon, Art," said Jerry as Art emptied the bag. He handed the bottle to McCaffrey, who pulled the wax seal from the top and uncorked the bottle. Jerry finished the juice he had been drinking and splashed some bourbon into his glass. Art reached in the freezer and pulled out the ice cube tray. Jerry put three or four cubes into his drink and handed the tray back to Art. Art opened his pint of Smirnoff's and took a sip. He went into his bedroom to change. He returned from the bedroom and McCaffrey started talking.

"Your mother's been regaling me with stories of her wild youth. Dancing and drinking in Kansas City, the whole sordid tale. Louis Armstrong and Big Bill Broonzy."

"Big Bill Broonzy is the man!" said Art. "I always remember my daddy singin' that song about if you white, how you all right," and thinkin' what the hell kind of world was I livin' in?"

Grace began to fill three plates with food. McCaffrey sat back and sipped his bourbon. By the time the food was on the table, Art was sitting in a chair ready to eat. Grace said a quick blessing and the three began to stuff themselves.

"How did the thing go with Rock?" asked McCaffrey. He was hopeful that Peter and Lucy were able to get some good leads from their "conversation."

"Good enough," answered Art. "Peter and Lucy were able to verify that it was Rock who pointed the cops towards Malcolm, just like Antoine and them thought."

"What about this asshole Samson?" asked McCaffrey. He looked at Grace. "Excuse my language, ma'am."

"It's okay," said Grace. "I heard worse in my life."

Art answered McCaffrey. "They tol' me that Rock said he heard some crazy shit at Samson's house the last time he was over there a week or so ago. Peter said he seemed afraid to talk about it, though. Like he was gonna get found out or somethin'."

"What was the gist of the stuff he heard?" asked Jerry. "Any clue?"

"That Samson was bragging about getting away with murder and that he was happy to see some nigger get the crime pinned on him," said Art.

"But this Rock punk won't say that for sure?" asked Jerry.

"That's pretty much it. He chicken. Peter was convinced that Rock thinks Samson will kill him if he finds out that he is even talking to any of Malcolm's friends. Oh yeah," remembered Art. "Rock said it was him and Jeremy who ripped the pot off Samson in the first place. He tol' Peter and Lucy that Jeremy had only been to Samson's place once so he couldn't have ripped him off by hisself. Rock said he goes over there a lot. To score and hang out."

"Samson probably would kill him," said McCaffrey. He poured himself another drink. He was going to have to get this Rock kid to tell his story under oath. Even then it might not carry much weight. Somehow he was going to have to get some scrutiny on this Samson jerk. He had an angle, but wasn't real sure it would go anywhere. There was an old college friend in the Maryland prosecutor's office who owed him a favor. When he was working in the prosecutor's office down in Loudonville, Virginia, Jerry had prosecuted this friend's father on a DWI charge and kept him out of jail, even though the old drunk had four priors and had paralyzed a passenger in the other car. He figured that this was a good time to cash in the favor. Any new evidence in this case wasn't going to be included as long as it remained below the state level. These good ol' boys in Snowdon and the county were gonna cover each other's ass until they died. And longer if they could. It was just like Virginia. Why charge a white man when there was a black one who could serve the time? He turned his attention back to the conversation between Art and his mother.

"Antoine called here today," said Grace. "He said Marion was back in town. They wanna come to the prison tomorrow with us."

"That'll make Malcolm happy," said Art. And give

him something to think about at night in his cell, he thought. "We gonna meet them there or what?"

"They gon' come here in the morning."

"I'd like to talk with Marion," said McCaffrey. "Maybe we can figure out a way to get her story into evidence. I don't know if it'll do any good, since these crackers don't want to corroborate Malcolm's story at all, but it would be good to have it in there."

"She be more than happy to talk," said Art.

"What about Antoine?" asked Jerry.

"Oh yeah," said Art. "Oh yeah." Grace served everyone another helping of food.

"By the way, Jerry," said Art. "I got a check for you. My boss loaned us some money to keep you around."

"You sure that's all right?"

"Yeah. I'll give it to you after dinner." The conversation turned away from Malcolm's case. Art and Jerry talked about baseball. Jerry raved about the Red Sox and even Art had to agree that it very well might be their year. He was impressed with Tiant. Bigger than the game was how Art put it. Like Satchel Paige. The mention of Paige got Jerry going.

"When I quit lawyering," he said. "I want to bring the Negro Leagues back into the public memory. White folks need to know that history and the history of some of the commissioners like Kennesaw Landis. He might as well have worn a sheet, he was so damned racist. Some of the white players, too. Ty

Cobb, for one. People all big today on talking about how bad the Nazis were in the '36 Olympics when Jesse Owens won all those medals, but they don't want to talk about how major league baseball kept black players off the field for close to fifty years."

Grace jumped in. "You know, Art's daddy loved baseball. The Monarchs were his team. He went to their games with a bottle every Saturday they was in town. Nothin' could prevent him from goin'—not a funeral, a wedding, nothin'. Heck, he even lost a job 'cause he went to the ball game. He tol' the white man who was his boss that he couldn't work Saturdays, but the white man didn't hear him and said you gon' be here or you ain't gonna have a job. Bernard, that's Art's daddy, tol' that man he was gonna have to find him a new worker then, 'cause he wasn't gonna work no Saturdays when the Monarchs was in town. When he tol' me that he lost his job and why, I was a mix of proud and angry. That man did that to me lots." She laughed.

"Don't look back," said Art. "'Cause someone or something might be gainin' on you. Them was Satchel's words that my daddy always say to me and my brother. Good words for a brother to heed."

The evening lasted until midnight. When Jerry called a cab, Grace had been in bed for a couple of hours. The two men watched television, drank, smoked, and talked until Art started nodding off. He had been up since six, after all. As soon as the cab came, Art fell asleep for the night.

Malcolm woke up Friday looking forward to his visit from Art and Auntie Grace. He was feeling better about everything after his conversation the day before with Mr. McCaffrey. He seemed like an all right guy and a good fuckin' lawyer. He had about as much faith as Malcolm did in the system, but, like he told Malcolm, he knew how to tweak it in such a way that it worked more than half the time. Let's hope, he said to Malcolm, that this is gonna be one of those times. Malcolm hoped like hell it was. He ate his prison eggs and sausage hungrily. Then he did forty pushups and some deep knee bends. The lawyer had suggested that he do some exercise to keep himself occupied and keep his body in shape. Prison food was notoriously bad for you. Fatty and starchy. After he finished his exercises, Malcolm sat down on his bed and waited. Visiting hours began at 11 AM. He picked up the novel Peter had sent along with Auntie Grace and started reading where he had left off. He usually didn't like science fiction, but this one was just different enough that it pulled him in. Stranger in a Strange Land. It was by Robert Heinlein and was about some half Earth, half-Martian cat who started a religion on earth that the government hated. The religion was into sharing sexual partners and communicating telepathically—kind of like that mind meld thing that Mr. Spock did on Star

Trek. Tripped out, but what else would Peter read?

He thought about Peter. Was he still hanging out with Lucy? Peter never seemed to waste much time on relationships. It was like he preferred to be alone. The sun was pretty bright shining onto the concrete floor outside the tier where his cell was located. As it neared 11 o'clock, he listened for his name. This time it was one of the first ones. He waited for the guard to let him out of the cell and lead him to the visiting room. At least they weren't putting him in shackles no more. He felt like a fuckin' slave at auction in those things. Hell, today they didn't even cuff him. When he got to the room he couldn't believe his eyes. Marion was there. He could hardly keep himself from running to the table she was sitting at. The guard whispered in his ear about how fine she was and Malcolm just thought—yeah, she fine and she mine. After sitting across from her, he said nothing for a couple minutes. They just looked at each other, their longing apparent in their eyes. Malcolm hated being in jail more than ever now. Marion committed herself to getting him out, even if she had to rent a helicopter and pull a jailbreak. They sat in their respective places for fifteen minutes and said perhaps fifty words. They didn't need to say more. Antoine followed.

"When she get here?" asked Malcolm. "Where she been?"

"Last night," answered Antoine. "She been in

jail, didn't Art tell you?"

"Oh yeah. Where she stayin'? Where's Leah?"

"At my place for now," answered Antoine. "Leah's takin' some special courses so she can get into Hunter College in the fall. Hey look, bro, we working on getting you outta here. Art got some news about your lawyer and that kind of shit. How you doin'?"

"Shit," answered Malcolm. "It's jail."

"Yeah." Antoine told Malcolm he'd be back and left. Art and Grace took the rest of Malcolm's time for their visits. As the attorney, McCaffrey was coming later since he could pretty much come and go as he pleased. When he did get there, he told Malcolm that he was still working on getting the ability to see the evidence the cops supposedly found in Malcolm's car. The prosecutors were dragging tail on his request. They probably hoped he wouldn't have a chance to see it until the pretrial hearing, which would make Malcolm's defense that much harder. McCaffrey didn't tell Malcolm about the parallel plan he had been cooking up to somehow get Samson to reveal his complicity or, even better, to get the state's attorneys to take over the case and pull a raid on Samson's place looking for evidence. It was too much of a long shot. McCaffrey knew it wouldn't be good to get Malcolm's hopes up without a hint of certainty that he could pull such a stunt off.

16

Mulhaney and Smith were in the lounge at the Howard Johnson's. One of the cocktail waitresses was sitting on Mulhaney's lap with her hand in his pants. She probably hoped to get off the next time she got picked up for drunk driving. Smith ignored Mulhaney and the waitress and stared into his drink. If Mulhaney were a woman, they would call him a slut, thought Smith. Ever since he and his wife divorced, Mulhaney had forgotten the meaning of the word discreet. Hell, he hadn't just forgotten the meaning, he had forgotten the word. It was getting downright embarrassing for Smith. Smith was a family man who held the belief that sex was something to be shared with one's spouse, not just any floozy who came along. Unfortunately there were enough cop groupies around that Muhaney could get a hand job or more whenever he wanted. If they wouldn't give it voluntarily, Mulhaney would just threaten to arrest them. It disgusted Smith. But, cops stuck by their fellow cops.

It was Friday evening and they were getting ready to pay a surprise visit on McRice. They knew the guard working this evening. The shift change had taken place that week at the prison, so that meant Mulhaney's cousin was working the weekend night shifts on Malcolm's tier. He'd let them in without a problem. Even better, he'd let them take in whatever they needed to intimidate the black sonofabitch. Things weren't looking as good as they had hoped they would be looking by this time. Malcolm refused to sign anything and now them niggers had found a Goddamn civil rights lawyer to defend him. The coloreds in the Grove and other colored sections of town were ignoring the police when they drove through. Hell, some of the teenage kids were flipping them off and throwing rocks at their cruisers. Mulhaney was pissed. Tonight was the night he was going to do something about it. The two cops ordered one more drink each. They tossed them back and left. It was dusk. By the time they reached Patuxent, it would be dark.

Mulhaney's cousin was ready for them when they arrived. He pretended to pat the two cops down for weapons and let them in to Malcolm's cell. Malcolm was half asleep. He jumped up with a start.

"Don't say nothing, McRice," said Mulhaney. "This guard is on our side. He ain't no friend of yours like all them niggers who work here." Mulhaney walked over to Malcolm's bed and pushed him hard in the chest. Malcolm fell back but caught himself before his head hit the wall. He stood up ready to fight. Suddenly, Smith was behind him. Malcolm felt some cold steel on his neck. He was pretty certain it was a pistol. He let Smith cuff him. Mulhaney punched him in the face. Malcolm felt the blood trickle down his lip into his mouth. He spit it out. Smith jabbed the gun into Malcolm's neck even harder.

"Sign the fuckin' confession, McRice," threatened Smith. "And you can live." He wished McRice would relent, just so the two cops could get this whole thing over with before it got further out of control.

"Fuck you," spat Malcolm. Malcolm kicked his feet back at Smith. He hit him in the crotch and his gun fell on the floor, but, at the same time, Malcolm went sprawling across the concrete floor of the cell. Smith was bent over holding his balls. Mulhaney began kicking Malcolm in the head. Smith found his gun. He was pissed off and hurting. He cocked the gun and was ready to fire it when the guard came back. He was breathing heavily and seemed scared.

"You guys gotta go!" he whispered loudly. "My fuckin' supervisor is comin' up here. He just called. I don't know what the hell he's doing here now, but he's comin'!"

Mulhaney kneed Malcolm in the balls and punched him in the face once again while Smith un-cuffed him. They were reluctant to leave, now that McRice had made it physical.

"If you ever make it out of this jail alive,

McRice," said Smith. "I'm gonna hunt you down and kill you and your hooker girlfriend." Smith hit Malcolm hard on the head with the butt of the pistol. Malcolm sank to the cell floor. The two cops left. As they turned and walked out of the cell, Mulhaney said quietly, "We're going after your family and your friends next, nigger."

McCaffrey had scheduled a meeting with Malcolm for the next day at noon. When he arrived at the prison he was told that his visit was canceled. McCaffrey refused to leave and demanded to see his client. The guard in charge of admitting visitors refused. McCaffrey demanded to talk to the person in charge of the prison. After half an hour of arguing and threats, he was brought to the warden's office. He demanded an explanation. The warden told McCaffrey that Malcolm was in the infirmary for wounds sustained during a seizure of some kind. McCaffrey demanded to use the warden's phone and called Grace.

"Does Malcolm have any history of seizures?" he asked her as soon as she answered. He knew the answer would be no. He had a terrible feeling that either the guards or those two cops had beaten Malcolm Friday night. "Thank you, Grace." He hung up the phone.

"I don't believe your assertion, Warden," said McCaffrey. "If I am not permitted to visit my client immediately either in his cell or in the infirmary I will leave these premises immediately and call my good friend who happens to be the city editor of the Washington Post. He's been interested in this case ever since I mentioned it to him a few days ago over drinks. It's just that he hasn't found an angle that will attract the front office's attention at his paper. But if I can mix your little prison into the story and say something about your guards letting rogue policemen into the prison at night after the administration goes home and that these rogue cops use their entrance into Patuxent Correctional Facility to beat and intimidate prisoners into confessing to crimes they may or may not have committed—well, you get my drift, don't you warden?"

The warden got his drift. He called for a contingent of guards to take McCaffrey and himself to the infirmary. When he saw Malcolm's swollen, scabbed-over face and his swollen crotch, McCaffrey knew exactly what had happened. He tried to talk to Malcolm, but he was unconscious from the painkilling drugs that were dripping into him.

"He better not die, Warden." McCaffrey said coldly. He stared at the warden. "Can you please escort me out of here now?" McCaffrey wasn't going to tell the papers just yet. He was going to tell Reverend Moore, Malcolm's family and friends, and the Maryland Coalition Against Racism and Police Brutality. They could tell the papers.

17

Monday morning. Snowdon Police Department steps.

There were close to 150 people walking back and forth in front of the police station. Most of them were members of the Zion Baptist Church of Snowdon. They carried signs and sang hymns. The majority of the signs carried some variation of a call for an end to police brutality and a re-opening of the investigation into Jeremy and Julie's murders. Others demanded Malcolm's freedom and that the DA drop the charges against him. Reverend Moore led the crowd. The members of the Coalition who were able to make the picket on such short notice were joining in the church people's songs, at least the ones who knew the songs were, anyway. Peter didn't know too many of the songs but he was trying. He, McCaffrey, Raymond and Reverend Moore kept their fingers crossed hoping that the media would show. This story had to get out. It had to be more than a flashlight that shone on the Snowdon Police Department—it had to be a fuckin' floodlight. Malcolm was half dead in prison and those assholes were getting free blowjobs from the waitresses at HoJo's. Peter knew the scoop about that. He had heard many a tale from some of the waitresses at the Pancake House about how the cops gave them coke or pot for sex, or sometimes they just promised to not bust the women for their drugs and whatever else they did. Some of the waitresses were cop groupies, but most of them were just scared of cops.

Five Snowdon policemen stood in front of the station with their nightsticks out. The building was a hundred years old. The dirty brick was chipped and the mortar was covered in moss. Four glass doors stood in its center. The police stood in front of them. This crowd wasn't going to rush the station or anything like that, but the cops were nervous. Peter wondered where Mulhaney and Smith were. Reverend Moore walked over to where the cops stood. He had a bullhorn and was getting ready to speak. The protestors stopped walking and looked toward Moore. The police were immediately backed up by another five officers who had been hiding inside the building.

"Brothers and Sisters," Reverend Moore began. "The Lord tells us the story of Abraham and Isaac. Most of us know this story. For those of you who don't, let me quickly recite":

The Lord said to Abraham, "Take your son, your only son, Isaac, whom you love, and go to the region of Moriah. Sacrifice him there as a burnt offering on one of the mountains I will tell you about."

Early the next morning Abraham got up and saddled his donkey. He took with him two of his servants and his son Isaac. When he had cut enough wood for the burnt offering, he set out for the place God had told him about. On the third day Abraham looked up and saw the place in the distance. He said to his servants, "Stay here with the donkey while I and the boy go over there. We will worship and then we will come back to you." Abraham took the wood for the burnt offering and placed it on his son Isaac, and he himself carried the fire and the knife.

As the two of them went on together, Isaac spoke up and said to his father Abraham, "Father?"

"Yes, my son?" Abraham replied.

"The fire and wood are here," Isaac said, "but where is the lamb for the burnt offering?"

Abraham answered, "God himself will provide the lamb for the burnt offering, my son." And the two of them went on together. When they reached the place God had told him about, Abraham built an altar there and arranged the wood on it. He bound his son Isaac and laid him on the altar, on top of the wood.

Then he reached out his hand and took the knife to slay his son. But the angel of the Lord called out to him from heaven, "Abraham! Abraham!"

"Here I am," he replied.

"Do not lay a hand on the boy. Do not do anything to him. Now I know that you fear God, because you have not withheld from me your son, your only son."

"That's the story, my friends.

"As God's children in this country in which we live, we have proven our fear of God a multitude of times, and we have proven our love. We have done as He wished. We have suffered the indignity of slavery and segregation, and we will suffer no more. We have offered our children to the Lord and they have been stolen from us, first by the slave owner and now by the prisons. We were told that the slave owner was a child of God, too, only to discover that he was doing Satan's work. Too many children done gone. Today our child Malcolm McRice is lying swollen and bloodied by the descendants of the slave-driver—the police inside this building. We have offered him like so many others and now we implore the Lord to tell these men—and yes they are men—these men in blue, to leave our children alone.

"Like the children of Israel, we have wandered in the desert for long enough. Today we take an oath in front of the Lord and in front of the world:

"We will not rest until Malcolm McRice is free and justice is served!"

Amen! Amen! The protestors cheered and raised

their signs in the air. The police tightened their ranks. Some local teenagers had gathered and had either joined in the protest or stood on the sidelines watching. Occasionally a car full of bigots drove by yelling obscenities and flashing their middle fingers at the marchers. Eventually, the protest dwindled to just a handful of older black women holding signs.

That night, the evening news showed a brief clip of the protest and provided their audiences with a fairly balanced assessment of the situation. Although none of the newscasts questioned Malcolm's guilt, they all remarked that questions were being raised about the nature of the investigation. One of the stations—Channel 5 in Washington, D.C.—suggested that pressure was building on the Maryland State Attorney's office to take over the case. This information had been provided to the reporter by McCaffrey, in hopes that this scenario would actually take place. He was scheduled to go to dinner with his friend in that office that evening. He hoped he wouldn't have to play the heavy, but he planned to use whatever persuasive tactics he needed to call in the favor this guy owed him. For Malcolm's sake, the prosecution needed to move out of the county.

It was also time to get the story from that kid Rock. McCaffrey needed to set that up. He figured Peter and Lucy could get the kid to the motel room McCaffrey was renting by the week now. Getting the kid to tell what he knew about Samson's involvement would be a good deal harder. Lucy said he was still running scared The trick was to convince the kid that he was better off telling his story to McCaffrey before the State's Attorney subpoenaed him and that Rock would be safer with Samson behind bars for life than he would be with Samson free. The one drawback to that argument was that, if Samson was a member of the Pagan motorcycle gang in good standing, they would try and kill Rock, since that was their standard way of dealing with snitches. Rock probably knew as much, which explained his fear. Of course, if they couldn't convince this kid by talking to him, Charles X's offer to provide some "information gatherers" was available, as Art had reminded him the other night while they were drinking and talking at his apartment.

McCaffrey was sitting at the bar in some Italian place on Route 1 in College Park. It was within walking distance of his motel. The bartender was a grad student regaling him with stories of the riots in College Park after the U.S. invasion of Cambodia back in 1970. McCaffrey was the only person in the entire lounge area. Fortunately, the bartender was a good storyteller. McCaffrey had been in New Haven that weekend in 1970 working frantically as a member of the liaison team between the Yale administration, the governor, the police, and the leaders of the demonstration taking place to free the Black Panthers

Bobby Seale and Ericka Huggins. Things were going relatively quietly, given the number of people who had cone to town and the nature of the police in charge. Naturally, the police hated the Panthers and anyone who supported them, but they were behaving. The governor had told his agencies to be ready for trouble, but not to start any. Then, that asshole Nixon made his speech announcing the invasion of Cambodia. The potential for trouble increased substantially the minute that speech ended. Campuses and city streets around the country were filled with protestors and buildings on fire. Shit, even high schools were going out on strike and GIs were refusing to work. From a revolutionary point of view, it was cool. From the point of view of someone who didn't want to see dead kids in the streets, it stunk. Sure enough, five days later four kids were dead in Ohio. Ten days after that, two more lay dead in Jackson, Mississippi. New Haven stayed reasonably calm and everyone went back to their respective schools and wherever else after the weekend, and the Yale administration breathed a sigh of relief. The shit hit the fan everywhere else in the country, though. Including College Park.

McCaffrey listened to the bartender for a few more minutes, then went to the bathroom. His friend was at the bar when he returned.

"Jim Lewis!" said McCaffrey, extending his hand. "Good to see you."

"Hey Jerry. What are you drinking?" He gestured to the bartender for a drink for McCaffrey. Once served, the two men found a table and sat down. After a few minutes of small talk, Jerry's buddy asked him what this meeting was about.

"You must have heard about the case I'm working on," said McCaffrey.

"The Snowdon double murder, right?" said Lewis. "You must be lovin' it. Better then H. Rap Brown, even."

"Not exactly, but I need some help," said Jerry. "I need your office to take over the investigation."

"On what grounds?" asked Jim. He seemed to bristle at the suggestion. "We don't usually usurp local investigations."

"I know, Jim," said McCaffrey. "Shit. I work in Virginia, which is ten times more parochial than this state." There was a waitress at their table. They ordered another drink and asked for a menu.

"So...." Lewis let the word dangle.

"So," continued McCaffrey. "I think I can produce evidence that will clear the accused. His girlfriend can testify that they were together all night on the night in question. They went dancing at a series of illegal clubs in Baltimore and some of the club owners and their bouncers are willing to testify that they saw the couple that night."

"You're gonna need more than that."

McCaffrey was wondering if Jim was just playing

prosecutor and making sure he had a case or if he was trying to cover up for the racist Snowdon cops. He had no idea where his politics had gone. Jim was never a radical, but he was pretty liberal during his college days—helping to organize antiwar protests and supporting affirmative action plans in student government. People change, though.

"I know," said McCaffrey. "I also have a friend of the male victim who was the individual who pointed the police in McRice's direction. He goes by the name Rock."

"How does that fit in exactly?" asked Lewis.

McCaffrey told Lewis the story of the break-in, the money Jeremy owed Malcolm and Samson's speed and alcohol-fueled tale of murder that Rock had related to Peter and Lucy a few days earlier. Lewis nodded his head. He was beginning to see his old friend's approach to the case.

"He told the police about the money the victim owed McRice for some pot deal?" asked Lewis.

"That's the guy." affirmed McCaffrey. "He's willing to tell what he knows, with or without any immunity. Just to repeat—he was definitely involved in the theft of some pot along with the male victim. The pot was stolen from a dealer in Snowdon who has ties to the Pagans motorcycle gang and who also attempted to stab McRice the Friday night before the murder."

"Why haven't I heard about this?" asked Jim Lewis. "I read the report and saw no mention of this at all."

"Because the police have refused to investigate this aspect of the case, despite my client's pointing them in that direction the first time he was interviewed—and I use that term loosely, given their recent beating of the man—before he was arrested. They told him, in so many words, that they had no idea what he was talking about and that, as far as they were concerned, he is their man and they would figure out a way to make certain he was convicted. Since then, they have shown up in his jail cell in defiance of prison regulations and attempted to force him into signing a confession. To his credit, he has refused, although it is becoming increasingly dangerous for him to do so. I visited the accused on Saturday and he had was in the prison dispensary. You should have seen the kid. He looked like he had been run over by a bulldozer."

Lewis said nothing for a few minutes. In the silence, McCaffrey wondered how much more he should tell his old friend. After all, he didn't want information about his potential courtroom strategy to fall into the prosecution's hands. The waitress came back with their drinks and the menus. The two men each ordered a sandwich and some fries. Lewis looked at his friend McCaffrey.

"I know you're calling in that favor you did for me, Jerry," he began. "And I don't blame you. I know you would probably never speak to me again if I refused. I don't blame you for that, either. So, let me put it to you this way."

He took a drink. Then he folded his hands and put on his prosecutorial face.

"I will petition to take over this investigation on two conditions." He kept a steady eye on his drink, unable to look Jerry in the eye. "The first is that you get me a recording of that young man's—what did you say his name was—Rock—story? Second, is that you keep the press out of this for at least a week. When is pretrial?"

"August 4th," answered McCaffrey.

"That gives us two weeks," said Lewis. "Can you do it?"

"You bet I can," answered McCaffrey. He smiled. "Just don't ask me how I got the recording."

"I won't if you don't ask me how I got jurisdiction." They raised their glasses and drank. "Besides, once my office gets jurisdiction, we'll re-open the investigation and bring this Rock in. If he's got anything solid, I'll have a special unit ready to pull a surprise raid on this biker dealer fellow. That's another reason we need to keep the press out—so we can get to any new suspects before they leave town or destroy any evidence that might be on their premises. I'll prepare the papers tomorrow and once you get me that tape I'll file them."

"I'll get the kid on tape by Wednesday—that's two

days from now. Do you want to talk to McRice's girl-friend?"

"Sure, let her know about it and we'll set up an appointment either at my office or her house."

"Great." McCaffrey was relieved. "Thanks, Jim. I appreciate this big time."

The two men ordered another drink and started catching up. Lewis had been married to the same woman for five years and had a son. McCaffrey had been divorced twice and was childless. Their musical tastes remained the same and so did their desire for an occasional hit of weed. Both were ecstatic about the Red Sox season so far. Lewis had gone to prep school in Boston and become a fan then. And, of course, both had their doubts that the Sox' success would last the season. It was the Red Sox, after all.

Lucy was hanging out at Peter's until he got home from work. She was listening to the second side of Dylan's Blood On the Tracks over and over again. Peter had got her into a game guessing what the lyrics might mean. There was something about the song "Lily, Rosemary and the Jack of Hearts." She was playing a game with the characters in the song, trying to assign each of the roles to people she knew. Peter struck her as the Jack of Hearts and Art had some of the attributes of Big Jim. At least the ones regarding his style and smarts. But what did that make her? Lily or Rosemary? She'd have to ask

Peter what he thought when he got home. And what was that drilling on the wall? She took a bong hit and laughed. It was Malcolm breaking out of jail. She giggled again. Peter walked in the door. He was tired and happy to see Lucy. He sat down next to her and joined in the game. His favorite song on the album was "Shelter From the Storm." There was something apocalyptic about it that just struck him. The imagery was similar to the imagery that Dylan used throughout his album John Wesley Harding— biblical, ironic, and dark. At the same time, there was a spirit in the song "Shelter From the Storm" that suggested warmth and security. "Try imagining a place that's always safe and warm." Peter saw the song as an allegorical tale of the so-called children of the sixties, especially the two lines that went: "I bargained for salvation an' they gave me a lethal dose. I offered up my innocence and got repaid with scorn." Then mother earth comes in and offers shelter from that storm. Him and Lucy had lots of fun playing the game. It was better than charades and less exhausting than softball. Peter removed his greasy shirt and snuggled up to Lucy. She smoothed the hairs on his chest and rested her head on his shoulder.

18

After catching him at a time when his defenses were down, Lucy had convinced Rock to tell his story to McCaffrey. He was in the car with Peter and they were heading to McCaffrey's motel. McCaffrey had bought a case of beer and a bucket of chicken for the conversation. They didn't want Rock going anywhere. In addition Charles X's two friends were at the motel room. They had instructions to say nothing. All they had to do was stay in the room and prevent Rock from leaving.

Rock was nervous. His hands were sweaty and he felt like he was stuck between getting killed by Samson or getting thrown in jail for lying and being an accessory after the fact. That's what Lucy had told him, anyway. She also told him that if Malcolm was let go and Rock wasn't involved in helping him get out he would be in deep shit. You don't send a man to jail for something he didn't do and expect him to forget. If Malcolm got convicted for the murders, Rock would be in even bigger trouble. After all, Art had some connections who weren't afraid to kill. Rock was nervous. He hoped this deal he was agreeing to could help him out.

They were now at the University Motel in College Park. Peter pulled into the lot and parked. The two men went up to McCaffrey's room. Peter knocked and McCaffrey let them in. He urged them to have a seat and to help themselves to a beer and some chicken. He did not introduce the two black men who sat in chairs near the door. Peter took two beers from the cooler and handed one to Rock. He raised his bottle: "To the truth." Rock said nothing.

McCaffrey introduced himself.

"Hi, I'm Jerry. You must be Rock." He offered his hand. Rock shook it half-heartedly. "I plan on taping our conversation. I also expect you to tell the entire truth exactly as you know it. If I have any doubts I'll ask you. Or Peter will. Okay? Or these men will." He indicated the two black men.

Rock shrugged his shoulders. He finished his beer and nervously reached for another one.

"Go ahead," said McCaffrey. "If it helps you relax, have a few."

McCaffrey popped a blank cassette into the tape recorder and turned it on. He spoke into the microphone. He stated the date, time, and the names of the people in the room. He identified Charles X's friends as Brother One and Brother Two. Then he sat down.

"Tell us what you told Peter and Lucy about the rip-off and the cops' interrogation of you," prompted

McCaffrey.

Rock began. "Jeremy came to my house pretty freaked out. I don't know what the date was but I remember that the Snowdon Carnival near the shopping center had just started. Anyhow, Jeremy was flippin' out because he had spent the money Malcolm had given him to buy a quarter-pound of pot on whatever. You know, beer, stuff for his girlfriend, and records. Nothing special, just everyday shit. Anyhow, Malcolm was pissed since it had been a couple weeks since he'd fronted the money. He was tired of Jeremy dickin' him around and told him that he better show up with the herb or the money 'cause otherwise Malcolm and his friends from Baltimore was gonna kick his ass bad. So Jeremy was scared. Like he always did when he was scared he came runnin' to me. I was always protectin' him from his fool stuff and from his mom's asshole boyfriends. So anyway, he comes over to my house freakin' heavy. We smoked some weed and thought about it for a little bit and then I told him I knew where we could rip off some pot that would cover what he owed Malcolm. It sounded good to both of us, so we rode our bikes out to this biker guy that I buy drugs from."

"Is this the fellow who goes by the name Samson?" asked McCaffrey. He handed Rock another beer and a couple pieces of chicken.

"Yeah. Anyhow, I knew Samson was gone to the

Poconos for a few days and I also knew he had some kickass pot that would shut Malcolm up once Jeremy gave him his fuckin' quarter-pound. I knew Samson's place pretty well and since me and Jeremy used to do burglaries all the time, I figured it would be easy as pie. And it was. We broke in an open window. Jeremy found the cabinet where the stash was and grabbed a bunch of pot. Then we left. The next day he paid Malcolm off and that was it. I was a little nervous about Samson finding out, but figured he wouldn't and if he did he would go after the guy who sold him the weed thinking he was short-changed. Unfortunately, it didn't happen that way. The next thing I heard was that Samson found out a black guy was sellin' the same kind of weed that Samson was sellin' and in Snowdon only one person at a time usually has the good weed. Everybody else is buying it from that person or selling Mexican. Samson called me to ask what I knew. I told him that it was Malcolm who was selling the weed and told him that Malcolm worked with me. So then Samson threatened and attacked Malcolm in the parking lot at work, which got people wonderin' what the hell was goin' on. I knew but I wasn't gonna say a fuckin' thing. Let things fall where they may was my thinking.'"

"Then Jeremy and Julie got killed. I had no idea who did it. You know, I just thought it was some random type thing and they had drawn the unlucky number or somethin'. I thought about Samson, but not really. Plus I didn't care who did it, just that I had lost a friend. I was walkin' around Snowdon the next day tryin' to figure out what I was gonna say if the pigs brought me in. I kinda figured they would since they knew me and Jeremy was super close. I was drinkin' in the culvert underneath Route 1 and got busted for that. Then those assholes Starsky and Hutch—"

"You mean the detectives Mulhaney and Smith?" interjected McCaffrey.

"Yeah, them fuckheads. Anyhow, they took me into one of them interrogation rooms and started askin' me questions about Jeremy and who did I think killed him and Julie. All I said was that Jeremy owed Malcolm a bunch of money. They did the rest. I don't like Malcolm anyhow, so I didn't give a shit what happened to him. Plus I figured it would take the heat off of me or anybody else. Those pigs fell for it like carp go after bread-and-butter balls. They hate niggers more than I ever could. Sorry guys...." Rock remembered the two brothers in the room.

"The cops told me to stay in town and then they let me go. I didn't think too much about it again until I heard Malcolm got charged with the murders. Like I said, I knew he didn't do it, but I didn't care if he took the fall, so I just tried to forget about it. That is, until I went over to Samson's place last week or the week before—I really don't remember which day or week it was, just that it was after the killings. I showed up at his door and he was pretty fuckin' cranked up. He let me in and we started partyin' hard. Lines of crank, pot, fuckin' liquor and beer. I mean we was doin' some serious gettin' wasted. Anyhow, he started talkin' about how funny he thought it was that Malcolm was gonna fuckin' do his time for killin' Jeremy and Julie."

Peter sat up and began to listen more intently. Rock hadn't told Lucy and him this part of the story. He had hinted at it, but hadn't provided any details. McCaffrey asked him to stop for a minute while he popped in a fresh cassette. Rock asked if he could use the bathroom. McCaffrey said only if he left the door open. Brother Number One stood up, ready to tackle Rock if he tried anything funny. Rock finished peeing and sat back down in his chair.

"Then he started describin' how he did the killings. He told me he went over there with a piece of pipe in his pocket and gloves on his hands. He said he knew the neighbors were gone and he didn't let nobody rip him off. He called himself the mighty Samson or somethin' like that. I was fuckin' scared, man. He was crazier than shit the night he tol' me all this, especially with all that crank inside his head. He had over an ounce of the shit and just kept doin' lines. He told me how Jeremy and Julie fought back and how he bashed them with his fists and the pipe. Then he said Julie hit him upside the head with the back of the toilet tank and that's when he finished them both off—after she hit him. Then, he said he cleaned up everything bloody he could find and stashed it away. I don't know where. He said somethin' about burying it. After he did that he left town again. Then when he heard about Malcolm takin' the fall, he came back. That's all I know."

McCaffrey looked at Rock. What the hell kind of society were our kids growing up in, he wondered? This kid, who couldn't be more than 20, had just told a tale so full of violence and disregard for human life. Yet, he told it like it was nothing—as if he had no conscience. Like he was a Green Beret or contract killer. Things don't look good for the future, thought McCaffrey. Not at all. At least he came clean. Maybe he did have some kind of soul, after all. Now, he needed to convince the kid to tell his story under oath. Maybe McCaffrey could promise that he wouldn't get prosecuted for accessory after the fact or some similar charge. McCaffrey told Rock to help himself to the beer. Peter would drive him home later. McCaffrey went to call Jim Lewis. He had the tape and was on his way to deliver it. Charles X's friends left with McCaffrey. He wasn't sure, but figured that bodyguards might be a good thing.

19

It was Wednesday afternoon. Jerry McCaffrey had delivered the tape the night before to Jim Lewis' house near Sykesville. After listening to it three or four times and making a copy that he placed in a safe spot, Lewis was convinced he had the evidence he needed to make his argument requesting jurisdiction be transferred to his office. He had visited Rock at his parent's house that morning and the kid signed an affidavit verifying the truth of the recording. Lewis was pretty confident that the McRice case was going to be his baby within the next several hours. He wanted to discipline those two yahoos in Snowdon, as well, but figured that part of the deal he would make with the higher-ups would include no mention of the Snowdon department's half-assed investigation or the beatings by the two officers. He honestly thought Mulhaney and Smith were just poorly trained, not racist. Jerry would have none of that, though, so the two of them had let it drop. Jerry believed that these two detectives were Klansmen in blue instead of white, but then Jerry was always less forgiving of stupidity than Jim fancied himself to be.

He was scheduled to make his presentation to the State's Attorney in an hour. Once the jurisdiction change was approved, he had a special unit ready to raid Samson's place in the woods. The warrants were signed and blank, which meant he could put anything he wanted in those blank spaces. His plan was to go along with the special unit to ensure that the raid was thorough.

Malcolm had no idea what had occurred in his case since his beating by Mulhaney and Smith. He was finally off the IV painkiller, but remained in the infirmary. No one was allowed to visit him there except for his lawyer. He had heard from the prison doctor that McCaffrey had hauled the warden's ass on the carpet over those two pigs being in the prison in violation of regulations. Malcolm smiled when he heard that but was secretly afraid that that only meant that the two cops would just kill him the next time they visited. If they did that, then they could make up whatever kind of story they wanted to cover their tracks. He was trying to focus on the light above him in the infirmary but couldn't. Must be the Demerol shot they gave him. He fell into a dreamless narcotized sleep.

By evening, Lewis had everything in place. The raid was scheduled to take place after 11:00 that night. He had permission to accompany the police. The office concurred with his decision to say absolutely nothing to the press or any other office. Indeed, the special unit would only be told their destination five minutes before they left. The group would be leaving from the trooper's barracks near Columbia, the planned city being built between Baltimore and DC. Samson's place was approximately seven miles from the raid's launching point. Lewis could feel the adrenalin slowly rising. He would be riding in a car at the rear, but was expected to conduct the search onsite. This meant he would be wearing a flak jacket and carrying a pistol. McCaffrey had been contacted with instructions to say absolutely nothing to his client or anyone else. There would be a press conference in the morning at the conference room usually utilized by the State's Attorney's Office for that purpose. After that, McCaffrey was free to say what he wanted. McCaffrey was still deciding whether he wanted to hold any type of media event or if he should wait until the charges against Malcolm were dropped. He supposed he should meet with the folks who had been the most active in the campaign and see what they thought. First, though, they had to find something that tied Samson positively to the murders. Otherwise, it was going to be a long trial with very little help from the state. He really hoped this wouldn't fuck up.

McCaffrey called Art's house to see if he was home. He was and invited McCaffrey over. Maybe they could watch an Orioles game or something. Peter and Lucy were coming over, too. Grace was doing something at the church.

"Bring some beer, Jerry," instructed Art. "I'll cook up some stew or somethin'."

"Sounds good. I'm on my way." McCaffrey hung up the phone and left the motel room. When he knocked on the door to Art's apartment he could hear Peter and Lucy giving Art a hard time about his clothes.

"Shit," said Lucy. "You lookin' like the Godfather of Soul."

"That man stole his name from me," said Art. "He may be the godfather, but I'm the father. I got more soul in my pinky finger than that man got in his whole being."

"Hell, he stole your hairdo, too," said Lucy. She pinched Art's belly, which stuck out a little like Santa Claus's.

"Get on uppa'..." sang Art in his best James Brown imitation.

Peter was thumbing through Art and Malcolm's records. He found My Favorite Things by John Coltrane and put it on. Then he pulled out a joint and lit it. Soon, everyone was laying back on a chair or the floor listening to Coltrane's take on the Broadway tune. Jerry remembered the very first time he heard this album. He was in college and had just smoked hashish for the first time. The music and the drug created a synesthesia he had yet to experience for the second time.

Antoine and Marion were eating dinner with Karin and Antoine's mom. Marion had tried to get in touch with the prison folks earlier, but had been put on hold three times in a row. It was obvious to her that they didn't want to talk to her. She hoped it wasn't because Malcolm's condition was worsening or, and she hated to even think about this, because he was dead. The only good thing about him being in the infirmary, according to Antoine, was that those cracker cops couldn't beat him up. Marion supposed that was a good thing. Karin pulled on her sleeve.

"Let's play cards, Marion." Karin was trying to shuffle the deck. The cards kept flying out of her hands and on to the floor. Marion chuckled at her attempts.

"All right, Karin. What game we playing?" At least cards would keep her from thinking the worst regarding Malcolm.

"Hearts. Mom and Antoine playin', too."

"I ain't playin' Karin," said Antoine.

"Oh come on, big brother," begged Karin. "Come on." She put her arms around his neck and began kissing his face.

"Yeah," teased Marion. "Come on big brother."

Antoine laughed. "All right. You convinced me, sweetie. Just quit kissing me!"

"Yay!" cheered Karin. "Now I just gotta convince Mama! Yay!"

Five minutes later, the four of them were playing Hearts.

Baltimore Sun

In Surprise Move, State Prosecutors Take Over Snowdon Double Murder Case

State Police Conduct Surprise Late-Night Raid on Suspect Not Previously Linked to Case

Annapolis, July 23 – State Prosecutor James Lewis announced a successful raid of the property of Samuel J. Johnson (30) at a noon press conference in Annapolis today. Johnson, also known as Samson, was charged with multiple counts of possession with intent to distribute marijuana, cocaine, methamphetamine and pcp. Several handguns, automatic weapons, and rifles were also found on the premises. Lewis acknowledged to the press that the warrant served on Mr. Johnson was in relation to the double murder case that still has the residents of Snowdon, Md. reeling in shock.

Police originally refused to say what Johnson's connection to the murders may be, but informed sources have told this paper that Johnson is believed to be the murderer of Jeremy Prehausen and Julie Epstein. Snowdon police had already arrested another man, Malcolm McRice, on those charges. These same sources told reporters that positive proof of Johnson's involvement in that crime was found on the premises. According to earlier unpublished stories and comments by members of the Snowdon Police

Department, the earlier evidence linking McRice to the murders was circumstantial and, according to sources within the department who prefer to remain anonymous, "shaky at best." The arrest and imprisonment of McRice has stirred local Black churches and civil rights groups to protest what they perceive to be racism in the Snowdon police force. Rumors have also circulated that McRice was beaten in his cell at least twice in an attempt by officers to extract a confession.

Members of the Maryland State Special Narcotics Unit, which conducted the raid of Johnson's property along with members of the Maryland State Police Homicide Division, told the press that over five pounds of marijuana, two ounces of methamphetamine, four grams of cocaine, and ten ounces of parsley sprayed with pcp were confiscated. In addition, police also seized 12,000 dollars in cash.

Johnson was surprised when over thirty heavily armed police surrounded his place late Wednesday night. He answered the knock on the door holding a rifle. "When he saw all those guns pointed at his face," said Asst. State's Attorney Lewis. "He dropped that rifle like it was burning his flesh." Johnson did not resist once law enforcement entered his house.

Samuel Johnson is rumored to be a member of the Pagans motorcycle gang. This could not be verified. However, police did emphasize that this gang does control much of the drug traffic in the Maryland-Virginia-Delaware area. In addition, the club is attempting to expand its influence beyond those states. The group is known for its violence and involvement in racist organizations such as the Ku Klux Klan.

As this article was going to press, Attorney Lewis told members of the media that his office was going to coordinate efforts with Prince George's County and Snowdon officials in the next couple of days. "It is expected," said Lewis. "That Mr. Johnson will also be arraigned on the murder charges once we get the lab results back and straighten things out between the various offices." When asked if murder charges would then be dropped against McRice. Lewis only said, "That sounds about right."

McCaffrey read the news article in the evening paper. He had a call in to Lewis, but had yet to hear back from him. He needed to know what the hell they found in those woods. The paper really didn't tell him much about that. He assumed that the lab was analyzing whatever they found looking for a link to Samson. All he knew for sure was that Samson wasn't going anywhere for a while. There were enough drugs seized in the raid to keep him behind bars for a few years. Meanwhile, McCaffrey had obtained the earlier evidence reports on Malcolm that the Prince George's prosecutor had been lagging on providing. The only stuff they found in Malcolm's car was a minuscule amount of pot and a few strands of hair that matched Julie's. The presence of the hair could be explained quite easily. Malcolm gave Julie a ride home from work three or four times a week. The weed proved nothing other than that Malcolm may or may not smoke pot. Even if Lewis and his crew did not find proof positive that Samson was the murderer, McCaffrey liked his chances in court a little better. As long as Malcolm didn't weaken and sign that bullshit confession.

20

It was Friday morning. The Samson arrest had been announced only two days earlier. Jim Lewis was on his way to the courthouse building in Hyattsville for a ten o'clock meeting. Jerry McCaffrey, Mulhaney and Smith, the Snowdon chief of police, and a member of the Prince George's County prosecutor's office were all scheduled to attend. Lewis was ready to file charges against the two cops. Assault, false arrest, and filing a false report were just a few of the charges he had in mind. In reality, he figured those little scumbags would get off with a slap on the wrist and a couple weeks suspension with pay. That was usually how it worked with the thugs who wore the uniforms—and he agreed with McCaffrey that these cops were thugs. Their chief would bring up their service record and their length of time on the force, as if that were to their credit. In Lewis' mind, it only proved how poorly the chief administered his force.

This situation wasn't unusual. Maryland, like the rest of the country, had miles to go when it came to modernizing their police forces. Even he could appreciate the rhetoric of groups like the Black Panthers when they called the local police, occupation forces. After all, most of the cops didn't live in the neighborhoods they policed and were white suburbanites who had no idea what life was like for a black person living in the United States Not that it was all the individual cops' fault. If fingers could be pointed, they should be pointed at those who were in charge, including Lewis' office. He hoped that by the time he retired there would be a change in the way police and citizens interacted. It was hard for him to support men who could just as easily have been wearing klan robes as police uniforms, but it was just as hard to support young people and others who had no respect for what the police were ideally supposed to be there for. Unfortunately, until the police administrators quit thinking like an occupation force and began disciplining their renegade officers, not much was going to change.

McCaffrey pulled into the Hyattsville courthouse parking lot just as Lewis was locking his car door. The two men walked into the building together. Lewis filled his buddy Jerry in on the lab results.

"You'll be glad to know," he began. "They got a bloody fingerprint from a piece of pipe that matched Johnson's. Lab guy thinks Johnson removed his gloves when he was burying the material. That matches your boy's story about the gloves being worn during the murder. There were also some of Johnson's hairs and skin remnants found on the female victim's clothes. Charges are being filed this morning by my office."

"What about my client?" asked McCaffrey. "When can he get out?"

"As soon as this meeting is complete," answered Lewis. "I've already contacted Patuxent Correctional."

"What about these redneck cops?"

"That's what this meeting is about, more than anything," said Lewis. "I don't expect them to get suspended or fired but I plan on reading the riot act to both of these assholes and their chief. In addition, they will be warned that if their department fucks up once more the state will take over their operations and a complete investigation of the entire department will take place."

McCaffrey laughed. He was skeptical but appreciated Jim's efforts. Personally, he would like to take the two motherfuckers out into the yard at Patuxent and let the prisoners have twenty minutes with them. "Thanks Jim. To be honest, I'd like to see them assholes in the unemployment line."

"Me too," said Lewis. "But the game isn't played that way around here. I figure this will be the best I can get."

"Shit, the game ain't played that way anywhere."

They entered the conference room where the others were already gathered. Lewis acknowledged their presence and asked everyone to sit down. McCaffrey sat in the back of the room near the door. Lewis began.

"As I speak, two counts of murder in the first degree are being filed against Samuel Johnson of Snowdon. These charges are the result of evidence obtained in the raid on his property on the night of Tuesday, July 22, 1975.

"This evidence included a bloody fingerprint on the alleged murder weapon—a 12 inch piece of steel pipe, and several of the suspect's hairs and pieces of his skin that were found on clothes that were worn by the female victim on the night of the murder.

"As you know, this raid was the result of the State's Attorney's office re-opening the investigation of these murders. This re-opening was due to the shoddy and incomplete investigation conducted by the Snowdon Police Department and the prosecutor's office of Prince George's County.

"As a person in law enforcement, I believe that in order for the community to respect us, justice must be served and, in order for justice to be served, every crime must be investigated fully without fail. I am appalled that this did not happen in this case. Indeed, from my vantage point it appears that the detectives in charge of the investigation decided early on that they would make the evidence match their prime suspect and, in so doing, ignore any evidence that might cause them to look elsewhere. I find this type of police work completely unprofessional.

"If these men worked in my department, they

would be out of a job as soon as the patrolman's association let me fire them. Now, I don't know if these detectives failed to conduct a full investigation because they were lazy, too busy, or—and I pray that this is not the case—because they fell victim to their personal prejudices.

"All I know is that there is a man sitting in Patuxent Correctional Facility right now who does not belong there and the reason he is there is because of these detectives' terrible police work. Furthermore, the beatings they administered to this man were completely out of line. My office will be conducting an investigation into these illegal actions and charges may be filed. I would hope that the Chief of the Snowdon department will clean up his own house immediately, since it would be better for the profession overall if we can keep these misdeeds in-house.

"However, my colleague, Mr. McCaffrey may have other ideas. Let me remind you—he has every right to file a civil suit seeking damages for his client, Malcolm McRice. If he does so, the newspapers will eat it up. I hope those in attendance here who will be affected by any such suit are taking heed of my words."

Mulhaney and Smith were pissed. They knew, however, that their best response would be to keep their mouths shut. Neither man wanted to lose his job just because of some liberal lawyer who wanted to score brownie points.

As far as Mulhaney was concerned, Malcolm deserved everything he got. The fuckin' nigger was a reasonable suspect. Why should they have believed anything he said? Smith was a little less certain. He and Mulhaney had already argued over the investigation being so shallow, but Smith deferred to Mulhaney's seniority.

He planned on talking to the chief about being reassigned to another partner. Mulhaney's personal habits regarding liquor and women had been bothering him for a while and making his home life difficult. This episode might be the perfect excuse to get out of Mulhaney's car.

"Any questions?" asked Lewis.

"When will the charges be dropped on my client?" asked McCaffrey. "And when will he be freed?"

"The murder charges have been dropped," answered Lewis. "He still has some marijuana charges pending. Perhaps a deal can be worked out on those."

"I want time served," said McCaffrey. "Otherwise we sue the pants off of these racist SOB's."

"The judge will certainly consider your request," said Lewis. "If there are no other questions, this meeting is adjourned."

Nobody said anything. People left the room. Jim Lewis caught up with the McCaffrey in the parking lot.

"You want to go get some lunch, Jerry?" he asked.

"Sure. I'll follow you." They got in their cars and headed out.

Baltimore Sun

Johnson Charged With Murders
Snowdon Detectives Suspended; McRice Freed

Snowdon, Md. – In a complete turnaround of events, Samuel Johnson was charged yesterday with the June 21, 1975 double murders of Jeremy Prehausen and Julie Epstein. A statement released by the Maryland State Attorney's office said evidence linking Johnson to the crime was found buried on his property when police searched it on Tuesday.

In a related event, the two Snowdon police detectives in charge of the original investigation were suspended with pay for their actions during the investigation. "It was one of the shoddiest examples of police work I have ever seen," said Deputy State's Attorney James Lewis. The detectives refused comment. The Snowdon police department was the target of protests in recent weeks by civil rights organizations and some church groups. It is believed that the detectives illegally beat Malcolm McRice, the original suspect in the case, while he was being held at Patuxent Correctional Facility. McRice's attorney, Jerald McCaffrey of Roanoke, Va., told the press that he was considering a civil suit over McRice's arrest and treatment. "These officers went way beyond the boundaries of the law," he said. "There is an expectation of fairness that must

be upheld if we are to maintain our democratic society. When that expectation is not met, especially by those hired to uphold it, the gate is open to totalitarianism."
McRice was freed yesterday afternoon. Family, friends and supporters gathered at the Patuxent Facility to welcome him. "It's nice to see justice take it rightful course every once in a while," said the Reverend Nathan Moore, of the Snowdon Grove Zion Baptist Church. "Of course, it wouldn't have happened without the work and efforts of hundreds of people. We thank them and the Lord." Moore was one of the leaders in the movement around McRice's case.
"I'm just grateful to the Lord that my baby's out of jail!" said Ms. Grace McRice. Ms. McRice is Malcolm McRice's great-aunt and has cared for him since he was an infant. Members of the Maryland Coalition Against Racism and Police Brutality—the civil rights organization that first put the case in the news —could not be reached for comment.
McRice will appear in court on Monday on an unrelated charge of marijuana possession.

Malcolm got six months probation on the marijuana charge. It seemed like the cops just didn't want to let him go completely and he was tired of dealing with the system. So, when they offered him the six months, he said yes and signed the papers.

After a week or two of hanging out and enjoying being out of jail, he went back to work at the Pancake House. The boss, Lewin, told him that he could work there as long as he needed to and not to worry about the money for the lawyer. Malcolm's plan was to get enough money together to leave Snowdon forever.

Marion had invited him to come live with her for awhile and he was pretty sure he would take her up on the offer. Maybe she really was the one. Art and his mom were moving into a house near Peter's abode. She was working with Reverend Moore and the ladies at the church on setting up a scholarship fund for youngsters from the church's neighborhood.

Peter had decided to take a couple weeks off from work and go to San Francisco to see if it was the place for him. Lucy was debating whether or not she wanted to join him. The love was still plenty warm between them, but California was pretty far away and she had this feeling that Peter might decide to stay once he got there. He had always seemed out of place in Snowdon, even back in junior high.

Rock's parents bought him a bus ticket the day after Malcolm was released. He was already on his way to his dad's brother's place in upstate New York near Albany. They figured a change of scenery might do the boy some good.

Detective Smith was spending time with his family and trying to get a job as a cop in another town.

Mulhaney found himself drinking Scotch at the Howard Johnson's lounge almost every night. He was still pretty pissed at the dressing down he and Smith had received, and, when he wasn't trying to seduce the single women he saw around him, he thought about revenge.

Fomite
Burlington, Vermont

Fomite is a literary press whose authors and artists explore the human condition—political, cultural, personal and historical—in poetry and prose.

A fomite is a medium capable of transmitting infectious organisms from one individual to another.

"The activity of art is based on the capacity of people to be infected by the feelings of others." Tolstoy, *What is Art?*

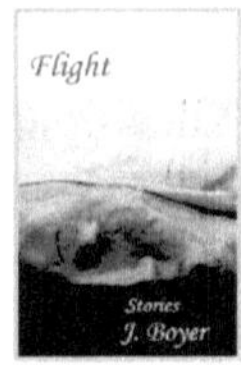

Flight and Other Stories - Jay Boyer
In *Flight and Other Stories,* we're with the fattest woman on earth as she draws her last breaths and her soul ascends toward its final reward. We meet a divorcee who can fly for no more effort than flapping her arms. We follow a middle-aged butler whose love affair with a young woman leads him first to the mysteries of bondage, and then to the pleasures of malice. Story by story, we set foot into worlds so strange as to seem all but surreal, yet everything feels familiar, each moment rings true. And that's when we recognize we're in the hands of one of America's truly original talents.

Loisaida - Dan Chodorokoff
Catherine, a young anarchist estranged from her parents and squatting in an abandoned building on New York's Lower East Side is fighting with her boyfriend and conflicted about her work on an underground newspaper. After learning of a developer's plans to demolish a community garden, Catherine builds an alliance with a group of Puerto Rican community activists. Together they confront the confluence of politics, money, and real estate that rule Manhattan. All the while she learns important lessons from her great-grandmother's life in the Yiddish anarchist movement that flourished on the Lower East Side at the turn of the century. In this coming of age story, family saga, and tale of urban politics, Dan Chodorkoff explores the "principle of hope", and examines how memory and imagination inform social change.

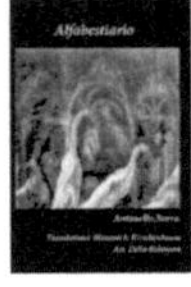

Alfabestiario
AlphaBetaBestiario - Antonello Borra
Animals have always understood that mankind is not fully at home in the world. Bestiaries, hoping to teach, send out warnings. This one, of course, aims at doing the same.

Fomite
Burlington, Vermont

Improvisational Arguments - Anna Faktorovich
Improvisational Arguments is written in free verse to capture the essence of modern problems and triumphs. The poems clearly relate short, frequently humorous and occasionally tragic, stories about travels to exotic and unusual places, fantastic realms, abnormal jobs, artistic innovations, political objections, and misadventures with love.

Loosestrife - Greg Delanty
This book is a chronicle of complicity in our modern lives, a witnessing of war and the destruction of our planet. It is also an attempt to adjust the more destructive blueprint myths of our society. Often our cultural memory tells us to keep quiet about the aspects that are most challenging to our ethics, to forget the violations we feel and tremors that keep us distant and numb.

Carts and Other Stories - Zdravka Evtimova

Roots and wings are the key words that best describe the short story collection, *Carts and Other Stories,* by Zdravka Evtimova. The book is emotionally multilayered and memorable because of its internal power, vitality and ability to touch both the heart and your mind. Within its pages, the reader discovers new perspectives and true wealth, and learns to see the world with different eyes. The collection lives on the borders of different cultures. *Carts and Other Stories* will take the reader to wild and powerful Bulgarian mountains, to silver rains in Brussels, to German quiet winter streets and to wind bitten crags in Afghanistan. This book lives for those seeking to discover the beauty of the world around them, and will have them appreciating what they have—and perhaps what they have lost as well.

Visiting Hours - *Jennifer Anne Moses*
Visiting Hours, a novel-in-stories, explores the lives of people not normally met on the page——AIDS patients and those who care for them. Set in Baton Rouge, Louisiana, and written with large and frequent dollops of humor, the book is a profound meditation on faith and love in the face of illness and poverty.

Fomite
Burlington, Vermont

Roadworthy Creature, Roadworthy Craft - Kate Magill

Words fail but the voice struggles on. The culmination of a decade's worth of performance poetry, *Roadworthy Creature, Roadworthy Craft* is Kate Magill's first full-length publication. In lines that are sinewy yet delicate, Magill's poems explore the terrain where idea and action meet, where bodies and words commingle to form a strange new flesh, a breathing text, an "I" that spirals outward from itself.

The Co-Conspirator's Tale - Ron Jacobs

There's a place where love and mistrust are never at peace; where duplicity and deceit are the universal currency. *The Co-Conspirator's Tale* takes place within this nebulous firmament. There are crimes committed by the police in the name of the law. Excess in the name of revolution. The combination leaves death in its wake and the survivors struggling to find justice in a San Francisco Bay Area noir by the author of the underground classic *The Way the Wind Blew: A History of the Weather Underground* and the novel *Short Order Frame Up*.

Short Order Frame Up - Ron Jacobs

1975. America has lost its war in Vietnam and Cambodia. Racially-tinged riots are tearing the city of Boston apart. The politics and counterculture of the 1960s is disintegrating into nothing more than sex, drugs and rock and roll. The Boston Red Sox are on one of their improbable runs toward a postseason appearance. In a suburban town in Maryland, a young couple is murdered and another young man is accused. The couple are white and the accused is black. It is up to his friends and family to prove he is innocent. This is a story of suburban ennui, race, murder and injustice. Religion and politics, liberal lawyers and racist cops. In *Short Order Frame Up*, Ron Jacobs has written a piece of crime fiction that exposes the wound that is US racism. Two cultures existing side by side and across generations--a river very few dare to cross. His characters work and live with and next to each other, often unaware of the other's real life. When the murder occurs, however, those people that care about the man charged must cross that river and meet somewhere in between in order to free him from (what is to them) an obvious miscarriage of justice.

Fomite
Burlington, Vermont

All the Sinners Saints - Ron Jacobs
A young draftee named Victor Willard goes AWOL in Germany after an altercation with a commanding officer. Porgy is an African-American GI involved with the international Black Panthers and German radicals. Victor and a female radical named Ana fall in love. They move into Ana's room in a squatted building near the US base in Frankfurt. The international campaign to free Black revolutionary Angela Davis is coming to Frankfurt. Porgy and Ana are key organizers and Victor spends his days and nights selling and smoking hashish, while becoming addicted to heroin. Police and narcotics agents are keeping tabs on them all. Politics, love, and drugs. Truths, lies, and rock and roll. *All the Sinners, Saints* is a story of people seeking redemption in a world awash in sin.

The Listener Aspires to the Condition of Music
- Barry Goldensohn
"I know of no other selected poems that selects on one theme, but this one does, charting Goldensohn's career-long attraction to music's performance, consolations and its august, thrilling, scary and clownish charms. Does all art aspire to the condition of music as Pater claimed, exhaling in a swoon toward that one class act? Goldensohn is more aware than the late 19th century of the overtones of such breathing: his poems thoroughly round out those overtones in a poet's lifetime of listening."
John Peck, poet, editor, Fellow of the American Academy of Rome

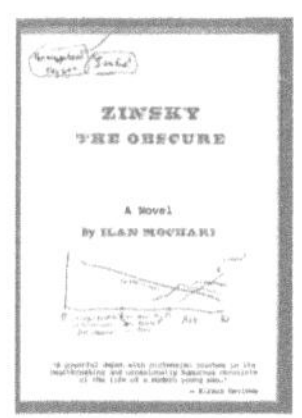

Zinsky the Obscure - Ilan Mochari
"If your childhood is brutal, your adulthood becomes a daily attempt to recover: a quest for ecstasy and stability in recompense for their early absence." So states the 30-year-old Ariel Zinsky, whose bachelor-like lifestyle belies the torturous youth he is still coming to grips with. As a boy, he struggles with the beatings themselves; as a grownup, he struggles with the world's indifference to them. *Zinsky the Obscure* is his life story, a humorous chronicle of his search for a redemptive ecstasy through sex, an entrepreneurial sports obsession, and finally, the cathartic exercise of writing it all down. Fervently recounting both the comic delights and the frightening horrors of a life in which he feels—always—that he is not like all the rest, Zinsky survives the worst and relishes the best with idiosyncratic style, as his heartbreak turns into self-awareness and his suicidal ideation into self-regard. A vivid evocation of the all-consuming nature of lust and ambition—and the forces that drive them.

Fomite
Burlington, Vermont

The Derivation of Cowboys & Indians - Joseph D. Reich

The Derivation of Cowboys & Indians represents a profound journey, a breakdown of The American Dream from a social, cultural, historical, and spiritual point of view. Reich examines in concise detail the loss of the collective unconscious, commenting on our contemporary postmodern culture with its self-interested excesses, on where and how things all go wrong, and how social/political practice rarely meets its original proclamations and promises. Reich's surreal and self-effacing satire brings this troubling message home. *The Derivations of Cowboys & Indians* is a desperate search and struggle for America's literal, symbolic, and spiritual home.

Kasper Planet: Comix and Tragix - Peter Schumann

The British call him Punch, the Italians, Pulchinella, the Russians, Petruchka, the Native Americans, Coyote. These are the figures we may know. But every culture that worships authority will breed a Punch-like, anti-authoritarian resister. Yin and yang—it has to happen. The Germans call him Kasper. Truth-telling and serious pranking are dangerous professions when going up against power. Bradley Manning sits naked in solitary; Julian Assange is pursued by Interpol, Obama's Department of Justice, and Amazon.com. But—in contrast to merely human faces— masks and theater can often slip through the bars. Consider our American Kaspers: Charlie Chaplin, Woody Guthrie, Abby Hoffman, the Yes Men—theater people all, utilizing various forms to seed critique. Their profiles and tactics have evolved along with those of their enemies. Who are the bad guys that call forth the Kaspers? Over the last half century, with his Bread & Puppet Theater, Peter Schumann has been tireless in naming them, excoriating them with Kasperdom....
from Marc Estrin's Foreword to Planet Kasper

Raven or Crow - Joshua Amses

Marlowe has recently moved back home to Vermont after flunking his first term at a private college in the Midwest, when his sort of girlfriend, Eleanor, goes missing. The circumstances surrounding Eleanor's disappearance stand to reveal more about Marlowe than he is willing to allow. Rather than report her missing, he resolves to find Eleanor himself. *Raven or Crow* is the story of mistakes rooted in the ambivalence of being young and without direction.

Fomite
Burlington, Vermont

Views Cost Extra - L.E. Smith

Views that inspire, that calm, or that terrify—all come at some cost to the viewer. In *Views Cost Extra* you will find a New Jersey high school preppy who wants to inhabit the "perfect" cowboy movie, a rural mailman disgusted with the residents of his town who wants to live with the penguins, an ailing screen writer who strikes a deal with Johnny Cash to reverse an old man's failures, an old man who ponders a young man's suicide attempt, a one-armed blind blues singer who wants to reunite with the car that took her arm on the assembly line— and more. These stories suggest that we must pay something to live even ordinary lives.

Travers' Inferno - *L.E. Smith*

In the 1970's churches began to burn in Burlington, Vermont. If it were arson, no one or no reason could be found to blame. This book suggests arson, but makes no claim to historical realism. It claims, instead, to capture the dizzying 70's zeitgeist of aggressive utopian movements, distrust in authority, escapist alternative life styles, and a bewildered society of onlookers. In the tradition of John Gardner's Sunlight Dialogues, the characters of *Travers' Inferno* are colorful and damaged, sometimes comical, sometimes tragic, looking for meaning through desperate acts. Travers Jones, the protagonist, is grounded in the transcendent—philosophy, epilepsy, arson as purification—and mystified by the opposite sex, haunted by an absent father and directed by an uncle with a grudge. He is seduced by a professor's wife and chased by an endearing if ineffective sergeant of police. There are secessionist Quebecois involved in these church burns who are murdering as well as pilfering and burning. There are changing alliances, violent deaths, lovemaking, and a belligerent cat.

The Empty Notebook Interrogates Itself - Susan Thomas

The Empty Notebook began its life as a very literal metaphor for a few weeks of what the poet thought was writer's block, but was really the struggle of an eccentric persona to take over her working life. It won. And for the next three years everything she wrote came to her in the voice of the Empty Notebook, who, as the notebook began to fill itself, became rather opinionated, changed gender, alternately acted as bully and victim, had many bizarre adventures in exotic locales and developed a somewhat politically-incorrect attitude. It then began to steal the voices and forms of other poets and tried to immortalize itself in various poetry reviews. It is now thrilled to collect itself in one slim volume.

Fomite
Burlington, Vermont

Suite for Three Voices - Derek Furr

Suite for Three Voices is a dance of prose genres, teeming with intense human life in all its humor and sorrow. A son uncovers the horrors of his father's wartime experience, a hitchhiker in a muumuu guards a mysterious parcel, a young man foresees his brother's brush with death on September 11. A Victorian poetess encounters space aliens and digital archives, a runner hears the voice of a dead friend in the song of an indigo bunting, a teacher seeks wisdom from his students' errors and Neil Young. By frozen waterfalls and neglected graveyards, along highways at noon and rivers at dusk, in the sound of bluegrass, Beethoven, and Emily Dickinson, the essays and fiction in this collection offer moments of vision.

Entanglements - Tony Magistrale

A poet and a painter may employ different mediums to express the same snow-blown afternoon in January, but sometimes they find a way to capture the moment in such a way that their respective visions still manage to stir a reverberation, a connection. In part, that's what *Entanglements* seeks to do. Not so much for the poems and paintings to speak directly to one another, but for them to stir points of similarity.

The Good Muslim of Jackson Heights - Jaysinh Birjépatil

Jackson Heights in this book is a fictional locale with common features assembled from immigrant-friendly neighborhoods around the world where hardworking honest-to-goodness traders from the Indian subcontinent, rub shoulders with ruthless entrepreneurs, reclusive antique-dealers, homeless nobodies, merchant-princes, lawyers, doctors and IT specialists. But as Siraj and Shabnam, urbane newcomers fleeing religious persecution in their homeland discover there is no escape from the past. Weaving together the personal and the political *The Good Muslim of Jackson Heights* is an ambiguous elegy to a utopian ideal set free from all prejudice.

Fomite
Burlington, Vermont

My God, What Have We Done? - Susan Weiss

In a world afflicted with war, toxicity, and hunger, does what we do in our private lives really matter? Fifty years after the creation of the atomic bomb at Los Alamos, newlyweds Pauline and Clifford visit that once-secret city on their honeymoon, compelled by Pauline's fascination with Oppenheimer, the soulful scientist. The two stories emerging from this visit reverberate back and forth between the loneliness of a new mother at home in Boston and the isolation of an entire community dedicated to the development of the bomb. While Pauline struggles with unforeseen challenges of family life, Oppenheimer and his crew reckon with forces beyond all imagining.

Finally the years of frantic research on the bomb culminate in a stunning test explosion that echoes a rupture in the couple's marriage. Against the backdrop of a civilization that's out of control, Pauline begins to understand the complex, potentially explosive physics of personal relationships.

At once funny and dead serious, *My God, What Have We Done?* sifts through the ruins left by the bomb in search of a more worthy human achievement.

As It Is On Earth - Peter M. Wheelwright

Four centuries after the Reformation Pilgrims sailed up the down-flowing watersheds of New England, Taylor Thatcher, irreverent scion of a fallen family of Maine Puritans, is still caught in the turbulence.

In his errant attempts to escape from history, the young college professor is further unsettled by his growing attraction to Israeli student Miryam Bluehm as he is swept by Time through the "family thing"—from the tangled genetic and religious history of his New England parents to the redemptive birthday secret of Esther Fleur Noire Bishop, the Cajun-Passamaquoddy woman who raised him and his younger half-cousin/half-brother, Bingham.

The landscapes, rivers, and tidal estuaries of Old New England and the Mayan Yucatan are also casualties of history in Thatcher's story of Deep Time and re-discovery of family on Columbus Day at a high-stakes gambling casino, rising in resurrection over the starlit bones of a once-vanquished Pequot Indian Tribe.

Fomite
Burlington, Vermont

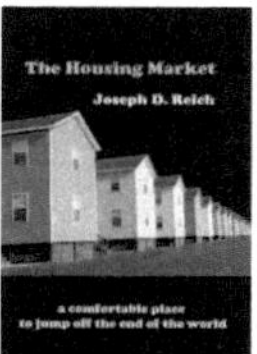

The Housing Market - Joseph D. Reich

In Joseph Reich's most recent social and cultural, contemporary satire
of suburbia entitled, "The Housing market: a comfortable place to jump off the end of the world," the author addresses the absurd, postmodern elements of what it means, or for that matter not, to try and cope and function, and survive and thrive, or live and die in the repetitive and existential, futile and self-destructive, homogenized, monochromatic landscape of a brutal and bland, collective unconscious, which can
spiritually result in a gradual wasting away and erosion of the senses or conflict and crisis of a desperate, disproportionate 'situational depression,' triggering and leading the narrator to feel constantly abandoned and stranded, more concretely or proverbially spoken, "the eternal stranger," where when caught between the fight or flight psychological phenomena, naturally repels him and causes him to flee and return without him even knowing it into the wild, while by sudden circumstance and coincidence discovers it surrounds the illusory-like circumference of these selfsame Monopoly board cul-de-sacs and dead ends. Most specifically, what can happen to a solitary, thoughtful, and independent thinker when being stagnated in the triangulation of a cookie-cutter, oppressive culture of a homeowner's association; A memoir all written in critical and didactic, poetic stanzas and passages, and out of desperation, when freedom and control get taken, what he is forced to do in the illusion of 'free will and volition,' something like the derivative art of a smart and ironic and social and cultural satire.

Still Time - Michael Cocchiarale

Still Time is a collection of twenty-five short and shorter stories exploring tensions that arise in a variety of con-temporary relationships: a young boy must deal with the wrath of his out-of-work father; a woman runs into a man twenty years after an awkward sexual encounter; a wife, unable to conceive, imagines her own murder, as well as the reaction of her emotionally distant husband; a soon-to-be tenured English professor tries to come to terms with her husband's shocking return to the religion of his youth; an assembly line worker, married for thirty years, discovers the surprising secret life of his recently hospitalized wife. Whether a few hundred or a few thousand words, these and other stories in the collection depict characters at moments of deep crisis. Some feel powerless, over-whelmed—unable to do much to change the course of their lives. Others rise to the occasion and, for better or for worse, say or do the thing that might transform them for good. Even in stories with the most troubling of endings, there remains the possibility of redemption. For each of the characters, there is still time.

Fomite
Burlington, Vermont

Signed Confessions - *Tom Walker*
Guilt and a desperate need to repent drive the antiheroes in Tom Walker's dark (and often darkly funny) stories:
• A gullible journalist falls for the 40-year-old stripper he profiles in a magazine.
• A faithless husband abandons his family and joins a support group for lost souls.
• A merciless prosecuting attorney grapples with the suicide of his gay son.
• An aging misanthrope must make amends to five former victims.
• An egoistic naval hero is haunted by apparitions of his dead wife and a mysterious little girl.
The seven tales in *Signed Confessions* measure how far guilty men will go to obtain a forgiveness no one can grant but themselves.

Meanwell - *Janice Miller Potter*
Meanwell is a twenty-four poem sequence in which a female servant searches for identity and meaning in the shadow of her mistress, poet Anne Bradstreet. Although Meanwell herself is a fiction, someone like her could easily have existed among Bradstreet's known but unnamed domestic servants. Through Meanwell's eyes, Bradstreet emerges as a human figure during The Great Migration of the 1600s, a period in which the Massachusetts Bay Colony was fraught with physical and political dangers. Through Meanwell, the feelings of women, silenced during the midwife Anne Hutchinson's fiery trial before the Puritan ministers, are finally acknowledged. In effect, the poems are about the making of an American rebel. Through her conflicted conscience, we witness Meanwell's transformation from a powerless English waif to a mythic American who ultimately chooses wilderness over the civilization she has experienced.

Love's Labours - Jack Pulaski

In the four stories and two novellas that comprise Love's Labors the protagonists Ben and Laura, discover in their fervid romance and long marriage their interlocking fates, and the histories that preceded their births. They also learned something of the paradox between love and all the things it brings to its beneficiaries: bliss, disaster, duty, tragedy, comedy, the grotesque, and tenderness.
Ben and Laura's story is also the particularly American tale of immigration to a new world. Laura's story begins in Puerto Rico, and Ben's lineage is Russian-Jewish. They meet in City College of New York, a place at least analogous to a melting

Fomite
Burlington, Vermont

pot. Laura struggles to rescue her brother from gang life and heroin. She is mother to her younger sister; their mother Consuelo is the financial mainstay of the family and consumed by work. Despite filial obligations, Laura aspires to be a serious painter. Ben writes, cares for and is caught up in the misadventures and surreal stories of his younger schizophrenic brother. Laura is also a story teller as powerful and enchanting as Scheherazade. Ben struggles to survive such riches, and he and Laura endure.

Four-Way Stop - Sherry Olson

If *Thank You* were the only prayer, as Meister Eckhart has suggested, it would be enough, and Sherry Olson's poetry, in her second book, *Four-Way Stop*, would be one. Radical attention, deep love, and dedication to kindness illuminate these poems and the stories she tells us, which are drawn from her own life: with family, with friends, and wherever she travels, with strangers – who to Olson, never are strangers, but kin.

Even at the difficult intersections, as in the title poem, *Four-Way Stop,* Olson experiences – and offers – hope, showing us how, *completely unsupervised,* people take turns, with *kindness waving each other on*. Olson writes, knowing that (to quote Czeslaw Milosz)) *What surrounds us, here and now, is not guaranteed.* To this world, with her poems, Olson brings – and teaches – attention, generosity, compassion, and appreciative joy.
— Carol Henrikson

Did you know that you can write a review on Amazon, Good Reads or Shelfari? Just go to the book page on the website and follow the links for posting a review. Books from independent presses depend on reader to reader communications.

48287CB00002B/514